A Sunday at the Pool in Kigali

———

A Sunday
at the Pool
in Kigali

GIL COURTEMANCHE

Translated by Patricia Claxton

Alfred A. Knopf   New York   2003

Originally published in French in Canada under the title
Un dimanche à la piscine à Kigali by Éditions du Boréal Montréal
in 2000. This tranlation was originally published in Canada
by Random House of Canda Limited, Toronto.
Copyright © 2000 by Éditions du Boréal, Montréal

Library of Congress Cataloging-in-Publication Data
Courtemanche, Gil.
[Dimanche à la piscine à Kigali. English]
A Sunday at the pool in Kigali / Gil Courtemanche;
translated from the French by Patricia Claxton.
p.   cm.
ISBN 1-4000-4107-4
I. Claxton, Patricia. II. Title.
PQ3919.2.C627D5613 2003
2003047442

Manufactured in the United States of America
First United States Edition

To my Rwandan friends swept away in the maelstrom

Émérita, André, Cyprien, Raphaël,
Landouald, Hélène, Méthode

To a few unsung heroes still living

Louise, Marie, Stratton, Victor

Finally, to Gentille, who served me eggs and beer and
could be dead or alive, if only I knew

I have tried to speak for you
I hope I have not failed you

Preface

This novel is fiction. But it is also a chronicle and eyewitness report. The characters all existed in reality, and in almost every case I have used their real names. The novelist has given them lives, acts and words that summarize or symbolize what the journalist observed while in their company. If I have taken the liberty of inventing a little, I have done so the better to convey the human quality of the murdered men and women. Those who planned and carried out the genocide are identified in this book by their true names. Some readers may attribute certain scenes of violence and cruelty to an overactive imagination. They will be sadly mistaken. For proof, they have only to read the seven hundred pages of eyewitness reports gathered by the African Rights organization and published under the title *Rwanda: Death, Despair and Defiance* (African Rights, London, 1995).

Finally, I would like to thank Patricia Claxton for the wonderful job she has done in translating my book into English, and for the skill and great care she brought to the task. As a result of our discussions, we made a few useful modifications and I took her counsel and the opportunity she offered to clarify some additional points. A good translation improves a text, and I feel that is certainly true in this case.

G.C.

Translator's Note

I have had the pleasure and privilege of working closely with Gil Courtemanche, following the original publication in French of *Un dimanche à la piscine à Kigali.*

In response to suggestions that readers might appreciate knowing more about the background of Rwandan politics, I have provided a few additional footnotes and now and then added a clarifying word or two to the body of the book, hoping to give a maximum of information with a minimum of disruption to the story. Some of this material was provided by the author.

The translation of all quotations of poetry by Paul Éluard and of a sentence by Albert Camus is mine.

Bibliographical references for the original excerpts will be found at the back of the book.

I would like to thank a number of people for their assistance with background and terminological information in their fields of expertise: Nouella Grimes, Antonino Mazza, Roger Titman, Eleanor Maclean of the Blacker-Wood Library of Biology at McGill University, Line Provost of La Clinique médicale l'Actuel in Montreal, Dr. Anne-Louise Lafontaine, Dr. David Claxton. Thank you to Gil Courtemanche for his cooperation and his confidence in me. Thank you also to Louise Dennys, Noelle Zitzer and Doris Cowan for their careful, courteous editing, and to our Australian publisher, Michael Heyward, for some astute and timely observations.

Patricia Claxton, Montreal, January 2003

A Sunday at the Pool in Kigali

Chapter One

In the middle of Kigali there is a swimming pool surrounded by deckchairs and a score of tables all made of
white plastic. And forming a huge L overhanging this
patch of blue stands the Hôtel des Mille-Collines, with its
habitual clientele of international experts and aid workers, middle-class Rwandans, screwed-up or melancholy
expatriates of various origins, and prostitutes. All
around the pool and hotel in lascivious disorder lies
the part of the city that matters, that makes the decisions, that steals, kills, and lives very nicely, thank
you. The French Cultural Centre, the UNICEF offices,
the Ministry of Information, the embassies, the president's palace (recognizable by the tanks on guard), the

crafts shops popular with departing visitors where one can unload surplus black market currency, the radio station, the World Bank offices, the archbishop's palace. Encircling this artificial paradise are the obligatory symbols of decolonization: Constitution Square, Development Avenue, Boulevard of the Republic, Justice Avenue, and an ugly, modern cathedral. Farther down, almost in the underbelly of the city, stands the red brick mass of the Church of the Holy Family, disgorging the poor in their Sunday best into crooked mud lanes bordered by houses made of the same clay. Small red houses—just far enough away from the swimming pool not to offend the nostrils of the important—filled with shouting, happy children, with men and women dying of AIDS and malaria, thousands of small households that know nothing of the pool around which others plan their lives and, more importantly, their predictable deaths.

Jackdaws as big as eagles and as numerous as house sparrows caw all around the hotel gardens. They circle in the sky, waiting, like the humans they're observing, for the cocktail hour. Now is when the beers arrive, while the ravens are alighting on the tall eucalyptus trees around the pool. When the ravens have settled, the buzzards appear and take possession of the topmost branches. Woe betide the lowly jackdaw that fails to respect the hierarchy. Birds behave like humans here.

Precisely as the buzzards are establishing their positions around the pool, precisely then, the French paratroopers on the plastic deckchairs begin putting on Rambo airs. They sniff all the feminine flesh splashing around in the heavily chlorinated water of the pool. Its freshness matters little. There is vulture in these soldiers with their shaven heads, watching and waiting beside a pool that is the centrepiece of a meat stall where the reddest, most lovingly garnished morsels are displayed alongside the flabby and scrawny feminine fare whose only diversion is this waterhole. On Sundays, as on every other day of the week at around five o'clock, a number of carcasses—some plump, some skeletal—disturb the surface of the pool, well aware that the "paras," as the paratroopers are known, are not the least daunted either by cellulite or by skin clinging to bones merely from habit. The women, if they knew what danger stalked them, would drown in anticipation of ecstasy or else get themselves to a nunnery.

This tranquil Sunday, a former minister of justice is warming up energetically on the diving board. He does not realize that his strenuous exercises are eliciting giggles from the two prostitutes from whom he is expecting a sign of recognition or interest before diving into the water. He wants to beguile because he doesn't want to pay. He hits the water like a disjointed clown. The girls laugh. The paras too.

Around the pool, Québécois and Belgian aid workers vie in loud laughter. The Belgians and Québécois aren't friends; they don't work together, even though they are working toward the same goal: 'development.' That magic word which dresses up the best and most irrelevant of intentions. The two groups are rivals, always explaining to the locals why their kind of development is better than the others'. The only thing they have in common is the din they make. There ought to be a word for the atmosphere surrounding these Whites who talk, laugh and drink in a way that makes the whole pool know their importance—no, not even that—just their vacuous existence. Let's use the word 'noisiness' because there's certainly noise, but it's continuous, there's a permanence to it, a perpetual squawking. In this shy, reticent and often deceptive country, they live in a state of noisiness, like noisy animals. They are also in continuous rut. Noise is their breathing, silence their death, and the asses of Rwandan women their territory of exploration. They are noisy explorers of Third World asses. Only the Germans, when they descend on the hotel in force like a battalion of moralizing accountants, can match the Belgians and Québécois in noisiness.

Important Frenchmen don't stay at this hotel. They dig themselves in at the Méridien with high-class Rwandans and clean hookers who sip whisky. The hookers at this hotel are rarely clean. They drink Pepsi while waiting to be picked up and offered a local beer, which may get them offered a whisky or a vodka later on. But these women are realists, so today they'll settle for a Pepsi and a john.

Valcourt, who is also Québécois but has almost forgotten it over the years, observes these things and notes them down, muttering as he does so, sometimes angrily, sometimes with tenderness, but always audibly. For all anyone knows or imagines, he's writing about them, and everyone wants someone to ask him what he's writing, and worries about this book he's been writing since the Project left him more or less high and dry. Sometimes he even pretends to be writing, in order to show he's alive, watchful and serious like the disillusioned philosopher he claims to be when he runs out of excuses for himself. He's not writing a book. He writes to put in time between mouthfuls of beer, or to signal that he doesn't want to be disturbed. Rather like a buzzard on a branch, in fact, Valcourt is waiting for a scrap of life to excite him and make him unfold his wings.

At the end of the terrace, walking slowly and grandly, appears a Rwandan just back from Paris. You can tell, because his sporty outfit is so new its yellows and greens are blinding, even for sunglass-protected eyes. There's sniggering at a table of expatriates. Admiration at several tables of locals. The Rwandan just back from Paris is afloat on a magic carpet. From the handle of his crocodile attaché case dangle First Class and Hermès labels. In his pocket, along with other prestige labels, he probably has an import licence for some product of secondary necessity, which he will sell at a premium price.

He orders a "verbena-mint" at such volume that three ravens depart the nearest tree. Gentille, who has just completed her social service studies and is interning at the hotel, doesn't know what a verbena-mint is. Intimidated, she whispers—so softly she can't even hear herself—that there are only two brands of beer, Primus and Mutzig. The Rwandan on his magic carpet is not listening and replies that of course he wants the best, even if it's more expensive. So Gentille will bring him a Mutzig, which for some is the best and for everyone more expensive. Valcourt scribbles feverishly. He describes the scene with indignation, adding some notes about the outrageousness of African corruption, but he does not stir.

"You little slut!" the Rwandan just back from Paris yells when confronted by his Mutzig that is not a verbena-mint. "I know the minister of tourism, you dirty Tutsi, sleeping with a White so you can work at the hotel!" And Gentille, whose name is as lovely as her breasts, which are so pointed they abrade her starched shirt-dress, Gentille, whose face is more lovely still, and whose ass is more disturbing in its impudent adolescence than anything else about her, Gentille, who is so embarrassed by her beauty she has never smiled or spoken an unnecessary word, Gentille cries. Just a few tears and a little sniff of the kind young girls still have in them before the smells of men take hold between their thighs.

For six months now Valcourt has thought of only one thing between the thighs of Agathe, who comes to his room when she has no customers rather than risk walking home to Nyamirambo in the dark. For six months now he has barely been getting it half up with Agathe because he wants to turn Gentille's breasts into a woman's breasts; six months in which the only thing that gets it up is seeing Gentille walking with those sweet breasts of hers among the tables on the terrace or through the dining room. Valcourt has but one plan in his head now—to thread Gentille, *enfiler* is the word he has in mind, a favourite of the writer Paul Léautaud whom he had discovered through a woman crueller than any of the words of that detestable writer, a woman who left him in pieces like a badly butchered carcass on a blood-smeared meat counter.

"I'm the president's nephew," bawls the Rwandan just back from Paris.

No, he's not one of the president's nephews. Valcourt knows them all. The one who plays the political science student in Quebec but in Rwanda organizes death squads that go after Tutsis at night in Remero, Gikondo and Nyamirambo. And the one who controls the sale of condoms donated by international aid agencies, and another who has AIDS and thinks the way to get rid of his poison is by fucking young virgins, and the other three, Eugène, Clovis and Firmin, who are soldiers and protectors of the hookers at the Kigali

Night, the "cleanest" of Kigali's hookers. The paras screw the clean hookers in the bush around the bar without condoms because the president's nephews tell them *they* fuck them without condoms and they aren't sick. And the rapacious French jerks believe them. As if they didn't know the Kigali Night belongs to one of the president's sons.

Gentille, who was shy already, now walks like a woman in mourning.

Valcourt orders "a tall Mutzig, *ma petite* Gentille." He almosts says something to comfort her, but she is too beautiful and he feels stupidly inarticulate. And soon it will be six o'clock and around the pool all the actors in the daily cocktail-hour ritual will have taken their places on stage in the same production as yesterday. And Valcourt will play his role, like all the others. The Mont Blanc fountain pen moves: "Now a fade-out to Blacks."

There's Raphaël and his bunch of pals who work at the People's Bank of Rwanda. They'll leave at midnight when the fourth-floor bar closes. And there's Monsieur Faustin, who will be prime minister when the president bestows democracy upon the children of his republic. Other opposition members of the government will join him—Landouald, minister of labour, who went into politics to please his wife, a liberated Québécoise, and a few others who will bow and scrape to right and left as they go back and forth three times to the buffet table. A Belgian embassy counsellor stops for a few minutes, diplomatically affecting an air of discretion in order to avoid saying anything about the peace accord and the transfer of power that the president accepts every six months and never signs, claiming he can't because it's the rainy season, or his wife is in Paris, or the last arms shipments have not arrived from Zaïre, or his secretary's husband is sick.

Every day for the past two years there has been endless talk around the pool about the change that is brewing; it's going to come tomorrow or Tuesday, Wednesday at the latest, they say. But this time it's true and the regulars are caught up in a great ripple of excited whispering. The husband of the president's secretary died of AIDS two days ago in Paris, where he had been in the hospital for six months. Émérita, taxi-woman, businesswoman, who pays the best black-market rate for the Rwandan franc, came to tell Monsieur Faustin. A doctor from Val-de-Grâce Hospital had arrived this morning and told the first secretary at the French embassy, who repeated it to Émérita—who runs little errands for him—knowing full well she would waste no time announcing the news to Monsieur Faustin. The late husband was a perfect fool, content just to make money with his exclusive Michelin tire import licence, but rumour has it that his wife does not owe her stunningly fast rise through the civil service ranks to her typing skills. The intelligence branch of the embassy, contacted by a brother of Madame La Présidente a few months ago, reassured this "neutral enquirer" that these things were all malicious gossip originating in the camp of the opposition.

No matter. In half an hour, when Émérita has finished her Pepsi after talking to Zozo the concierge, a swarm of taxi drivers will leave for the city. Tonight, from Gikondo to Nyamirambo, not forgetting Sodoma, the well-named hookers' quarter, they'll be imagining—then saying outright—that the president is dying of AIDS. Tomorrow they'll be saying it in Butare and the day after in Ruhengeri, the president's own fiefdom. In a few days when the president is the last to hear he's dying of AIDS, he'll fly into a rage and heads will fall. Here, rumours kill. They're checked out afterwards.

On the same plane with the doctor and his fatal news there arrived ten copies each of *L'Express* and *Paris Match* which will be swapped around for a month, and French cheeses in slightly over- or underripe condition which will be consumed amid great trimestrial pomp and circumstance in the hotel dining room.

Around the pool, two important subjects are being discussed. The Whites are consulting the list of cheeses and writing their names on the reservation sheet. People will come from as far away as the Gorilla Sanctuary on the Zaïrean border for the traditional cheese tasting, at which the first wedge will be cut by the French ambassador himself. At the tables occupied by Rwandans, the majority of whom are Tutsis or Hutus of the opposition, the tone is hushed. The subject of conversation is the president's illness (which is already taken as acknowledged fact), the probable date of his death, and who will succeed him. André, who distributes condoms for a Canadian NGO and as such is an expert on AIDS, calculates busily: according to rumour, the president has been fucking his secretary for three years; if he's been doing it often and his secretary's husband is already dead from AIDS, and the gods are with us, then President Juvénal has at most a year left. His listeners applaud wildly.

Only Léo is not joining in the applause. Léo is a Hutu who says he's a moderate so he can get to screw Raphaël's sister. Léo is a journalist at the television station that doesn't exist yet, that Valcourt was supposed to set up. Léo is not a moderate, it's just that he's got a bone on for Immaculée, Raphaël's sister. Though he comes from the North, where the president was born, Léo recently joined the Social Democratic Party, the party of the South. At the pool bar this act of courage has impressed quite a few and Léo is making the most of it. Mind you, the very thought of undressing Immaculée would instill conviction in many small minds. But Léo is also a Tutsi through his mother. With the simmering conflict in mind, Léo is seeking the camp that will save his precious skin and let him realize his dream of becoming a journalist in Canada. Rwandans are good at putting on a front. They handle concealment and ambiguity with awesome skill. Léo is a caricature of all this: Hutu father, Tutsi mother. Tutsi body, Hutu heart. Social Democratic Party cardholder and speechwriter for Léon, the Hutu extremist ideologue, known as the Purifier or Avenging Lion. Country talk, clothes of a fashionable Parisian. Skin of a Black, ambitions of a White. Fortunately, thinks Valcourt, Immaculée feels only scorn and disdain for Léo though he zealously plies her with flowers and chocolates.

Valcourt has not joined his Rwandan buddies as he normally does in the evening. Gentille's distress is keeping him at his own table. The stupidity of the Rwandan just back from Paris disgusts him. But he has become a bit weary of the obsessive conversation of his friends and even more of their overblown, florid, pretentious, often old-fashioned language. They do not speak, they declare, declaim, not in verse but in slogans, formulaic dicta, press releases. They talk of massacres they foresee with the certainty of weather forecasters, and of the AIDS eating at them as if they are prophets of the Apocalypse. Valcourt knows plenty about massacres, brutality and

AIDS, but sometimes he'd like to talk about flowers or sex or cooking. He hears Raphaël announcing, "We have come to the end of time, eaten away by two cancers, hatred and AIDS. We are a little like the Earth's last children. . ." Valcourt covers his ears.

The Canadian ambassador arrives and without so much as a nod to anyone goes and sits at the table nearest the buffet; Lucien is wearing his favourite T-shirt again, the one sporting the legend, "Call Me Bwana." Lisette, the consul, is in despair since having her golf bag stolen and is in a grouchy mood. Imagine her distress. She is left-handed, the only left-handed player among the members of the Kigali Golf Club, whose ill-kept fairways wend through the little valley overlooked by the arrogant high-rise of the National Council of Development, the luxurious villas of the regime's favourites, the Belgian Club, and the ambassadors' residences. Golf is her only pleasure, her only civilized activity in this godawful country she abhors. An appointment to Kigali when one has been in the Canadian Service for seventeen years is an invitation to hand in one's resignation. But some people are blind, deaf and pigheaded. The embassy here is only a branch, in fact, a dependency of Kinshasa, which is an even more unbearable city than Kigali. But when one doesn't know anything but the art of lying politely, one is better off living in Kigali than answering the phone in departmental offices in Ottawa. Lisette suffers in luxury.

The laughter from Raphaël's crew is short-lived. The president's three brothers-in-law appear, followed by the hotel's Belgian assistant manager and five soldiers of the presidential guard. But all the tables are taken. The former minister of justice scurries, still dripping water, to invite them to sit with him, but his table is in the sun and the gentlemen wish to sit in the shade. All the suitable tables are occupied by Whites, or by Raphaël's friends, who of course will not budge. For the assistant manager, a tricky situation. It is saved miraculously by the manager, who happens along at this moment and displaces his own wife and in-laws to make way for the three pillars of the Akazu.*

And now Canada's presence is complete: the commander of the UN troops has just arrived. The major general is a miracle of mimesis, a perfect incarnation of his country and his employer too, rather the way masters who adore their dogs end up looking and behaving like them. Unassuming, apprehensive, ineloquent and naive, like Canada. Meticulous, legalistic, a civil servant and exemplary bureaucrat, as virtuous as "le Grand Machin" itself (as General de Gaulle was pleased to call the United Nations). What he knows of the world is airports, the grand hotels of Brussels, Geneva and New York, and strategic studies centres. Of war, he knows what he has seen on CNN, read in a few books and experienced through military exercises he has directed, and invasions of several countries he has conducted on paper. About Africa finally, he knows its colour and several of its smells to which he has still not become accustomed, although he dexterously wields canisters of "Quebec spruce" deodorant and douses himself with Brut, an eau de cologne highly prized by the military and the police. Yet behind his salesman's

---

* Meaning "house" or "family." At this time, the word designated the family of the president, especially his wife Agathe's three brothers who controlled most of Rwanda's wealth, both legitimate and ill-gotten.

moustache and sad eyes, the major general is an honest man and a good Catholic. He is deeply touched by the obvious piety of the dictator and his family and the frequent company they keep with bishops. These are upright people. Their few excesses ought to be ascribed to a certain African atavism rather than the insatiable venality and bloodthirsty cruelty they are so maliciously accused of by all those ambitious Tutsis who pretend to be playing by the rules of democracy but in fact aspire only to set up a new dictatorship. This was explained to the major general at length by the archbishop of Kabgaye one morning after the solemn high mass which Canada's UN commander had attended with his new personal secretary, a nice young man named Firmin who had studied in Quebec and who enjoyed the valuable advantage of being a nephew of the dictator. On the way back, Firmin confirmed what the archbishop had said, forgetting to add that the rotund representative of His Polish Holiness was personal confessor to the dictator's family, the Habyarimanas, as well as a member of the executive committee of what had been the only political party before the international community imposed the Arusha peace accord, and with it an official opposition.*

---

* In 1990, the Tutsi-led Rwandan Patriotic Front (RPF) launched a military campaign against President Juvénal Habyarimana's government. After protracted negotiations, with the support of countries of the Organization of African Unity, the Arusha peace accord was signed in August 1993. It called for a Transitional National Assembly with a predetermined number of seats per party and a transitional government, pending elections. To help achieve national reconciliation, the UN Security Council created the UN Assistance Mission for Rwanda (UNAMIR) to ensure respect of the terms of the peace accord. Despite the negotiated peace, a Tutsi-led rebel force remained across the border in Uganda to the north, and sporadic cross-border fighting continued.

A man of duty, the major general is an unprejudiced man, and he is not displeased about being in central Africa. He could have been sent to Somalia or Bosnia. Here there's no peace but at least there's no war, for all the sporadic fighting on the Ugandan border. It's almost as restful as a posting to Cyprus. In fact, he views this mission as eighteen months of well-deserved rest, far away from all the UN paperwork and bootlicking. In New York they ordered him to interpret his mandate as narrowly as possible. He has been given minimal military resources, in case he should be tempted to show too much initiative. On account of which the major general has already forgotten—or almost—that the United Nations forces are expected not only to ensure respect of the peace accord but also maintain order in the capital.

A grenade explodes. Just far enough from the pool for it to be somewhere else. Only the major general is startled. He is not yet used to this peace that kills on a daily basis. He has spilled a little soup on his uniform and looks anxiously around him. No one has noticed his nervousness. Reassured, though sweating profusely, he dips his spoon back into his black bean soup.

Twelve French vultures dive into the pool all at once; three women have just slipped into the water. Sometimes vultures turn into crocodiles.

Valcourt closes his notebook. The vaguely surrealistic play being acted out at the pool day after day ceased to interest him some time ago. The plot is heavy-handed and the characters behave as predictably as in a TV soap opera. He wonders if he hasn't put in enough time here in Kigali. He wanted to live somewhere else; he's done it. He feels this evening as though he's swimming round and round in an aquarium.

He orders another beer from Gentille whose head is still bowed, though the Rwandan from Paris is no longer there.

Chapter Two

One tenth of April, when Montreal had begun to celebrate spring but was still buried under forty-five centimetres of snow, all Bernard Valcourt knew of Rwanda was where it was on the map and the fact that two ethnic groups, the Hutus, the majority by far, and the Tutsis, about fifteen per cent of the population, were locked in an undeclared civil war. He was drinking in the bar of a hotel after attending a conference on development and democracy in Africa. The snow might stop after a few beers and he could walk home. And then, there was nothing to go home for. Since his daughter had left, the way all daughters do when they fall in love, and since Pif, his cat, so named because he was the brother of Paf,

had died like his sister of simple, stupid old age, loneliness was all his apartment had to offer him. A few
nice women had unhooked their bras, one or another
had slept over and had breakfast, but none had passed
the morning test. Since his wife died five years ago, he
had known only one great passion—and it was so
mad, so all-consuming and magnificent that he hadn't
known how to handle it. Passion feeds on abandon.
He had not yet reached that state of total freedom
that obliterates fear of the unknown and allows one
to soar. As for his work as a Radio-Canada producer,
it was looking increasingly like a monotonous chore, a
tedious burden.

A tall, good-looking man with a beard, who had bab-
bled some platitudes about the media in Africa, came
over and introduced himself.

"Claude Saint-Laurent, director of democratic development for the Canadian International Development
Agency. May I sit down?"

And he ordered two beers. He explained that
Canada, a country of small importance in the concert of
nations, nevertheless exerted an influence in certain
regions of the world that could determine their future
and above all their access to democracy. This was the
case with Rwanda. With other partners, the Canadian
government had agreed to finance the establishment of
a television station in Rwanda. Its primary mission
would be educational, particularly in community health
and AIDS.

"We begin with hygienic necessities, with programs
on prevention, on dietary matters, then the information
gets into circulation, and information is the beginning
of democracy and tolerance."

Bullshit, thought Valcourt.

"Would you be interested in being co-director of this television station?"

Valcourt said yes without thinking it over even two seconds.

He gave his furniture to the St. Vincent de Paul Society and his pictures to his daughter, sold his apartment and all but two of his books, keeping only Camus' *Essais* and the *Oeuvres complètes* of Paul Éluard, the Pléiade edition. Two months later he was drinking a Primus beside the pool in the middle of Kigali.

He had been living two years now in this heterogeneous, excessive city. He no longer had much faith in the television station project. The government kept finding reasons for putting off its launch. When closed-circuit programs were shown there was always the same complaint: "There's not enough stress on the government's role." When the government was satisfied with the propaganda inserts, it was the donor countries, Canada, Switzerland and Germany, that balked. Valcourt and the station had come to a dead end. But one thing had impassioned Valcourt. He had discovered with horror that over a third of Kigali's adults were HIV positive. The government was denying its own statistics. Those stricken with AIDS were living in infamy, shame, concealment and delusion. Only a few people were trying to face up to the disaster and, paradoxically, they were parish priests and nuns. Devout, virginal nuns from Lac-Saint-Jean, Quebec City and the Beauce were gathering in prostitutes and teaching them about the virtues of condoms. Parish priests, and lay brothers too, had the pockets of their cassocks bulging with plastic packages, which they handed out beneath the photograph of the Pope watching protectively from the walls of their offices. In his spare time on weekends and holidays, when he could quietly bring out a camera, Valcourt was making a documentary film on AIDS and these heroic, pious transgressors.

From the moment of his arrival in Kigali he had been deeply moved by the landscape, the hills sculpted by thousands of gardens, the mists caressing the valley floors, and by the challenge he was being handed. At last he was going to be useful, was going to change the course of things. My real life is beginning, he said to himself.

But Gentille's life? When does that really begin?

The story of Gentille—who still has her head bowed and is drying her tears, watched inquisitively and lustfully by the barman—has two beginnings.

The first was in a time when her country was called Ruanda-Urundi. Germans had settled there, but a war that no one in her country had heard of changed the Germans into Belgians. Kawa, Gentille's great-great-grandfather, had been told that these soldiers, these civil servants, these teachers and these priests gowned all in white were coming to the land of a thousand hills to make it a protectorate. An important league, which no one had heard of either, a league of kings, ministers and other powerful people, had asked the Belgians to protect Ruanda-Urundi. They had brought with them the Great Protector, a mysterious and invisible god divided into three, one of which was a son. To shelter their god, the Great White Robes had built huge houses of red brick and smaller ones for themselves, and other houses too where people could learn to read and also learn about the life of the son of the Great Protector. Kawa, who was Hutu and wished to obtain a position for his eldest son at the court of the Tutsi king, enrolled his son at the school but would not have him baptized because the king, the mwami Musinga, was resisting the pressure from the Great White Robes. However, the Belgians did not want a mwami who believed in Imana the creator and in Lyangombe, and who practised *kuragura,* or divination and ancestor worship. Monseigneur Classe, the head of the Great White Robes, arranged for the son of the mwami, Mutara III, to become king on condition that he abandon his old beliefs. Mutara III was baptized on a Sunday in 1931. On Monday Kawa went to the school with his son and asked the priest to baptize him Célestin, which was the name of the Belgian burgomaster of his commune. This was how Célestin, several days before his death, had recounted the story of his conversion to his own son, Gentille's grandfather.

Once enrolled at the university in Butare, Célestin began to read all that the Great White Robes had written. These people must truly have been communicating with God, for in their books one could discover the story of all humanity. He learned of course that the Earth was round. He was not surprised. If the Sun and Moon are round, why would the Earth be flat or square? Célestin was intelligent and was soon making use of what he learned. From being with them as much as from reading their books, he quickly understood that the Belgians considered themselves superior. He was not upset by this discovery. From the beginning of time, individuals, clans, tribes had paraded their superiority, proclaimed it on the hills and in the valleys. Some used force and others used trade to assert themselves, but always, each in his own way and each on his own hill, the Hutu and the Tutsi had stayed polite but distant, garnering a little of each other's wisdom and carrying on their business with respect for one another.

Célestin was Hutu, and only the haste of his father to have him baptized had opened the doors of the university to him—this conversion plus the two cows that Kawa, a prosperous farmer, had promised to give the mission every year in thanks for its generosity. Célestin asked his father if his own generous offer had been made first. No, his father replied slowly after reflecting several minutes, the two generosities were born simultaneously.

This was how Célestin received his daily lesson in concealment, a kind of half-lie practised by men of the hills since life began. He who lives on a hill distrusts strangers. He lives in isolation and knows neither friend nor enemy. So he gives himself time to understand and, in the meantime, he pretends. Often he takes a whole lifetime and only says what he thinks on his deathbed. In this country this is sometimes how, after years of keeping company, of cheerful conversation, gifts and being kowtowed to, a White can learn that he has never been liked. Whites say that Ruanda-Urundi is the kingdom of liars and hypocrites. They do not understand the first thing about the permanent insecurity of the men of the hills. The Whites have guns. The Blacks have secret thoughts.

Kawa wanted Célestin to know another life than life on the hill. He wanted him to be an "intellectual."

This is what someone is still called today who can read and pile up paper instead of milking a cow or goat. He would go and live in Astrida,* the capital, and become rich trading with the colonials. A legitimate plan, which did honour to a loving father, but one whose full complexity was still beyond his grasp. It was Célestin, an insatiable reader, who made it possible for his father to get an inkling of the difficulties that lay ahead in his advance toward prosperity and social prominence.

Célestin had brought home a big book written by a Belgian doctor who was a specialist in indigenous cultures. In his country he was considered a great Africanist. The Belgian king, queen, ministers, high and low civil servants, all learned everything they knew of the mysterious continent from this book. There was no greater authority on Rwanda than this doctor. He knew the history of all the kingdoms of Africa and the characteristics of each of its peoples. He described each scientifically, applying the leading theories of morphology and anthropology, as they had recently begun to do in Europe, particularly in Germany. Célestin's teacher, Father Athanase, had explained all this to him when placing the precious volume in his hands. If Célestin wanted to become an intellectual, he said, it was time for him to discover which were the pure races so he could model his attitude and behaviour on them. This would do much for his social advancement.

Reading this book disrupted his entire life and the lives of his family, his children, grandchildren, and great-grandchildren, of whom the most beautiful and most intelligent would be baptized Gentille.

* Butare today.

He learned that the Hutus had inhabited the region of the Great Lakes since time immemorial and that they were probably descended from the Bantus, who were savage warriors from Lake Chad and had founded great kingdoms, like those of the Monomotapa and the Kongo, as well as the great Zulu chiefdoms in South Africa. It was they who, long before the birth of Jesus, introduced metallurgy to the region as well as a pottery technique still being practised today.

The Tutsis, who had reigned over Ruanda-Urundi for centuries, had come from the North, from Egypt or Ethiopia. A Hamitic people, they were not true negroes but probably Whites darkened by centuries of sun. Their tall stature, the paleness of their skin and the fineness of their features attested to this noble ancestry and their distant relationship with the civilized peoples.

"The Hutu, a poor farmer, is short and squat and has the nose characteristic of the negroid races. He is good natured but naive, coarse and unintelligent. The Hutu is deceitful and lazy, and quick to take offence. He is a typical negro.

"The Tutsi, a nomadic cattle grazier, is tall and slender. His skin is light brown on account of his northern origins. He is intelligent and skilful at trade. He has a sparkling wit and a pleasant disposition. Colonial administrators in Ruanda-Urundi would do well to obtain the assistance of Tutsis for tasks which in their judgment they may entrust without danger to natives."*

When Célestin read these words to his father, Kawa uttered a fearful cry. All was crumbling around him: his

* Sasserath, *Le Ruanda-Urundi, étrange royaume féodal,* quoted by Jean-Pierre Chrétien in *Burundi, l'histoire retrouvée,* Karthala, 1993.

pride as a Hutu patriarch and the ambitions he had been harbouring for Célestin. He himself no longer existed and his son was worth no more than a leper. On the hill, he was already being looked on with suspicion. Yes, now he realized why. For Kawa was very tall and his nose was neither large nor flat like the noses of his six brothers and forty-nine cousins. His skin was darker than the skin of Tutsis he knew, but when you saw him from behind or far away, or in a dark place, you could not tell the difference. He did raise cows like the Tutsis, but only chance and a crazy bet his father had made a long, long time ago had put him on that course. He was neither lazy nor stupid. People complimented him on his humour and admired his instinct for trade, and certain Tutsis of rank readily took him into their confidence.

If the doctor who had written this book was right—and who could doubt it?—Kawa and his parents and grandparents and children were neither Hutu nor Tutsi. Unless some ancestor had been mistaken and, throughout all these seasons past, they had been Tutsis without knowing it. If they really were Hutus, on the other hand, they were deformed, bastards of some kind, and their future held only obstacles and disappointments. Kawa asked Célestin to pray to his new god, and for good measure invoked his own, Imana. One can never be too careful. Neither seemed to have a solution for his dilemma. He would have to consult the ancestors, even though the practice, *kuragura*, had been forbidden by the bishops and burgomasters.

Kawa did not sleep a wink all night. Ten times at least he rose and went to walk in the banana grove, hoping for a sign from the sky or a sudden inspiration that would spare him from having to go and consult his

distant cousin, one of the most venerated *umumpfumu**
of the Kibeho district. In vain. The stars were deaf that
night, the sky blind and silent.

His cousin's name was Nyamaravago, in honour of
the queen mother who at her baptism later had taken
the name Radegonde. She had been practising divination since the death of her husband, he too a diviner,
who had transmitted to her all the secrets of interpret-
ing saliva, and pats of butter dissolving in boiling
water. The too easy and unreliable sacrifice of chickens
they left to lesser diviners.

He set out long before the first ray of sunshine lit up
the eucalyptus trees. He had brought his finest cow as
a gift for his cousin to make sure she would be
favourably disposed. When he arrived at her house the
sun was already announcing the end of the day. A dozen
or more worried, ill or wounded people were patiently
waiting, sitting in the shade of the rugo hedge surrounding the big round hut decorated with abstract
motifs. The urgency of his case, or perhaps the ties of
blood, or even more the cow which uttered a piercing
moo of fatigue on arrival, ensured that Kawa waited
only a few minutes.

Without speaking, but his eyes brimming with
questions, he took his place on the mat woven with a
black arrowhead design. Nyamaravago, seated facing
him, had not even raised her head when he entered.
She was humming almost inaudibly, her eyes closed,
breathing slowly. A serving girl presented him with a
large bowl of water. He washed his hands and face. He
was offered banana beer, which he drank slowly, and

---

* Witch and diviner combined.

then rinsed his mouth with water. He closed his eyes and prepared himself to listen.

His cousin spoke of the rains which had fallen very heavily, and of the buzzards which were more and more numerous, meaning that people were throwing away a lot of food, then of her husband who had visited her three nights before. She enquired after Kawa's stomach, which had been ill and which she had treated several months before. Yes, the cramps had disappeared as soon as he had returned home to his hill. An oil lamp, a gift from a rich patient, was lit. The cousins talked for at least an hour. Five minutes of words followed by meditative silences. At last, she who communed with the spirits invited him to state the reason for his visit, the more important, it would seem, for the fineness and fatness of the cow. Kawa had not come for himself but for his children and the children of his children. He feared that great misfortunes would fall upon them and that all his descendants were cursed. And if he was in such despair, it was because a big book written by a White diviner confirmed his anxieties.

"It seems we are not what we are, nor what we appear to be," he concluded, "and the future of my children will be bearable only if they become what they are not." Even with the gods and ancestors, caution and discretion are permissible. A man who tells all is a naked man. A naked man is weak.

He spat into a small calabash. His cousin soaked a strip of wood in his saliva and added a little goat's grease. She heated the strip over the flame of the oil lamp. She examined the forms created by the heat and closed her eyes. The serving girl brought a big bowl filled with boiling water. Nyamaravago put two little dabs of butter into it. Once the butter was melted, she closed her eyes once more and said, "Your children and the children of your children, as long as they live in the land of the hills, must change their skins like snakes and their colour like chameleons. They must always fly in the direction of the wind and swim with the river. They will be what they are not, otherwise they will suffer from being what they are." Silence fell. Kawa trembled. Ants could be heard walking on the mat. The cousin slowly raised her right hand. Kawa, without his cow, took the path back to his hill.

Here is where the story of Gentille, who is yet to be born, begins a second time.

When he reached home, Kawa said not a word of his journey and even less of his worries or the painful decision he had taken in order to save his progeny and their yet unborn descendants.

In the land of hills, the father's origin determines the ethnic group of the children. A Hutu father has Hutu children, a Tutsi father has Tutsi children, regardless of the origin of the mother. Kawa's daughters would need only to marry Tutsis for their children to be part of the race chosen by the gods and admired by Whites. This ought to be easy to bring about. Kawa was rich and knew many less well-endowed Tutsi families who would gladly agree to improve their lot by a few cows in exchange for a son. But for the males of the family, fate condemned them to remain Hutus in Tutsi bodies. And their origin and that of their children would forever be written on their identity papers. What a nightmare. What a tragic fate. Schools forbidden, scorn from Whites, careers and ambitions blocked. Kawa would not allow his sons and the sons of his sons to be officially inferior beings forever, negroes among negroes.

Father Athanase confirmed his darkest fears when he reminded him that God loves all his children equally, that the true greatness of man is within and that the first shall be the last, implying, Kawa understood, that the Batwas* would enter heaven first, followed by the Hutus, then the Tutsis. He did not dare ask the holy man why the children of God did not love the Hutus and Tutsis equally, why true greatness in this country was physical and why, here on earth, the first are always first. The man of the hills, who does not like to lose face, takes care to save face for the person he is talking to. Which is why he never revealed his transaction with the burgomaster.

To the burgomaster he offered several cows, several goats and his most beautiful daughter, who had just turned fourteen. The White refused to issue new identity papers transforming Kawa's Hutus into Tutsis. However, he would take the girl in exchange for the silence he would keep forever regarding Kawa's improper and shameful proposal. This is how Clémentine (whose buttocks and breasts nourished fantasies in the men of the hill, whatever their ethnic group) became the property of a very ugly, pimply-faced Belgian who came and abused her from behind every time he was in the neighbourhood. She died at seventeen from a blood disease that came, it was whispered, from the cocks of unwashed men.

Kawa's other five daughters married Tutsis, thus saving their descendants from shame and infamy. Kawa

* Pygmies.

still had enough cows to find Tutsi wives for his four sons. He chose his daughters-in-law for their stature and paleness of skin. He wanted them slimmer and taller than average, as long and sinuous as snakes, hoping that the Tutsi blood would kill the Hutu blood. Now there was only Célestin left in the house. Célestin was looking after his father, who was wasting away with illness and melancholy since the death of his wife several weeks after Clémentine had died. All the children had left the hill, fleeing the disapproving looks of uncles, aunts and nephews who felt betrayed by this family that had decided not to be what it was. By now Kawa possessed almost nothing. Not even goats. To arrange the last marriage he had had to give up the banana grove. All he had left was the big house and a small field of beans. He and Célestin had been eating beans for a year.

Célestin was not married. He was going to the seminary at Astrida, walking ten kilometres every day there and back, even though he had been offered room and board. He could not leave his father alone on the hill. As an exceptionally gifted student, he had been allowed to continue his studies in spite of his origin. Of the three hundred seminarists, thirty were Hutus, which was how it was in all the country's schools. Célestin was hesitating between the priesthood and teaching. But the bishop decreed that the country was not yet ready to accept a priest of the inferior ethnic group; he could be a brother or a teacher. Kawa's decision was final. Célestin would become a teacher in the city, which would allow him to have profitable associations. And Kawa set out to find him a wife. Célestin was his heart of hearts, the repository of his hopes. Of all his children, he was the tallest and palest. The

Belgian doctor who wrote the big book, learned as he
was, would never guess that Célestin was a Hutu, if
not perhaps for his nose which was a little wide.
Kawa finally found the nose he needed on the neighbouring hill. A nose so fine one would have thought it
had been cut with a razor. A nose with skin so pale
that her family thought Ernestine was sick. A nose so
straight on a body so long and thin that the wind had
nowhere to catch. If the superior blood did its job, the
children of Célestin and Ernestine would be more Tutsi
than the Tutsis. And with Célestin's massive, solid body,
they would be as strong and handsome as gods. Before
making his request, he returned to his old cousin.
Without either cow or goat, he was entitled only to the
saliva, but even that cost him the little bean field.
Nyamaravago said, "You have travelled too far and the
little strength left to you is waning. You think you have
found the key to all your dreams. Open the door and die
happy with your hopes."

The marriage cost the house. Ernestine and
Célestin made their home in Astrida, and Kawa settled
under the fig tree that shaded what had been his house.
Ernestine's father allowed him to live there. He was
brought a handful of beans every day. He died a few
weeks after the marriage, saying to a distant cousin
who happened by, "The children of my children will be
white, but will they recognize me?"

This was the story told by Célestin, Kawa's grandson, to
Gentille, who told it piecemeal to Valcourt. As Valcourt
listened, he sat in the only armchair in the little red-
mud house she shared with a girlfriend in the Muslim

quarter of Nyamirambo, several kilometres from the hotel. A single room, the floor partly covered by two mats. A rickety armchair he had fled to so as not to be standing too close to Gentille. A table and two chairs. Two cardboard suitcases containing all the girls' possessions. On the wall, three colour lithos: the Virgin, the Pope and the president. What was he doing here, still trembling and sweating from every one of his pores, billions of inexhaustible little fountains?

He had just spent another worthless Sunday at the pool. When all the ravens and then the buzzards were perched and the sun had disappeared suddenly behind the wall of eucalyptus trees, when there was no one left but him—as happened every Sunday—and he was growing despondent at the thought of starting another worthless week, Gentille approached his table.

"Monsieur, I beg you, Monsieur," she whispered rather than said, "the governor must be told that I'm not a Tutsi. I don't want to lose my job. I'm a real Hutu. I've got papers to prove it. I'm afraid of being taken for an *inkotanyi*."*

Valcourt pooh-poohed racist theories that claimed to deduce a person's origin from the shape of a nose or a forehead, or the slenderness of a body. But, unwittingly a prisoner of these stereotypes himself, he was surprised to find he didn't really believe her. She was crying softly, resolutely, avoiding his eyes as Rwandans often did. Shyly she came a few tiny steps closer, repeating, "Monsieur, Monsieur, help me." And then suddenly he caught her scent. He was overcome, knocked askew, invaded from every quarter, fingers

* "Cockroach," in Kinyarwanda.

trembling, legs jellylike, body wet, as if hit by an attack of malaria, but with an erection so sudden and painful he let out a low moan. Whatever held all his body parts together to make a human being of him had dissolved. All that was left was an uncontrollable mass of enzymes, glands and molecules.

No, he was not sick, he heard himself say. Yes, he would like a glass of water. No, she mustn't go and get anyone. He just had to be left alone. She promised to come back after tidying up the bar, to show him her identity card. Too much life racing through rusty veins and muscles, too much blood in a heart that had forgotten how to handle sudden ecstasies, too much air in lungs accustomed to breathing stingily.

Gentille really was Hutu according to her identity card. But he still didn't believe her. She wanted to talk to him, but not at the pool or in his room either. Just going to his room would mark her as a hooker and only worsen the constant harassment, for which her beauty alone was responsible; for there was no more silent, cautious, self-restrained woman than Gentille. It was getting late. Valcourt knew she would have to spend half her day's pay to take a taxi. Otherwise, she would have a good hour's walk through a city that the curfew transformed every night into a hunting ground for soldiers and their usually drunken militia acolytes who dispensed HIV like parish priests their indulgences.

He drank a Primus that was as warm as his burning forehead. What could he do for Gentille? Nothing. Sophisticated as he was, a man of the left and an enlightened humanist who knew all about mixed marriages and the transmission of ethnic origin in Rwanda, he didn't really believe her. If an anthropologist needed a photograph to illustrate the archetype of the Tutsi woman, he would have shown him Gentille's. If he, a White who considered himself unprejudiced and free of any preconceived hatreds, did not believe her, what Rwandan would take this piece of cardboard seriously when it declared the opposite of what she showed to such perfection? An accommodating, high-placed lover, a relative or a lecherous civil servant, must certainly have obtained forged papers for her. As for the president's phony nephew who had planted this anxiety in her, Valcourt promised, if ever he saw him again, to swear to him that Gentille was a real Hutu. In any case, danger was on all sides. A discontented Belgian, a drunk and infatuated German, a passing soldier, a love-struck civil servant. All of them possessed her potentially, and all of them could kill her. Increasingly, in Kigali and even more in the countryside, life hung on a word, a whim, a desire, a nose too fine or a leg too long.

And her legs, partly revealed by the way she had hitched her blue skirt onto her knees, were perfect, her ankles smooth and graceful. Valcourt ran his eyes slowly over every part of her body, grateful for the semi-darkness that allowed it undetected.

"You're nice with me. You listen to me and you've never asked anything of me. You're the only White who's never asked me . . . to . . . you know what I mean. You can stay here tonight if you want. I'd like it."

No, she was not afraid to stay alone. She wanted to thank him, and then, there was something else, but she would rather not talk about that now. Thank him for what? What she had just said, for his respect, for never having touched her on the sly, or as if by accident.

Especially for not having done what all the other customers did when signing their chits, saying, "I'll be in my room all evening," showing her their key to make sure she memorized the room number.

"Gentille, I'm not completely different from the customers around the pool. I . . . I want . . . I want you too, you know."

Valcourt felt trapped by his own frankness. For he was firmly convinced that if he did have a chance to lift Gentille's blue skirt up to her navel, it was because he was not like the others who never hid the way they ate her up, sucked at her with their eyes, touched her on the hand or hip as if by accident, called her over and offered her a drink, protection and all the money she wanted.

"You want to be with me? You want to sleep with me? As much as all the others?"

That was it. All her fears were confirmed. Now she understood everything. Like all the others she mistrusted and avoided, he was undressing her, fucking her every time he looked at her. That was it, Valcourt told himself. So why not tell the whole truth? Why keep in what had been tormenting him for these months he had been looking at her?

Her breasts, her mouth, her ass (this was the word he now used, certain to offend her modesty), her dewy-morning, café-au-lait skin, her eyes, her shyness, her sculptural legs, the way she walked, her scent, her hair, her voice, yes, everything about her drove him a little crazy, even if he'd never dared approach her. Yes, like all the others, he wanted to fuck her. There it was, and he was sorry and swore never to talk about it again and he was leaving now, not just saying he was sorry but asking her to forgive him. He went toward the door without conviction.

Again the scent of her washed over him. Paralyzed him. A pornographic smell. Not titillating perfumes or powerful and exotic spices, but a dark smell of flesh, heavy hair and warm, moist sex.

"And I thought you didn't like me and didn't want anything to do with me. You can have me whenever you want. I'd like to be loved by a nice White like you."

Exactly what she should not have said. She wanted a White, a White like any other. A promise of wealth, maybe a visa for somewhere else; and if the blessed Holy Virgin answered her prayer, marriage with a White and a house in a cold country, a clean one. He could hear Raphaël this afternoon at the pool, saying, "Anything to leave this shitty country."

Temporary or permanent mating was a salutary transaction, according to Raphaël. "Forget your White man's love language," he kept telling Valcourt. "Sex with a White man is a lifebuoy. A dress from Paris or from Lévis"—Raphaël had done a financial internship at Quebec's Mouvement Desjardins—"a duty-free piece of jewellery, a little money so you can leave the Muslim quarter and move up the hill into a house with a hedge and a guardian. Then, God willing, liberation, paradise, a shack in Canada or Belgium or France or Tashkent, as long as there are no more Hutus and Tutsis, just Whites who look down on Blacks. Intolerance doesn't kill. Buy me a beer, I'm broke."

"Gentille, I don't want to be a White who gives gifts," Valcourt said. "If you want to leave, I can help you get a visa, but you don't need to sleep with me. Even if it seems ridiculous, all I want is for you to love me a little."

He left without looking back, surprised by his own confession. Love was the only feeling he had ceased to hope for and he had been doing fairly nicely without it. And here he was asking for it.

Chapter Three

On the way home he had to stop three times at
makeshift roadblocks set up by young militiamen of the
government party. Beers in one hand, machetes in
the other, eyes rolling up in their sockets, legs
unsteady. The party had also been distributing a little
marijuana to boost militia fervour. Valcourt had heard
about these idle young men whom the Rwandan
National Movement for Democracy (RNMD) rounded
up and trained, but he was seeing them for the first
time. Officially, they belonged to a youth movement.
Like Boy Scouts, a senior civil servant had told him.
For some time they had been turning up extemporane-
ously in districts of Kigali, particularly Gikondo. They

didn't worry him. "The French are our friends." Thank
you, President Mitterrand, for supporting Franco-
Rwandan friendship.

On her red and green mattress, Gentille cried. He hadn't
understood at all.

Think Gentille. Draw Gentille. Talk about Gentille. With
anybody. But most of all, nurse the sharp pain stabbing
his gut. Build up his feeling of absence and loss. Dream.
Dream. Or else, so as not to die from delusion, find out
that Gentille has been sleeping with all the Whites willing to pay, and then tell himself, I should have known.
And yet she lives so poorly. Her shyness seems so real.
But here, shyness is an acquired behaviour. How could
he be sure she was telling the truth?

At this hour, Olivier, the dining-room maître d', was
probably casting a dejected and disenchanted eye at his
distinguished guests, whom loneliness and Primus or
Mutzig were turning into vulgar, aggressive billygoats.
Valcourt could confide in him, especially since he was
Gentille's boss. Olivier was gentle and fond of laughter.
He did not put on the smarmy lackey obsequiousness so
often found amongst the staff of African luxury hotels.
He respected his employees more than his guests—
although no guest would have suspected this, and even
less the hotel's Belgian management. Only Bertrand,
the chef from Liège, marooned in Rwanda for love of a
Rwandan, then love of her hill, then of the whole coun-
try, knew this. Olivier always ended the evening in
Bertrand's company. The two had only one subject of

conversation, Rwanda, which they both loved passionately but without the blindness of passion. To use an expression that Valcourt prized, they were "men of good counsel," men worth consulting.

With them, he could talk about Gentille.

The hotel bar was shoddy, like a C-grade-movie cocktail lounge in a suburb of Dayton, Ohio, or Shawinigan, Quebec. Dark drapes covered the windows. Armchairs in black leatherette, round Formica-covered tables and two U-shaped banquettes facing a television set that was blathering CNN. Finally, six bar stools that were uncomfortable and too high, occupied by the lonely regulars, drunks most of them, and at midnight, invariably, Bertrand and Olivier.

"Well! The Canadian! A Primus! I've kept you the cold meats left from the German embassy reception. What a long face! You know, in Belgium we'd say a 'mussel face,' all soft inside the shell. Okay, okay, you don't look like you're in the mood for jokes. Take your beer and go see your friend Raphaël. He's been waiting two hours for you." Bertrand jerked his head toward one of the U-shaped banquettes.

Valcourt didn't want to see Raphaël. He would have liked to devote one little hour to his own personal distress.

Raphaël and Méthode were asleep on the far banquette. The two of them had been inseparable since their childhood in Butare, then at school, at the People's Bank, at Lando's restaurant, and with the girls they shared systematically. Two brothers. Even more inseparable in the last two years, since Méthode had found out he had "the sickness," as if not naming AIDS kept it farther away.

Méthode wanted to die at the hotel. In luxury, as he'd said. He especially wanted not to die in the Kigali Hospital Centre's internal medicine building, where two or three lay dying in a single bed, where they'd run out of aspirin three weeks ago, where the Belgian doctors were using this vast reservoir of patients to prepare the scientific papers that would open doors for them at the annual International AIDS Conference. This year the research had reached an even higher pitch of intensity: the conference was being held in Tokyo.

For luxury, Raphaël's small income from his job at the People's Bank couldn't be counted on. It had disappeared almost completely as soon as Méthode developed a mycosis that had to be treated with Nizoral (a week's pay for a week's medication), and each time he was hospitalized. When he was in hospital, to comply with the dictates of the International Monetary Fund, the prescribed costs plus the cost of food and nursing had to be paid. Raphaël had sold his motorbike. Three mycoses, two perfusions and two hospitalizations later and the value of the handlebars was all that remained of Raphaël's nest egg.

Méthode had only a few days left. A week, perhaps two. Raphaël carried him without effort, the way one carries a child, up to Valcourt's room. Méthode now weighed only about forty kilos. An insubstantial, fragile assemblage of memories and vague evocations of what once had been arms, legs, a neck. Only the immensity of the eyes in a face after Giacometti recalled the gentle, handsome ebony head that women used to love.

Méthode gave a weak smile when he heard the sound of water filling the bathtub. A hot bath. This was his first wish. "With lots of foam." The foam was to be

found at the neighbour's in room 314, an Italian consult-
ant by the name of Lisa who dressed from the boutiques
on the Via Condotti in Rome and, for a visiting con-
sultant, had the curious habit of spending her days at
the pool waiting for the leader of the delegation to
return from his work at the World Bank. The latter, a
Christian Democratic deputy whom a whiff of scandal
had caused to be recycled into international development, was conducting a secret meeting of consultants
with Lisa when Valcourt came to ask if she wouldn't
give him a little foaming bath oil.

"At this hour?"

"Yes, it's for a dying man."

This kind of reply, which he had been practising for
some time with ferocious pleasure, brooked no repartee,
provoked embarrassed silence in his interlocutress, and
established a healthy distance.

Méthode wanted to die clean, drunk, stuffed with
food and in front of the television. A triumphant end for
a life of thirty-two years, an end he was no longer afraid
of because he would rather die of AIDS than be hacked
up by a machete or shredded by a grenade. "That's the
fate waiting for all Tutsis. We have to leave or die before
the Holocaust." Since the sickness had been keeping
him in bed, Méthode had been reading everything he
could find about the Jews. Tutsis and Jews—same fate.
The world had known the scientific Holocaust, cold,
technological, a terrifying masterpiece of efficiency and
organization. A monstrosity of Western civilization. The
original sin of Whites. Here, it would be the barbarian
Holocaust, the cataclysm of the poor, the triumph of
machete and club. Already, in the province of Bugesera,
corpses were afloat on Lake Mugesera, drifting toward

the Kagera, the legendary source of the Nile. This was the way to send the Tutsis back to where they came from, to Egypt—as loudly declared by Monsieur Léon, who owned a fine house in Quebec and here was behaving like a little Hitler. It would be dirty, ugly, lots of severed arms and legs, women with bellies ripped, children with feet cut off, so these Tutsi cockroaches could never again walk and fight. Méthode wasn't sad about dying. He was relieved.

Raphaël and Valcourt sit on the edge of the bathtub looking away while Méthode talks. A faint, muffled voice that needs a push to begin each sentence. Where he finds the strength for the push, God knows, but he finds it and then hurries as if to arrive before running out of breath.

"You blind or what? . . . You can't see? Everyone's pissing off. Before, we pretended, we lived, for a few hours anyway; we talked, for a few minutes anyway." Silence, breathing that reaches down almost to his feet for its base. Silence, breathing that comes from as far away as the belly of the earth and rumbles like a volcano. "Today, somebody comes in, we say, he's Tutsi, Hutu, he's got AIDS . . . We're often wrong, but it doesn't matter. We live so much with fear it makes us feel better to finger the enemy, and if we can't guess who he is, we invent him."

Silence. He tries to continue, but all his friends can hear is the gurgling of an animal being strangled, then his head falls to the side, like a goat's at the end of a long, broken neck, a comatose head slipping into the foam that fills the bathroom with voluptuous smells and perfumes.

Raphaël and Valcourt both wish Méthode were dead already.

It is not to be on this night.

Méthode whistles, emits some throaty rattles, snores, hiccups, then falls into a sleep that is not far from death. Raphaël settles on the other bed without unmaking it, seated rather than stretched out, his eyes fixed on the television which, with breathless admiration, is giving an account of the latest autumn-winter fashion creations.

"They've all got AIDS, those girls," Méthode murmurs. "Thin like me, huge eyes like mine, and arms and legs like mine too . . . I want a real woman before I die, with breasts that bulge out of her dress, and hands and a bum, a real bum."

He still has desire, and desire is suffocating him as much as his tuberculosis-riddled lungs. In his throat a rattle says, "A real woman." Then the rattle falls asleep.

On the balcony, Valcourt is trying to sleep in a low chair made of plastic like all the others. There's plastic everywhere in this hotel plunked down in a land full of wood.

"Claudia Schiffer's beautiful?" Raphaël asks Valcourt.

"No, I like Gentille better, now let me go to sleep."

"You don't sleep beside a dying man. You keep watch. And then, we have to find him a real woman . . . you know, with a negro's breasts and ass and thighs. He's not modern like me . . . he still likes negro women. We'll go and ask Agathe tomorrow. He's always wanted Agathe."

———

In the morning, life wakens as if a whole city were emerging from a coma, astonished to be alive even as it counts its dead. Many people in this country have the courtesy or forethought to die during the night, as if they did not wish to disturb the living.

Before the humans, long before the roosters and the jackdaws, the dogs raise the first cry; a whole clamorous, howling fauna whose wails and lamentations pierce the pockets of iridescent mist that fill the hundred valleys running this way and that through the city. On the balcony of room 312, perched on Kigali's highest hill, a soul at peace with itself could easily think it was in paradise, looking down on these tattered clouds that hide the thousands of oil lamps being lit, the babies and old people coughing their lungs out, the stinking cooking fires, and corn and sorghum cooking. This mist, which little by little takes on all the colours of the rainbow, acts as a protective Technicolor cushion, a filter that lets only shadows, sparkles, and faint and fleeting sounds pass through from the real world. This, thinks Valcourt, is how God must see and hear our constant activity. As if on a giant movie screen with Dolby quadrophonic sound, while drinking some kind of mead and nibbling on celestial popcorn. An interested but distant spectator. This is how the Whites at the hotel, instant minor gods, hear and figure Africa. Close enough to talk about it, even to write about it. But at the same time so isolated with their portable computers in their antiseptic rooms, and in their air-conditioned Toyotas, so surrounded by little Blacks trying to be like Whites that they think Black is the smell of the perfumes and cheap ointments sold in the Nairobi duty-free shop.

A grenade explodes, probably the last for the night because the mist is dissipating. This is the hour when killers go home to bed.

A man so young and handsome should die fulfilled, if only through his eyes. For only his eyes and ears (his friends would have to think of music) might still bring him some pleasure. He wanted to fly away with the memory of "a real woman." Agathe—who wanted to change her first name because it was the same as the president's wife's—would do the trick. She had bigger breasts than Jayne Mansfield and more ass than Josephine Baker. Plus a smile like a billboard permanently positioned on her face, laughing eyes, unruly hair, and a mouth as juicy as grenadine. A capable woman, Agathe, proprietor of the hotel hairdressing salon—proprietor, yes, and also madam, for while women did come here to have their hair done, generally in a European style, it was also here that the girls' territory and prices were negotiated, and many other things too, like the marijuana that came directly from the forest of Nyungwe, the private domain of the president, brought weekly by a libidinous colonel who required payment in kind and without a condom. Agathe, in whom a terror of poverty and contemplation of the "wealth" of Whites had implanted a firmly entrenched capitalist sensibility, called this "risk capital." She was obeying the laws of the marketplace.

From the Avenue of the Republic encircling the hotel came sounds of hotel staff approaching, soon to begin their sixteen-hour day, footsteps already heavy. In a few movements repeated for the thousandth time, they would slip into a white shirt, a bow tie and a smile too broad that must stand up to sixteen hours of temperament, condescension, impatience, ill-concealed mistrust and sometimes a kind of Third Worldism so pleasantly warm that the employee would paint his situation the blacker to please the lonesome White. To start a real conversation, the latter would do better to ask, "How are your children?" than, "Do your children have enough to eat?"

No one ever wondered why the employees' smiles showed so many teeth and so little in their eyes. Valcourt called this "the dichotomous smile."

There was a knock at the door. Raphaël was snoring. Méthode's breath was rattling in his throat. Zozo, who was just beginning his day, knew everything. He had come to see the patient and also to warn everybody that the hotel management would not be pleased to have a respectable hotel room turned into a hospital room for a guest suffering from a shameful sickness and one furthermore so contagious. He liked Méthode, but not to the point of letting him die in his hotel. The other staff might refuse to work on this floor and certainly wouldn't do the room. The hospital would be a better place. He offered to put Valcourt in touch with a cousin who worked at the hospital and reminded him that hotel policy, with which he himself disagreed profoundly, was now very strict.

"An additional night must be paid for every person not registered who spends the night in the room of a guest, even if the guest is a good guest like you, Monsieur Bernard. Unless, of course, the additional night is occasioned by a lady friend of yours, Monsieur Bernard. And my cousin is a graduate nurse and has a lot of influence."

Zozo was always anxious to be of service because he had to feed a great many children and could not manage it on the pay of a minor flunky. Only his clientele's generosity enabled him to keep the whole brood alive. And so, as a result of his love for his family and a few thousand francs slipped to him by Valcourt "for the children," the Kigali Hospital Centre was relieved of several bags of aqueous solution and a bedpan. The cousin was not in fact a graduate nurse but a stock-keeper in the pharmacy. He wielded no influence but, resourceful and wily, kept his extended family supplied with medicines and bandages.

Élise, a Canadian nurse more stubborn than a mule and more generous than a field of poppies, administered the perfusion. Méthode would die in a private room at the hotel, as he wished. A steady stream of visitors began to arrive. Immediate then distant relatives, friends, colleagues at work and finally vague acquaintances. Méthode would smile sometimes. He did not know that so many people loved him. A medical inspector, accompanied by a policeman, had come and seen that no by-law had been infringed, especially having discovered in conversation with Raphaël that he himself was related to the dying man. He was pleased to deliver a certificate attesting that the patient could not be moved. He went through the motions of refusing the five thousand francs offered him, but thought about his many children and the fact that he had not been paid for three months. Worse, his small medicine business was doing badly. The pharmacy had been out of aspirin for a month and had not had a glimpse of an antibiotic for two weeks. He had tried to sell off some of the anti-tuberculosis medicines but without much success, because the missionaries were handing them out free and there were almost as many missionaries as there were tubercular patients.

The Belgian manager, Monsieur Dik, who had summoned the medical inspector but forgotten to offer him a gift, arrived with his large pustulous nose at the door left open to accommodate the constant coming and going. He was greeted by Agathe, who regularly offered him her mounts and hills of firm flesh in recognition of friendship or rent in arrears. Madame Agathe made use of her opulent body the way others use their chequebooks. He had fondled, caressed, sucked the breasts she had presented to him one after the other the way one offers cakes to a greedy child. He had pawed her buttocks and slipped his hands between her humid thighs. And he had come while doing it. But he had never seen Agathe naked. Frugally, she did not waste her assets and saved some of her capital for grand occasions. When the manager cried, "Monsieur Bernard, this cannot go on . . . ," she clasped the little man to her bosom and literally carried him into the bathroom.

"Monsieur Dik, I'm taking you to paradise." And she closed the door.

Five minutes later, still quivering with pleasure, the manager came to speak to Méthode with all the respect and studied compassion that courtesy and circumstance required.

Then Méthode's mother arrived and the visitors withdrew. Marguerite Izimana's face, like an emaciated cat's, was deeply furrowed, her eyes empty and her gaze fixed. She sat on a straight chair and took Méthode's hand; he gave a faint smile of recognition. She did not look at him. She alone of the whole hill had known that her son was suffering from "the sickness." She was not ashamed, no, but she did not wish to be troubled by the gossip, the rejection, the judgments and the scorn. If Méthode was dying of a shameful sickness it was because he was born in shame. The shame of poverty, of discrimination, of university education denied, grants refused, of land and house so tiny that he had soon left for the city, the shame of being unable to marry because of poverty and inadequate housing, then a girl for a few brochettes and a beer, a girl to help forget fear and time in jail, a girl for a quick little orgasm, that's not a sin, that's an imitation of happiness. This is what she was thinking as she murmured what ought to have been prayers. And then, to die at thirty-two, or at forty butchered by drunken soldiers, or at forty-two of malaria, or at fifty-five, like her, of weariness and heartbreak . . . What's the difference?

"Dying is not a sin" was the only thing she had come to say to him, and she gently placed her other hand on her son's glistening forehead, whereupon he closed his eyes and let his last tear fall. The last tear is death's beginning.

Finally soothed and free, Méthode repeated, "Dying is not a sin." Then, slightly raising his head, "We must tell them," he said. Marguerite Izimana nodded and turned to Valcourt. In her eyes there was neither appeal nor interrogation, just a command. Awed by this dark solemnity, Valcourt stepped forward.

"You want to speak to me, Méthode?"

"Yes, but not just to you, to a lot of people . . . on the television . . . with the film you wanted to make with me. Let's make the film. I'm going to rest, build up my strength, then we'll make the film and you'll show it to them. And then . . . I'll go."

Méthode closed his eyes and his mother closed hers. The two settled down calmly to wait.

Méthode emerged from his sleep, his stupor, his silence or semi-coma—how could anyone tell which?—only in late afternoon, jerked from his limbo by the harsh, strident calls of the jackdaws and buzzards arriving as the Whites returned from their aid work and deal-making. Méthode's mother, like a seated tombstone figure, had not moved, had not let go of her son's hand for a second. Only her shoulders, which would hunch suddenly whenever Méthode's breath became more gasping, showed there was life left in a body made of knots, bones and skin stretched and dry, creviced by thousands of fine wrinkles, like the furrows the country people plow on their hills.

On the long, low dresser along the wall facing the two beds, Valcourt had ordered food and a bar set out.

"We're going to eat, drink and fuck," said Méthode, adding with the smile of a kid surprised by his own audacity that he was glad his mother didn't understand French.

Then in Kinyarwanda:

"Maman, don't be sad, I'm going to have a beautiful death."

"For a young man, there's no such thing as a beautiful death. Or a death that makes sense. All children's deaths are ugly and senseless."

André, who had learned in Quebec how to make Rwandans aware of condoms and abstinence, was the first to arrive for this funerary feast, which Méthode called the Last Supper, though he was quick to add, with a little laugh broken by coughing, that he did not

take himself for Jesus Christ. Then came Raphaël with
some colleagues from the bank, and Élise, her arms full
of flowers and her handbag full of morphine, which an
understanding and ill-paid friend had obtained for ten
dollars American. Finally Agathe, accompanied by three
of her girls because a party without free girls is not a
party. The girls would not kiss the dying man or even
shake his hand. Méthode was too charmed with everything to insist. On the contrary. He was delighted the
girls thought they might catch the sickness, even with
the merest touch of their lips or fingers. Fear had got to
them, and though unjustified, it was a fear, a terror
almost, that he and so many of his friends had never
felt. His death would not have been in vain.

When the first fevers had taken him, he had thought
of malaria. The first diarrhea attacks had not surprised
him. Sick goat's meat or polluted water. The ten kilos he
lost in a few weeks were certainly food poisoning, that
rotten goat he had eaten at Lando's, or maybe the grilled
tilapias at the Cosmos that had left an aftertaste. The
sores in his mouth hadn't surprised him either, any more
than the tuberculosis that floored him so suddenly. He
took a room in the intellectuals' building at the Kigali
Hospital Centre so as not to have to share a bed with
someone who had diphtheria or pustulant scabies. The
sickness appeared to him along with the face of a
Belgian doctor, the head of internal medicine, who knew
well that it was penetrating everywhere, multiplying
faster than rabbits, and that this was giving him a long
head start on his Western colleagues. All these patients,
this constantly replenished horde of ignorant people at
his disposal, and the sickness progressing at lightning
speed but with its own characteristics here—all of it

could lead to an important discovery, and even wealth. For example, the almost total absence of Kaposi's sarcoma in Blacks, and the frizzy hair becoming straight and supple like blades of grass or the hair of Whites. AIDS might hold the secret of a miracle cosmetic product that would make its inventor a billionaire in Belgian francs. Think of all those African women dreaming of having hair like Claudia Schiffer's! The Belgian doctor, who had never been sick, dreamed of his Mercedes while listening to Méthode describe his latest health problems. He didn't need to listen, not really. He had already seen enough, from the colour of his eyes, from his thinness, from the sores scattered around the insides of his cheeks because Méthode had only been able to afford one week's treatment with Nizoral. And then that tuberculosis. "A classic symptom," the textbooks said. AIDS 101.

"Perhaps you should have the Test."

The Test. There was only one test they were talking about when the tone of voice put a capital on the word. They did the others without telling you and gave you the results if ever you screwed up the courage to ask a question of a KHC doctor. But *the* Test was not done at the KHC; Québécois aid workers in a building near the hospital were responsible for that. And when the White doctor sent you to them, the reason was clear.

Élise understood instantly when she saw Méthode sit down painfully in her little office and say in a low voice, "I've come for the Test."

Two years in Rwanda; hundreds, thousands of AIDS patients. The same cautions tirelessly repeated, the words a thousand times said announcing the end, the encouragements whose effectiveness she doubted, this permanent companionship with the death of people

she learned to love day by day as they confided in her—
nothing undermined her determination.

Élise was a specialist in life which she devoured
with gusto in order to forget that her routine contact
was death. She offered her plump but firm little body
to anyone who would remind her of life triumphant.
She had loved a South American terrorist, fought for
abortion on demand in the 1970s in Quebec, and was
convinced that in this far-off country, in this festering
hell, she could make a difference. Back home, everything was so easy. Here, everything had to be started
from scratch. With Méthode, this meant finding the
words, the phrases, the smiles that would set him com-
fortably and with dignity on the short path leading to
the end. Élise and Méthode had thus become friends,
confidants and almost lovers, as ordained by lympho-
cytes and mycoses, to the tempo of tuberculosis and
attacks of diarrhea. Méthode's disintegration drew
them together. Never had a patient moved her this
much. Méthode did not know it. He took Élise's atten-
tions as the bounden duty of the White aid worker come
to help the negroes, though he was fond of his nurse,
rather as one loves a sister. Until he understood that
Élise was ready to commit a crime so that he could die
when he was ready, when he had had enough of turning
into a skeleton, an imitation mummy.

She had said to him, "When you're fed up with being
in pain, tell me. You'll fly away like a little bird. Softly."

Élise was there. Heavy-hearted but smiling. With
her vials of morphine, her syringes and a huge glass of
whisky in her hand. Méthode would do what he had
promised and then leave, borne on the chemical wings
she would give him. Méthode, who so loved life, was

happy to be able to die this way. He whispered to Raphaël, "Even rich people in the United States don't have beautiful deaths like this." And to Valcourt he said, "I'm going to do you a good film that'll make you rich." And he dozed off again while Agathe was wondering whether, before going to paradise, he wouldn't like a last knowing, expert manipulation of that damned member that was now taking him to the grave because it had dipped here, there and everywhere unprotected. Dying without one last orgasm, she said to one of her hairdressers, is like dying alone and loveless. The hairdresser agreed and volunteered to help this young man, who once had driven all the young girls of Kigali wild, get it up. However, she would wear gloves to present her last sexual respects. She was HIV positive and knew it, but she did not want to become twice positive.

She sat down beside the thin body, next to Méthode's mother, who was still holding her son's hand. With her gloved hand she groped under the sheet and found a small penis, all shrivelled up, and began to caress it with skill she had never before used, professional hooker that she was, experienced as she believed herself to be. With a delicacy and unhurried tenderness that was a blend of respect and manual adoration.

"Give him a nice big one before he leaves for heaven, my girl," said his mother. But Mathilde knew that a hand was not going to be enough. She would have to do what she had always refused to do for insistent European johns; heaven was not within reach of a hand but of a mouth.

The friends put down their glasses, Agathe quickly swallowed her canapé. All gathered religiously around the bed, holding their breath and admiring. It was the mother who drew back the sheet and untied the belt of the bathrobe. It was the mother who placed her hand on Mathilde's head, who pushed it gently between the two bones passing as legs and said, "Suck it, suck it, so a last drop of life can come out of him." And Mathilde took the inert member in her wide mouth and worked it with her tongue and lips. Slowly, the way clay is thrown on a potter's wheel, her patient sucking restored a semblance of shape to the penis of the living dead man. Méthode murmured, "I have no penis left, I have no sperm left. Your tongue is like a serpent bewitching me, but my tongue is still alive, let me drink you." Without a word, Mathilde undressed, and supported by his mother and Raphaël, applied her crotch to Méthode's mouth. Exhausted, sated, satisfied, fulfilled, trembling, she collapsed on Méthode, who uttered a loud cry of pain.

The party was over. Élise stayed to administer the death, but most of all to love Méthode all the way to the last second. Méthode's mother left for her hill. She did not want to see her son die and hoped he would fly away with his mind at peace, without having to bear the additional pain of a final separation.

Méthode was sleeping. Valcourt set up the camera facing the bed in a position that would film the dying man from above. When he woke, the camera would make a single, slow panning movement. First it would remain fixed on the long-limbed body for five seconds, then for another five seconds would slowly pan up to the face, close in for a further five seconds, slowly, very slowly as in a funeral march, and stop. All that would then be seen would be a close-up of the diminished face and the immensity of those eyes, which would speak more eloquently even than the mouth.

Chapter Four

———————

Gentille came five minutes before starting work at six in the morning. She did not knock. She came in and went to Valcourt who was sitting on the bed beside Méthode's corpse.

"My condolences," she said, holding out her hand to him.

"Thank you. You're not too tired?"

"No, I'm okay. You know, I think I may be related to Méthode. My parents and his come from the same hill. He's Tutsi and I'm Hutu, but that doesn't mean anything."

Valcourt wasn't really listening, he was lost in her breasts, which were exactly at eye level. He wanted to say, Gentille, I love you. He wanted to put out his hand, he wanted to stand up and take her in his arms. He did none of these things. She left without another word.

With a yardstick Zozo had brought, he measured Méthode and left for the coffin market, which shared space with the iron market beside a barracks. The coffin makers could no longer keep up with the demand. They had been making beds, tables and chairs until very recently, but the death market, spurred by grenades, guns and AIDS, was growing exponentially. In Kigali, a coffin is a wooden box made of a few badly squared boards, sometimes decorated with a crucifix in a burst of extravagance or folly brought on by the pain of bereavement. Valcourt chose the wood carefully: fine boards that were pale in colour and free of knots. He gave the dimensions and asked that the box be delivered to his room. Next he went to see a sculptor friend who sold multicoloured giraffes and elephants to the two or three tourists a week who still came to Rwanda to see the gorillas and volcanoes.

"Make me a disco cross for Kigali's best DJ."

There were around a hundred people in the hotel conference hall. In the aisle separating the two sections of straight chairs was the wooden box, not even varnished. Some relatives and close friends had come, but also colleagues from work at the People's Bank and the minister responsible for the financial institution, flanked by two young soldiers nonchalantly carrying their Uzi automatic rifles, courtesy of Israel via France and Zaïre. All Agathe's girls were present, as were Lando and his Québécoise wife, and several men who remained discreetly at the back of the room and were quickly associated with the Rwandan Patriotic Front, the clandestine army of the Tutsis. For Méthode, it was rumoured around the pool, had been a member of the undercover army, like Raphaël.

On the left behind the minister sat the few officials and Hutus close to power who felt obliged to attend this bizarre funeral. On the right were all the Tutsis, the Hutu friends of the Liberal Party and the Social Democratic Party, and all the women Méthode had laid.

A television set occupied a place of honour over the coffin. The emaciated face appeared with huge burning coals for eyes. The lips barely moved. It was the eyes that spoke.

"My name is Méthode. I work at the People's Bank. Weekends I'm disc jockey at Lando's discotheque. My favourite music is country and love songs. I'm Tutsi, you know that, but above all I'm Rwandan. I'm going to die in a few hours, I'm going to die of AIDS, a sickness the government says didn't exist a few years ago, when it was already destroying my blood. I still don't understand much about how the sickness works, but we'll say it's like a country that catches all the defects of its sickest people, and each of these defects turns into a sickness that attacks a different part of the body or the country. That's pretty well what I've learned about it, it's a kind of madness in the human body, which succumbs piece by piece to all its weaknesses.

"To those who love me, I want to say that I didn't die in pain. A friend kissed me and told me I would wake up in heaven. I died in my sleep. I felt nothing. In fact, it's as if I didn't know I was dead. But I know that if we carry on this way, a great many of you will suffer frightful pain and die appalling deaths.

"But I want to talk some more about the sickness. We refuse to talk about it, and staying silent kills. We know that a condom protects, but we big strong black men go through life as though we're immortal. My friend Élise calls that magic thinking. We tell ourselves the sickness won't happen to us and we fuck and fuck like blind men, with our cocks naked in the belly of the sickness. I'm telling you, and this is why I want to talk to you before I die, that millions of us are going to die. Of AIDS, of course, of malaria too, but most of all from a worse sickness for which there's no condom or vaccine. This sickness is hate. In this country there are people who sow hate the way ignorant men sow death with their sperm in the bellies of women, who carry it away to other men, and to the children they conceive . . . Could I have a little water?"

A hand holding a glass of water appears in the picture. Méthode drinks and chokes. He takes some more, more slowly.

"I'm dying of AIDS, but I'm dying by accident. I didn't choose, it was a mistake. I thought it was a White's or homosexual's or monkey's or druggie's sickness. I was born a Tutsi, it's written on my identity card, but I'm a Tutsi by accident. I didn't choose, that was a mistake too. My great-grandfather learned from the Whites that the Tutsis were superior to the Hutus. He was Hutu. He did everything possible so his children and grandchildren would become Tutsis. So here I am, a Hutu-Tutsi and victim of AIDS, possessor of all the sicknesses that are going to destroy us. Look at me, I'm your mirror, your double who's rotting from inside. I'm dying a bit earlier than you, that's all."

The minister stood up and shouted, "It's a disgrace!" He stormed out. The effect was to wake his two body- guards, who had fallen asleep. The dignitaries, the Hutus and the two representatives of the Swiss embassy, which was subsidizing the People's Bank, followed.

"I'm dying happy because I've spoken at last. Goodbye and may the Lord bless you."

Standing at the back of the wide, cold, ugly hall, Gentille was crying. When Valcourt came to see her she said, "Méthode's right. Promise me you'll take me with you when you leave, I don't want to die."

Valcourt put his trembling hand on her cheek. "I promise."

His world flipped. Uttering two words had brought him back to life. He had come here to live at a leisurely pace, with no goal, ambition or passion. All he had wanted was to go to the end of his own path without deceit, but at the same time without getting involved or taking sides in anything. One day he had written, "We are inevitably prisoners of the words we speak." Oscillating between anxiety and happiness, he set off with the gang to get drunk at Lando's, prisoner of the last words he had spoken.

He had barely sat down before he began to miss Gentille, who had not been able to leave work. He got up and left the friends crowding around a long table, which in a flash was covered with big Primus bottles, and went to sit in a corner at a rickety table. It rapped on the cement floor every time he leaned on it as he watched the Lyon–Monaco soccer match being televised by Radio-Française Internationale.

Lando came and joined him with a bottle of Johnny Walker Black and two beer glasses, which he filled. They were going to get very drunk.

"Méthode dreamed of going to Quebec, the way his friend Raphaël did. You don't know how he envied him for having done it. In a way I can understand that. It's fun to be there. You're so far away from everything."

Landouald then talked about Quebec's Grande Allée and the people of the city, gently poking fun at their small-town reserve, and about his political science professors at Laval University. When he had talked to them of Rwandan excesses, corruption, violence, his Québécois Third World–enthusiast profs had told him he was talking like "a colonial."

"I sometimes had the strange impression that the oppressed Blacks were the ones driving round in their Volvos and I was just a naive little White who wanted to exploit Africa."

Valcourt smiled and emptied his glass. His friend did likewise but without a smile.

"You should leave, Bernard. Our friend Méthode was more observant than I thought. He was right. The big bloodbath is brewing, bigger than all the others Rwanda and Burundi have seen. Our only chance is the Blue Berets and your Canadian general. But as Hélène says— mind you, she's a separatist—he's a real Canadian, an imitation Swiss, a civil servant who follows procedure to the letter. Here, if you follow procedure, you're a hundred corpses late. Drink up. Come and see."

Lando held Bernard by the shoulder. Since he was tall and limped, there was more weight than grip. They walked the length of the bar and crossed the restaurant parking lot to the traffic circle. It was well past the curfew. In theory, only "humanitarians," which is to say Whites, doctors and of course soldiers, still had the right to be out and about. "The vultures," as Lando called them, were patrolling the traffic circle. There were around twenty of them. They were neither policemen nor regular soldiers.

"Hello, gentlemen of the presidential guard," called Lando. "I drink to the health of Rwanda. Would you like to drink with us? No, you would not like to drink with us. You are Hutus, real Rwandans, and I am a villainous Tutsi, a false Rwandan. You are only awaiting the command that will kill me. That is not tonight, I know, but which of my friends will you kill when he leaves here? Which one will you follow patiently all the way home so he can die in front of his children and neighbours?"

The soldiers burst out laughing. Then came the abusive language and insults: all Tutsis were sons of bitches and Lando more than all the rest, he's not a negro anymore because he sleeps with a White. The dull thud of a grenade exploding came from downtown. Flames licked at the purple sky near the national stadium, a neighbourhood where mostly Tutsis lived. Lando gripped his friend a little tighter.

"You still don't understand. Good little Westerner that you are, all tied up with fine sentiments and noble principles, you're witnessing the beginning of the end of the world. We're going to plunge into a horror never seen before in history. We're going to rape, cut throats, chop, butcher. We're going to cut open women's bellies before the eyes of their husbands, then mutilate the husbands before the wives die of loss of blood, to make sure they see each other die. And while they're dying, coming to their last breath, we'll rape their daughters, not just once but ten times, twenty times. And the virgins will be raped by soldiers with AIDS. We'll have the savage efficiency of the primitive and the poor. With machetes, knives and clubs we'll do better than the Americans with their smart bombs. But it won't be a war for television. You won't be able to stand fifteen minutes of our wars and massacres. They're ugly and you'll think they're inhuman. It's the lot of the poor not to know how to murder cleanly, with surgical precision, as the parrots of CNN say after their briefings from the generals. Here, we're going to kill in a great, wild excess of madness, beer and pot, in an unleashing of hate and distrust that'll be beyond your capacity to understand, and mine as well. I say 'we' because I'm Rwandan and because the Tutsis will do it too when they get the chance. I say 'we' because we've all gone mad."

"I don't want to leave."

"You're crazier than I thought."

"No, I'm in love. It's the same thing."

From Sodoma, the hookers' quarter, a bucolic landscape can be seen several hundred metres away. A hill where the earth is always freshly turned and dotted with pretty flowers. The view is beautiful from Sodoma. A CIDA official on a visit to ascertain whether the money Canada was giving to the fight against AIDS was being well spent said to his Rwandan escort:

"So you have community gardens too?"

He has to be forgiven. On this hill there's a constant coming and going, with people hoeing, digging and turning the earth. From a distance it looks as though they're working at small plots, carefully and methodically cultivated, such as one sees on vacant lots in poor districts of Montreal.

"No, that's the new cemetery," replied the escort. "There's no room left in the others."

The cross Valcourt had ordered was perfect, twisted like a dead tree, all yellow, blue and green, with a body not of Christ but of Johnny Cash, not a perfect likeness but recognizable because the sculptor had engraved the name.

Valcourt was there, and Élise, and Father Louis, the calm, stubborn old priest from Champagne, who by himself cared for more AIDS sufferers than all the humanitarian organizations in the country. They listened to Johnny Cash while two teenagers finished digging a hole deep enough to hold the box. They kept turning their heads to look in all directions but no one else arrived except other groups coming to bury their own dead. Then a few soldiers came prowling like jackals, just close enough to be noticed. At this mid-morning hour in this city of five hundred thousand souls, ten gaping holes awaited their boxes, and there would be ten more later, around midday. There would be scores of others by late afternoon, when the sun would beat less directly on the coffins.

A muddy black Volvo appeared. Lando's car. Lando got out with a huge bouquet of flowers, which he let drop into the bottom of the hole. They mustn't wait any longer for anyone else to come, he said. At the bank, he explained, employees who might be tempted to be absent had been threatened with dismissal. The private radio station, Radio Mille-Collines, which had just begun broadcasting, was announcing that a terrorist named Méthode had died the previous day and the local militia would consider anyone seen at his burial as an accomplice to be eliminated. And then, during the night, Raphaël's house had been burned. Raphaël had taken refuge at Élise's. Élise had said nothing about this, not wanting to alarm anyone. She shrugged an apology, and Father Louis said a few words in Latin, which he persisted in using in moments of solemnity or when he was officiating for friends. Then he sprinkled the box with holy water and said:

"Méthode, you do not need my benediction or my prayers. All you asked of life was simply the pleasure of life. And you have died of it. While you have committed a thousand mortal sins, your words yesterday may ensure your redemption . . ."

He broke off because he had seen Gentille approaching. She had just passed the group of soldiers, who were insulting her profusely. In one hand she held her black leather shoes and in the other a bouquet of blue irises. She walked in a straight line, resolutely, like someone with a mission to accomplish.

"I took the morning off," she whispered to Valcourt. "I had to be here with you. I didn't really come for Méthode. Forgive me for being so frank." She took his hand and gave it a little squeeze. The soldiers came closer, laughing.

Dozens of jackdaws wheeled patiently over the cemetery. In the distance a family approached, carrying a body on a stretcher, and behind them other mourners, tired out from climbing the hill. Six bodies now were waiting for the gravediggers to finish with Méthode's and dig holes for them. A dismal cacophony rose skyward—a confusion of hymns, hysterical weeping, and the roaring of engines and blaring of horns from dilapidated trucks on the Mombasa–Kampala road, the AIDS freeway. For in the valley between the cemetery and Sodoma stood the smoky, smelly truck stop. You parked your truck, you climbed the Sodoma hill to drink a few Primuses and shoot your wad, and a while later you ended up in a hole on the hill opposite.

Father Louis resumed his sermon.

"We are here to honour the dignity of a man who dared to speak out. I am here to tell him that the gates of paradise are open for him. Can we reproach a man for dying because he wanted to love? My faith reassures me but leaves me powerless to act, except, like Méthode, through words. And so I say that here in Rwanda we are approaching the limits of humanity, we are in danger of falling into insanity, into a madness that will be beyond our own understanding. I would like to reassure you and I cannot."

The priest straightened his shoulders and with sweeping gestures traced a benediction that cut across the sky, as though blessing the entire country.

Once the hole was filled with earth, they put a circle of stones around the psychedelic cross. Gentille placed her bouquet of irises and then they all piled into Lando's Volvo, since the truck that had brought them had left to get another wooden box.

Near the mosque on the way out of Nyamirambo, some young men of the Hutu militia were running about among the cars and minibuses trying to sell one of the many extremist rags whose publication the regime encouraged. Lando stopped and bought a copy of *Ijambo.*

"What are our killers saying today?"

And he handed the badly printed little weekly to Father Louis.

"They're talking about Raphaël, who owes his advancement only to his sisters who he's put into the bed of the White manager of the People's Banks. And about you, Lando, who, to thank the manager, Raphaël and Méthode for the credits you've been given by the Banks, have provided them with rooms in your hotel for entertaining prostitutes . . . Tutsis, of course."*

"Gentille," Lando said, "you've got yourself in a heap of shit. You can't go home, not for now anyway."

Gentille said not a word because she was busy letting Valcourt know discreetly that if her thigh was pressed against his it was not because of the car's cramped space, any more than the fact that her elbow had gradually slipped into the bend of his arm. Valcourt was not a fool. He was living in this country partly because he had often waded blindly into murky waters for no more than an insistent thigh or an innocently nestling elbow. He had got carried away for a lot less— a glance, a smile, a way of moving. In Montreal he had followed one of those dancers who float almost on the surface of life all the way down into the black hole of heroin. He had fled successfully in time, but had remained bruised and broken in the most vital of a man's possessions, confidence in the object of his love. How warm was this thigh! How fragile and delicate this elbow! But Valcourt had not left his country in order to live more or better. All he had craved was the right to drowse in peace. And here he was being woken, jolted like a child being told he'll be late for the party. He had promised, of course. He would not abandon Gentille, he

*Summary of an article that appeared in the weekly *Ijambo* in November 1991.

would keep her with him, protect her, a little like an adopted daughter. This was the lie Valcourt told himself, paralyzed by the fear of re-entering life fully, and perhaps even more of being unable to give those breasts the caresses they expected, or that sex—whose scent and taste he had already invented—a sex that could satisfy it. He was sweating huge drops and shivering at the same time.

"Are you all right?" she said, taking his hand.

He said nothing but did not withdraw his hand, which she squeezed gently. He squeezed hers, closed his eyes, rested his head back against the seat. God was offering him the most beautiful of his daughters. Never had he felt so old, so close to the end, but at the same time so free. This scared him more than anything. He had always believed that absolute freedom was a prison. Never had he been so afraid of the acts he was going to perform, for he was having forebodings about them already. He was measuring the depth of the happiness promised him, and of the pain into which he was willingly, knowingly, rushing headlong.

He squeezed Gentille's hand a bit tighter, then looked straight into her eyes for the first time. She gave a shy little smile with her moist lips. He closed his eyes, hoping that everything would freeze then and there, that life would stop at this precise moment. Then his body relaxed. Muscle by muscle. He could have described the exact sequence, as if a twisted skein were undoing itself before his eyes, each thread taking its proper place in an orderly, harmonious tapestry.

They did not say a word all the way to the hotel. Lando, with a sad smile, had observed the whole scene in his rear-view mirror.

"Come on, friends, we're all going to celebrate Méthode's life. You're my guests. My goat brochettes are better than the European buffet at the Mille-Collines, but they do have a more sophisticated wine list."

Gentille walked across the parking lot toward the hotel entrance. Valcourt stopped to watch her rearranging space into graceful, sensual curves. She turned, worried not to see him beside her.

"Okay?"

"I'm watching you walk and I like it, it scares me how much I like it."

They entered the lobby hand in hand. Zozo froze. So did the assistant manager who was passing by, though it did not prevent him from saying:

"Mademoiselle Gentille, you are dismissed for unauthorized absence."

"If you only knew how little they care," Lando shot at him scornfully.

Gentille and Valcourt went up to Valcourt's room. He gestured at the bed by the sliding door opening onto the balcony.

"You'll sleep there tonight."

"What about you?"

"In the other bed."

"I'll feel farther away than if I was sleeping at home."

"No. I'll hear you breathe while you're sleeping. You'll hear me snore. Your smell will get into the sheets and penetrate the walls and carpet. You'll smell my scent, which is now only what's given off by lotions and toilet waters and aging skin. You may soon get tired of it. You Blacks often say we Whites give off a dead-body smell, a medicinal smell. Our emanations make you think of test tubes and laboratories. And then, I need time, Gentille. We shall see, we shall see."

"You don't love me."

"I love you too much already. And what do you know about love, little girl? Because that's my whole problem. You're only a little girl."

"I'm not a little girl. I'm twenty-two and here, at my age, a girl has seen a lot of things. And you never understand anything because you complicate everything. You think, you take notes. I know, I've been watching you ever since I started working here. You talk and you argue. When the others laugh out loud and shout in fun, you just smile. When you laugh you don't make any noise, or hardly. When you get drunk, you do it alone in your room. I know, because Zozo knows everything and tells me everything, because he thinks I'm going to love him when he gets to be head steward. He'd do anything for me. I've asked him hundreds of questions about you. Even if the girls often sleep in your room, I know you've never slept with any of them, except Agathe, and I know you're not a real man with her. I've talked to all the girls. They think you like them but look down on them, because they offer themselves and you never take them, even for free. No, I don't know anything about White men's love. I only know Whites who look at me with big round eyes, like the eyes of the tilapias on the plates I serve, and when I come with their second beer, they say, 'I could help you, you know, we could have a beer and we could talk about it.' Rwandans come right out with it. 'You're beautiful, you know, will you come with me tonight?' And they'll put a hand on my back or my bum. I say no and they keep on laughing and having fun.

But the White acts like I've offended his manhood. He stops smiling and sweet-talking. He orders his third beer by pointing at the empty bottle. And he leaves without saying thank you or good night. And the tip, forget about it. The next day he acts like he never asked me to sleep with him.

"When you came and drove me home, what I wanted to tell you was I liked you because you'd never asked me to go with you. I know I'm beautiful because people have been telling me that since I first had breasts, since I was twelve. But I don't know what it means to be so beautiful. It's not a blessing, anyway. It's a curse. On my hill, they've all tried to have me, uncles, cousins, friends of uncles and cousins. A few were more delicate or nicer about it, they said the kinds of things you see in French or American movies in bars where they have TV. Before throwing me down on the mat they would take my hand, like in the movies. That would last a few seconds. I'd get taken in. They'd have their pleasure and leave, laughing and telling me, 'You're good, Gentille.' Then there were the others who didn't ask permission. They just did it. So what I wanted to tell you the other night was, I thought you didn't like me because you'd never asked me to go with you. And I wanted to because you'd always been polite and nice, nothing else, just polite and nice."

"And White . . . and rich."

Why couldn't he understand what seemed so simple to her? Of course she wanted to be loved like a White woman, like in movies where all you see are caresses and long kisses, bouquets of flowers and men suffering from broken hearts. No, she didn't want him to suffer, but she'd like to know her man would be capable of it.

"I know Rwandans who suffer too when their love affairs go wrong," he said.

She didn't know any.

"I want you to teach me the White people's love."

"I can only teach you my own. And sometimes it's pretty black."

A terrified woman began to scream in the next room. Then came sounds of a scuffle, more screams and chairs being overturned on the balcony, then finally a long, piercing "No-o-o-o" that ended in a dull thud. On the metal awning over the pool bar lay the body of Mélissa, the ugliest and skinniest of the hotel's prostitutes.

"Aah, the bitch! The disgusting whore! She jumped just to piss me off."

A fat, naked Belgian was waving his arms on the next balcony. A few paras trying to upgrade their suntans looked up. Two tourists stopped swimming briefly, then resumed their studied crawl.

Gentille shouted, "Mélissa! Mélissa!"

Valcourt said, "Do you still want me to teach you the White people's love?"

Mélissa lay close to death three floors below on the white-hot aluminum.

Gentille screamed, "He tried to kill her! Call the police!"

"Just a dirty, drunken whore," the pot-bellied Belgian protested.

However much Gentille might yell and Valcourt argue and threaten, the hotel management never called the police. The head of security at the Belgian embassy, who was lunching at the pool bar, took the matter in hand. His colleague, he explained, had been attacked by a cheap little prostitute who had tried to rob him, he had defended himself, and the unfortunate accident had ensued. The embassy, where they knew how to do things right, he continued, would take care of the poor woman and pay all hospital expenses. The huge tottering beer-barrel, parading his little comma of a penis in the corridor, nodded to confirm his superior's every word. In conclusion, the embassy official said to Valcourt:

"Monsieur, you have all the bad friends here a man could have. You're taking risks . . . Tell me, why don't you just leave these people to their fate?"

At the hospital they searched through all the buildings, stepping over the pallets and mats, describing Mélissa to the staff. In Emergency they were insistent, raising their voices. No Mélissa had been admitted to the KHC that day.

Mélissa's body was never found. The fat Belgian spent two days at the embassy and then went home to Belgium. At the bar, another girl who had been waiting for months for permission to begin active service had taken her place. The day after the incident, which had already ceased to be a subject of conversation, Valcourt and Gentille went to the public prosecutor's office to lodge a complaint. The assistant chief prosecutor received them out of respect for Valcourt, the citizen of a donor country and above all a neutral country like Canada, a country that asked no questions and gave with its eyes closed, a perfect country in short.

Valcourt laid out the facts in a few words, stressing that the body had disappeared after members of the Belgian security service had promised to take it to the hospital. Why not question them? Where was the Belgian counsellor? The official interrupted, spreading his two hands like a parish priest preparing to bless his flock or deliver a long sermon. The representative of the republic understood the Canadian's effort, but . . .

"We too are seeking the path to greater democracy, even if we have not been practising it as long as you. We too believe in the rule of law and practise it, although sometimes in our own ways that may surprise others but must be respected. You are appealing to this rule of law and showing confidence in us. I am delighted at this mark of respect for our democracy. It is apparent that you have not fallen victim to the propaganda of the Tutsi cockroaches who take such advantage of our generous republic. Although I venture to say that you keep curious company, that you are a friend of that Raphaël of the People's Bank who gives his sisters to Whites in order to obtain benefits from them. You also organized the rather spectacular funeral of a certain Méthode who, before dying, attempted to destroy the tourist industry of this peaceful country by raising the spectre of a sickness that exists so little here that our citizens do not even know its name. I am telling you now that I am attributing these errors of judgment to too great a need for superficial friendship, to the vicissitudes of loneliness. Tutsi women are quick with a laugh and into bed. I understand how an expatriate might succumb to these charms and be carried away to the point of blindness. But that is not what concerns us. Incidentally, Monsieur Valcourt, I studied in Canada, you know. Yes, at Laval University. But the French spoken there was so close to some kind of incomprehensible creole that I liked my negro French better and completed my studies at the University of Butare . . ."

By now Valcourt knew all too well the pleasure derived from solemn sermons, pompous speeches and long orations by so many African "intellectuals" to dare interrupt.

"Yes, I know, it was a Canadian priest who founded the University of Butare, and many of your citizens still teach there. One day you will perhaps explain to me why, here, they endeavour to speak correctly, and we generally manage to understand them, while in your country . . . But I digress . . . So there you were in a room at the Hôtel Mille-Collines with a young woman, I must admit, pardon my candour, Mademoiselle, a young woman of remarkable beauty, I would go further and say, of exceptional beauty. Quite obviously a Tutsi, and perhaps a minor. We will need to verify. . ."

The prosecutor scribbled a few words, then removed his Armani glasses.

"This young woman has just been dismissed from her employ. She had no reason to be in your room, if not to practise the profession in which, they say, the Tutsis excel. You know, Monsieur Valcourt, that these people do not like either the Belgians or the French, anyone in fact who has helped the Hutu majority take back its rights that were usurped by the Tutsi cockroaches . . ."

Valcourt and Gentille protested. She had attained the age of majority and was a Hutu, and certainly not a hooker. The official snapped irritably that there were more forged than authentic papers being made up these days.

"Look at her, Monsieur . . . that narrow nose, that milk-chocolate colouring and that figure. Look at her and you will see clearly that she is descended from Ethiopians. So, you are in your room. You hear loud voices, you rush out onto the balcony. A Tutsi prostitute is lying on the awning of the pool bar and an unhappy member of the Belgian diplomatic corps is shouting himself hoarse, distraught at this suicide attempt which could compromise not only his honourable career but also his family's serenity. But, swayed by love I dare say, Monsieur Valcourt, you see some sinister motive in it. You run to the hospital without knowing whether that girl, Mélissa, needed to be hospitalized. You insult worthy physicians, including the Emergency Room director, and then you come here to accuse a Belgian diplomat of involuntary homicide, and the police officers who came to get the girl—who was still alive, you remember—of complicity. In fact, if the girl has disappeared as you claim, you are accusing the police of sequestration or perhaps, though I dare not believe it, of murder and obstruction of justice through concealment of incriminating evidence, namely the dead body of the said Mélissa. I assure you that the girl, whose behaviour can rightfully be qualified as shameful, having placed a friend of our country in a position of embarrassment, quite simply returned to her hill by the first minibus. Do you still wish to file a complaint?"

Gentille squeezed Valcourt's hand fiercely for a few seconds, allowing the sounds of the market to kill the silence that had fallen. Long enough for them to hear a hundred small slices of boisterous, harmless life.

"Yes," Gentille said, "I want to file a complaint . . . against the Belgian and against the people who came to get Mélissa."

"Since you are alone in wishing to go to law, as my learned colleagues say, I will ask you to remain here to comply with the formalities and answer the questions of our investigators. As for you, Monsieur Valcourt, I shall not keep you further." ˙

"You don't understand, Monsieur Assistant Chief Prosecutor. I am the one who is filing the complaint, and asking for an inquiry into the attempted murder of Mélissa, and her disappearance."

"You are very fond of Rwanda, I know, Monsieur Valcourt, and also of Rwandan women, as I observe, but for you to remain here Rwanda will have to be fond of you."

"And you are Rwanda, perhaps?"

"Yes, Monsieur Valcourt, in a certain fashion. You can return tomorrow to comply with the formalities. We are rushed off our feet today."

Yes, they were rushed off their feet. From the next office came hysterical laughter. In the waiting room a group of militiamen, those *interahamwes* seen strutting about in increasing numbers, were amusing themselves hitting a teenaged boy. Some policemen were standing by, laughing. Three civil servants sat behind small school-type desks, slowly pushing pencils.

Valcourt and Gentille were walking down the steps toward the market when they heard:

"Monsieur Valcourt, your television contract is still in force, is it not?"

Chapter Five
_____

Across from the Justice Ministry office is an orgy of
colour and noise, of bustle and loud, cheery voices. A
kind of concerto to life. Small life, undistinguished,
ordinary, wretched, boisterous, simple, rough, dumb,
merry, life of whatever kind. Kigali's main market,
a lurid, spectacular tableau saying in its fashion that
an indestructible Africa exists, an Africa of close
proximity, elbow-rubbing, small business, resourceful-
ness. The Africa of endurance, persistence and endless
conversation.

   Before Valcourt and Gentille stretched a long red
scar, as red as the red on flags that kill, like the
red, yellow and green Rwandan flag. Thirty metres of

tomatoes, thirty women selling tomatoes. Valcourt, who had never seen a red as vibrant, came often to sit on the steps of the prosecutor's office and look at the scene. He had asked cameramen to shoot long fixed sequences of these tomatoes, then panoramas and zoom-ins and zoom-outs. And then the same shots, with the same movements, of the spice stands, where little pots of ground peppers and saffron were lined up as in a field of poppies and daisies. His student cameramen could never understand his fascination with scenes showing nothing but tomatoes, pepper and saffron.

"Come, I want you to meet Cyprien."

Cyprien sold tobacco leaves, which he displayed on a little mat opposite the tomatoes which were vastly more popular than his tobacco, for tobacco was more and more a luxury product. He did not hold it against the tomatoes and particularly not against the tomato vendors, whom he cruised constantly though he was married and the father of three children. His ambition was to have fucked them all before dying and he was already not far from having succeeded. The former truck driver couldn't set eyes on a woman without wanting to have her. Cyprien had AIDS but hardly anyone knew it, not even his wife, so that his last two children were also HIV positive. He had got his place at the market thanks to Father Louis, who financed a program of small loans that enabled certain AIDS patients to carry on a business. Cyprien was happy. His serenity and detachment in the face of imminent death had fascinated Valcourt. But when Valcourt began talking to him about it, bombarding him with questions as only journalists and betrayed wives can do, Cyprien could not understand his astonishment and curiosity. One day, having run out of answers that

Valcourt kept finding too simplistic or attributed to the traditional reserve of Rwandans, he said:

"But, Monsieur Valcourt, don't people die in your country?"

Cyprien was going to die the same way he came to the Kigali market to sell his tobacco. The end meant no more to him than the beginning or the middle. Here, Valcourt was beginning to understand, dying was simply one of the things you did one day.

"Monsieur Valcourt, I'm glad to see you. We're going to make the film soon?"

Cyprien was one of some fifty people, most of them HIV positive, with whom Valcourt had become friends, close friends in some cases, while doing research for the film on AIDS he was losing hope of ever finishing. He had approached them and questioned them with such patience and respect that these cautious, even secretive people now confided in him with a familiarity and candour that made his heart glow. Explaining why he had conceived a child with his wife despite his illness, Cyprien had told him:

"Monsieur Valcourt, it was an accident. That day I'd sold all my tobacco in an hour. I was so happy I went and drank beer at the Cosmos. And there was this girl I'd wanted for such a long time. I had her with a condom the father gave me. Then I went home a bit drunk. But I still wanted some more. That girl wasn't very good and my wife's very, very good. I didn't have another condom but I wanted it so much and my wife too. God won't punish me because my wife and I wanted some pleasure. You see, it was an accident."

Valcourt repeated for the tenth time that the film project was making headway.

"Will you take me home, Monsieur Valcourt?
Business isn't good today, and most of all the customers
aren't good quality. Look behind you."

Ten metres away, four young militiamen wearing
the cap of the president's party were twirling their
machetes. The market's cheerful, noisy anarchy had
ceased, the way the birds in a forest fall silent when a
predator creeps near.

Georgina, Cyprien's wife, had made tea but they were
drinking warm Primus. Valcourt watched the three children intently as they played on the small, well-trodden
patch of earth that served as both garden and play-
ground. There were a few tomato plants and some
beans struggling to grow in the shade of the little hut of
reddish mud. The children were like any others. They
were making up games with a tin can, kicking it one
moment then holding it to their ears like an empty shell
and hearing sounds that made them laugh hysterically.
Valcourt was not seeing children, he was seeing dead
bodies on reprieve. Hardly aware of what he was doing,
he searched their faces for evidence, signs of their illness. On each visit he asked questions about their
diarrhea attacks or their weight. Had they had fever
recently? He was doing it again this afternoon, particularly wanting Gentille to observe, but she just
laughed like the children.

"Gentille, how can you laugh so easily?"

"Because they're funny. Because they're having fun.
Because right now it's hot and nice. Because you're
here. Because the beer's tickling the insides of my
cheeks and I like Cyprien and Georgina. D'you want

more reasons? Because of the birds, the sea that I can't see and have never seen, because of Canada, which maybe I'll see one day. Because I'm alive and the children are alive and because right now things are good for us. D'you want more reasons?"

Valcourt shook his head. Gentille was right.

"Monsieur Valcourt," Cyprien began, "I'm going to tell you what always gives you such a long, serious face. I'm going to be very straight with you because you know everything about me. You've got everything out of my head with your questions. You even know my sickness better than me, and you explain it to me. Yes, as you say, we're close friends. Funny way to be close friends—you know when I put on a condom and when I don't, and I don't even know how old you are. But that doesn't matter. What I want to say is, you get us thinking. We feel from your eyes what you see in your head. You see dead bodies, skeletons, and on top of that you want us to talk like we're dying. I'll start doing that a few seconds before I die, but until then I'm going to live and fuck and have a good time. You're the one who talks like a dying man, like every word you say is going to be your last. You mustn't take it wrong, but that's what I think and I'm saying it. Monsieur Valcourt, have another Primus, have a good time with us, then go back to the hotel, eat, fuck the beautiful Gentille, and go to sleep snoring like a cat. And leave us to die peacefully alive. There, my friend, that's what I've been wanting to tell you for a long time."

Valcourt received the lesson like a boxer taking a devastating punch. He was KO'd.

But Cyprien wanted to confide something else to him. With an indication to Gentille that she should go and join Georgina and the children in the house, he spread his arms to embrace all of Kigali. To the left lay the city centre, with the hotel overlooking it from the highest hill; on the right was the Ruhengeri highway; and opposite, on the other hill, the iron market, which was shrinking to make room for coffin-makers. Slightly farther to the right was the red-toned, almost medieval mass of the prison. Then Cyprien explained. His cousin had told him that the president had set up a training camp in a college in Ruhengeri, and the brothers of the Christian colleges had not protested. Hundreds of young fanatics like those who had been playing with machetes in the marketplace were being trained there. Every day along that highway—he pointed—army trucks filled with militiamen were arriving in Kigali. They were being billeted in different neighbourhoods with party sympathizers, and at night were throwing up roadblocks and checking the identity of anyone passing. They were roaming the streets with papers, filling them with marks after asking whether the houses were Tutsi or Hutu. Sometimes, a bit drunk or stoned on hash which the soldiers doled out to them, they lopped arms or legs off a few stray Tutsis. Recently, in his own neighbourhood, someone had been setting fire to Tutsi houses. The arsonists came from elsewhere, no one knew them, but they never mistook their targets. At "the bar under the bed"* nestled in the spot where the road turns and climbs toward the city, Cécile, whom Cyprien liked to fondle on his way home from the market, had shown him lists left by a militiaman who had

---

* A local term for a popular convenience: a bed with a case of beer stored underneath for the further entertainment of the proprietor's clientele.

wanted to fuck but had no money. The names had come from the section head, Madame Odile, a hysterical woman who beat her children when they played with Tutsis. The list held 332 names. Almost all Tutsis. The rest were Hutu members of opposition parties. This is what Cyprien wanted to tell Valcourt. And something else too.

Another cousin, a member of the president's party, was working as a guard at the prison.

"We've begun the work at the prison," this cousin had confided to Cyprien. "It's important work for the survival of Rwanda, which is threatened by the cockroaches. We're eliminating them as soon as they arrive."

But there was a lot more still to come. The militiamen were passing out machetes in the neighbourhood. Certain section heads had even been given machine guns. And there was beginning to be talk of bumping off Whites. For example, the priests who organized co-operatives, and who took care of Tutsi refugees. No one was going to be safe, not even Valcourt.

"In the marketplace, the militiamen were shouting that all your friends were going to be cut up into little pieces and you'd never see Canada again, because you're a friend of Lando's. And I'm not saying what they promised to do to Gentille. Now that I haven't said it, you know."

"If you're telling the truth, Cyprien, my friend, and unfortunately I believe you, they're going to cut you up into little pieces too. You have to leave here, and you mustn't go back to the marketplace."

"Monsieur Valcourt, in your head, I'm already dead and gone. And you're right. A few months more, a year maybe. Every day I carry on, I'm stealing time from

God, who's waiting for me and doesn't hold a few acci-
dents against me. But you don't stop wanting to live and
do things right just because you're dying. And I'm one
that does things right. A friend's a friend. I'm staying
with you to make your film. And something I haven't
told you—Cécile showed me the list because my name's
on it. She likes me. She's the one I was with at the Cosmos, who I had my last accident with. She wanted me to
get out of here too, and go somewhere near Butare
because it's safer."

When the sun goes down over Kigali, the beauty
of the world brings joy to the beholder. Great flocks of
birds delicately embroider the sky. The wind is gentle
and cool. The streets are transformed into lazily slipping, brightly coloured ribbons, thousands of people,
like swarms of ants, leaving the city centre and slowly
climbing their hills. On all sides smoke rises from cooking fires. Each column that shows against the sky
speaks of a tiny house. Thousands of laughing children
run about in the earthen streets, kicking burst footballs
and rolling old tires. When the sun goes down over
Kigali, if you're sitting on one of the hills surrounding
the city and still have the remains of a soul, you cannot
do otherwise than stop talking and watch. Cyprien put
his hand on Valcourt's shoulder.

"Look. Everything's beautiful from my house. This is
why I want to die here, watching the sun put Kigali to
sleep. Look, it's like red honey running out of the sky."

Gentille came and sat beside Valcourt. They stayed
this way in silence, the three of them, until nightfall,
hypnotized by the murmuring city curling up for the
night in the folds of sun-painted shadows, first golden,
then red, and finally brown. They felt that their lives,

until now more or less shaped by their own decisions, were escaping them totally. They felt borne along by forces they could name but could not understand because they were foreign to them, had no place in their genes, or their frustrations, or their failures, because never, in their worst excesses of hatred, had they ever imagined that anyone could kill the way one hoes a garden to get rid of weeds. The hoeing, the work, had begun. Still, they were not giving up hope.

Dogs were barking as though speaking, as though warning humans: "Watch out, men are turning into dogs and worse still than dogs and worse still than hyenas or the vultures on the wind making circles in the sky above an unwary herd."

Cyprien began speaking again. Valcourt, he said, was trying to teach him how to live while waiting to die. He wanted to teach the White that you could live only if you knew you were going to die. Here, you died because it was normal to die. Living a long time was not.

"In your country you die by accident, because life hasn't been generous and leaves like an unfaithful wife. You think we don't value life as much as you. So tell me, Valcourt, poor and deprived as we are, why do we take in our cousins' orphans, and why do our old people die with all their children around them? I'm telling you in all humility, you discuss life and death like great philosophers. We just talk about people who are living and dying. You consider us primitive or ignorant. We're just people who don't have much, either for living or dying. We live and die in messy ways, like poor people."

Over the Kigali prison, the breath and sweat of thousands of men cooped up one against another was raising a cupola of mist.

Cyprien knew much more than he wanted to say about the massacres brewing. He knew the caches where guns and machetes were being stockpiled, the barracks where the militia was training, the gathering places in most of the city's neighbourhoods. He had never liked the Tutsis. He thought they were arrogant and laughed too much, but he adored their women's slender waists that he could girdle with his two great hands, their milk-chocolate skin and their breasts as firm as juicy pomegranates. That was his downfall in the eyes of his Hutu neighbours and friends, that and his friendship with this White, who hung out only with Tutsis and talked about freedom when instructing the journalists for the television station that still wasn't producing any television. He liked this Valcourt, who could listen for hours and hours and talk without ever preaching. But he was also a little sorry for him. Valcourt was as arid as a desert, like dead earth that rejects seed. He was being eaten away by the hopelessness of living, the malady that afflicts only those who can afford the time to think about themselves. Valcourt was dead though alive, while Cyprien was alive though dead. Cyprien had been using this equation to resolve the endless questions he kept putting to himself after their meetings. Perhaps the beautiful Gentille would administer the electric shock that would bring the White back to life and allow him to die properly. Only the living know how to die.

The staccato sounds of a volley of gunfire cascaded down the neighbouring hill, and sleeping dogs woke and resumed their tortured-beast yowlings. Cyprien walked back and forth on the small terrace, thinking about the horrors looming in his country. He did not feel like help-ing this country that deserved only to die, it had gorged so greedily on lies and false prophecies. He could do nothing for his family, who were already dead, condemned by AIDS. His relatives? His friends? They were already waving their brand-new machetes recently arrived from China, and practising cutting up Tutsi meat after smoking a joint or drinking a few beers distributed by the section heads.

"Valcourt, you love Gentille?"

"Yes," Valcourt replied calmly as if he had known it for years and it was right and natural that it should be so. "Yes, I love her," he repeated, as if the three were dining together at a quiet, favourite restaurant, as though they were the same age and there was nothing they could not talk about.

Gentille had not moved, not even quivered, but already she was tumbling into another world, the world of movies and novels, because all her life she had never heard these words except in movies or read them except in the works of romantic novelists she had studied at the Butare Social Service School.

"Valcourt, you love her to sleep with or you love her to live with?"

"Both, Cyprien, both."

Gentille laid her head on Valcourt's shoulder, and Valcourt bent his so that their hair mingled. As if in eruption, all the juices of life ran between her trembling thighs. An orgasm from tenderness and words.

"You're not feeling well?" Valcourt asked gently, feeling her shiver.

"Oh yes, maybe too well. For the first time in my life, I know I'm living real life. When they taught me poetry at school, they told me words could lead to ecstasy. Here, feel."

For her this life was different anyway, for not minding Cyprien's presence, she took Valcourt's hand and guided it to the wetness of her crotch. Valcourt was alarmed by all this energy, these mysterious forces of body and soul that he had unleashed. It was not the joy of having said *I love you* that gripped him at this moment, but despair of keeping her. For she would leave, of that he was certain.

"Valcourt, your Gentille is Tutsi, even if you swear she isn't. Her death's already written in the sky. So if you love her, you'll pack your bags, you'll forget the film and the television station that'll never make any television because we're too poor, you'll forget Rwanda and tomorrow you'll take the plane."

Gentille protested. She was not a Tutsi.

"You can tell me that and it's okay, I won't go and repeat it to anybody. You've got a nose that's as straight and sharp as a knife, skin the colour of café au lait, legs as long as a giraffe's, breasts so pointed and firm they stick through your blouse, and buns, buns . . . that drive me wild. I'm sorry, but there it is. You've got a Hutu card because you bought it or you slept with an official, but at a roadblock, when you're intercepted by a gang of little Hutus as black as night, they're not going to look at your card, they'll see your buns, your legs, your breasts, your pale skin, and they're going to bang that Tutsi and call their friends so they can bang her too. And you'll be lying in the red mud with your legs spread and a machete against your throat, and they'll have you ten times, a hundred times, till your wounds and your pain will have done with your beauty. And when the wounds and bruises and dried blood have made you ugly, when there's nothing left but a memory of a woman, they'll throw you in the swamp and, while you lie there dying, insects will eat at you and rats will nibble at you and buzzards will tear at you. I want to terrify you, Gentille. We have to stop living like we can keep on living normally."

A bus careened down the hill with squealing brakes and rattling sides. Men were singing off-key in chorus and laughing like hooligans coming home from a football match.

"That's our killers going by," said Cyprien. "Militiamen arriving from the North to do 'the work' in the capital. You hear what they're singing? 'We're going to exterminate them.' Gentille, they're talking about you and anyone who touches you, knows you or loves you. Get away from here. Not from my house. Get away from this lousy country. Hate comes to you with birth. They teach it to you in the cradles they rock you to sleep in. At school, in the street, at the bar, at the stadium, the Hutus have heard and learned only one lesson—the Tutsi is an insect that has to be stamped out. If not, the Tutsi will steal your wife, he'll rape your children, he'll poison the water and the air. The Tutsi woman will bewitch your husband with her backside. When I was little, they told me the Tutsis would kill me if I didn't kill them first. It's like the catechism."

From the Remero district, near Lando's, the echo of a grenade, then of a second and a third, rolled down one hill to the next, punctuating Cyprien's words as if to amplify them.

Gentille, although she was hearing, was not listening. She was feeling like a woman at last, honoured, admired and loved, no longer merely a body, an object found to be beautiful, a bauble to be bought or a desire to be satisfied. A few words had brought her here, only a few words. And this place was as frightening to her as it was enchanting. The man who had brought this wetness to her thighs with just his words would surely leave her. It was written in the sky, in life. After he had had his pleasures and orgasms, once he had explored her breasts and ass and legs and private places, when he knew his way by heart around them with his fingertips and impatient penis, he would realize that he'd fallen for a poor little country negress who didn't know anything, who couldn't talk about the world, or about life, or especially about love. She was convinced he would not be able to put up much longer with this hysterical country where madness was settling in as the normal condition of life. She knew he would leave her, in a few weeks, a few months at best. It was inevitable.

Cyprien's wife had made brochettes of chewy goat's meat, which they ate slowly with tomatoes, onions, green beans and warm Primus. They didn't talk much, content to be together and sharing the same destiny for a few hours. After the meal, Cyprien insisted on going with Valcourt and Gentille as far as the hotel because the militia had already set up roadblocks and Gentille could have problems. Some young girls had already disappeared.

The first roadblock was less than a hundred metres from Cyprien's house. A tree trunk across the road, a brazier, a dozen men under the command of a policeman who had swapped his gun for a machete. These were neighbours who respected Cyprien even if they distrusted him. They let the three pass without causing problems. The policeman was a cousin. Another one.

Just before the downtown area, a second roadblock. The men guarding it seemed more excited and more dangerous. They were dancing in front of two tree trunks that they had thrown across the road, waving machetes and clubs with enormous spikes driven through the heads. Valcourt stopped the car several metres before the roadblock. Cyprien got out and went to speak to two young men who were weaving about unsteadily. He brought them back to the car. The two militiamen would look at nothing but Gentille. They made her get out of the car and pranced around her making obscene gestures and calling their companions. Valcourt got out, holding his Canadian passport and his government press card. Cyprien kept arguing, his identity papers in his hand.

"Look, they're friends of mine, going home. She's Hutu, he's Canadian, not French or Belgian."

There were now a dozen around them, all drunk or stoned on hash. A little bearded fellow in a Chicago Bulls sweater with Michael Jordan's name on the back spoke to Valcourt.

"The Canadian likes Tutsi hookers with phony Hutu cards. That's not good for you, chief. Not good. This is a Hutu country, chief. If you don't want to end up in the Kagera River with all the Tutsis, get yourself a Hutu woman. I'll let you through tonight, but you'll have to pay a little money for the training and patriotic education of militias."

Valcourt handed over a sum and the bearded fellow gave him back his passport but not his press card or Gentille's identity card. To recover these cost the entire five thousand Rwandan francs Valcourt had on him.

Valcourt tried to persuade Cyprien to spend the night at the hotel, but Cyprien said he would rather leave the two of them alone together and did not want to leave his wife and children unattended in these troubled times.

"And then, a thirty-minute walk under a full moon is a great joy. Don't worry, I know everybody. Give me a beer for the walk."

He could avoid the roadblocks by taking some of the footpaths that wove about the hills like a complex circulatory system. But he hankered to follow the paved main road and meet up with people he'd call cheery greetings to, asking what was new in their neighbourhood, or how a distant cousin was doing. Clutching his big bottle of Primus from which he'd taken only a single swig, Cyprien was looking for a fling. Surely he'd find a free woman along the way who, for a share of his beer, would burst out laughing and spread her big, warm, moist thighs for him. Sex had done him in, but that was all he lived for. And after that woman, he'd wake up his own and maybe have another accident with her because it had been a long time, and because he threw away the condoms he was given every time he had a medical exam, or handed them round to children to use as balloons. He was so afraid of dying without having slept with all the women he could have in a normal life that he thought of nothing else. His day was organized around sex. He had plundered literally half the marketplace without ever a thought that he could infect the tomato or tilapia vendor of the moment. This country was doomed, he figured. What was the difference if a machete or an infected cock did the job? Yes, there was a difference. A cock was kinder than a machete.

One day Élise had raged at him because he had been sleeping all over without a condom.

"You're a murderer!" she shouted in her small office beside the hospital. "You're killing all those women!"

He was killing them maybe, but they laughed and squealed when he patted their bums and slipped his hand up their skirts. And they gave great cries of pleasure when he penetrated them while massaging their breasts. That was a much more beautiful death, he said, than death by machete.

Cyprien had not found a free woman on the road homeward. He was even thinking of turning back to the city, he needed so badly to relieve his aching balls and persistent erection. I'm not dead yet, he told himself, laughing. Then he thought of Fabienne, his friend Virginie's sister, who kept "a bar under the bed" just beyond the roadblock. A nitwit who yakked non-stop like a magpie, even with her legs in the air and you wearing yourself out on her belly, trying to make her shut up or come. You never knew. But since she always asked for more and the second time you didn't pay, she enjoyed a certain renown. In the neighbourhood she was called the Glutton because she was always hungry for a man and took them all, even on credit, unless they were Tutsis.

They were having a ball at the roadblock. A radio with the volume on full was diffusing disco to the farthest corners of the neighbourhood. Shadows danced and leaped crazily, silhouetted against the lurid light of two fires lit in big metal barrels. The militiamen were singing of the glory of the president's party, the eternal superiority of the Hutus. The refrain went: "We're starting the work, and the work's going to be done right." "Work" was the term always used in the propaganda. It also referred to the *corvée collective*, an annual community service when the residents of each commune were supposed to take part in the work, the *corvée*, which consisted of cutting down weeds and cleaning up along the sides of the roads. No one nowadays understood the word to mean overgrown weeds. But as long as the calls to violence remained in the realm of parable or poetic hyperbole, friendly countries would not be worried about the inhumanity France was condoning and feeding with its arms and military advisers. In the designs of the great powers, these Rwandans were of negligible weight, people outside the circle of real humanity, poor, useless types whom the glorious French civilization, with monarchical arrogance, was ready to sacrifice to preserve France's civilizing presence in Africa, a presence already threatened by a major Anglophone plot.

Cyprien wanted Fabienne, right here and right now, as the great French chief might have said, the president of France who had armed and trained these men—men who were separating Cyprien from Fabienne and his pleasure. When they caught sight of him laboriously climbing the hill, the militiamen began shouting and gesticulating.

"Come party with us, Cyprien, come on. Move it, Hot-Nuts, your wife's back here, she's waiting for you and wants you."

Just beyond the two tree trunks blocking the road, his wife was lying with her skirt pulled up onto her belly. Two young militiamen, laughing hilariously, were holding her legs apart and a third was holding her head still. A breast was hanging out of her torn, bloodstained T-shirt. The roadblock commander held a revolver to Cyprien's temple and led him to Georgina's side.

"We've tried everything but nothing works. Your wife has no pleasure. Even I've been on and women like me. Nothing, not even a little sigh of pleasure. She can't be normal. We've had her two at a time, one by the front, the other by the back door. And we did it hard. Big bangs with big cocks, then we used a stick. Nothing, just crying and horrible screaming, even insults, not one little bit of pleasure to thank us for finding her so beautiful and appetizing. Now, you know all the secrets of the Whites and Tutsis you hang out with, so you're going to show us, Cyprien, you're going to show us what a man's got to do to make your wife come."

As the first effects of shock began to fade, Cyprien was relieved. He was not going to die in sickness, but in pleasure.

"I'll show you how to do it," he said.

He undressed completely. The militiamen holding his wife stood aside, intimidated by the nakedness of this man who stared them straight in the eyes and bent calmly toward Georgina.

"Wife, better to die of pleasure than of torture," he said to her.

Slowly and most of all with a delicacy he did not recognize in himself, he removed her skirt, then her T-shirt in the colours of Rwanda. On his knees between her thighs, he looked at her at length while the militiamen howled their impatience. He lay down on her and began to kiss her, in the curve of her neck, on her ears, on her eyes, her cheeks, the corners of her lips, delicately, only the tip of his tongue expressing his desire, while the militiamen booed the dreary spectacle. The little bearded fellow came up and slashed him savagely across the back with his machete. Cyprien felt his blood running down like a hot river between his buttocks and wetting his testicles. Never had he had such an erection. He sat up and, for the first time in his life, plunged his head between his wife's thighs and sucked, kissed, ate. He had almost no strength left. He penetrated her, and just as he was about to come, the policeman fired. His body gave what seemed like a hiccup and he fell on his back beside his wife. Sprayed with semen, the policeman began to bellow.

"Kill me now," Georgina implored. "Kill me now, please."

The policeman, furious, pulled down his pants and lay on her. He gave an initial thrust and then a lot more as if trying to ram all the way through her. Georgina expressed neither pain nor pleasure. Not a sound, just staring with eyes empty and already lifeless. The policeman got up in disgust. They executed the woman without enthusiasm, swinging their machetes from the shoulder as if to finish off a dull job. The two bodies looked like abattoir refuse, carcasses clumsily cut up by unskilled butchers. The men had had their fill of pleasure and violence. As they left the roadblock, after putting out the fires and pulling aside the two tree trunks until tomorrow, hungry stray dogs crept in and feasted on this flesh that the humans were offering them with such casual generosity.

Chapter Six

I speak from the depth of the chasm
I speak from the depth of my abyss . . .

We are the first cloud we two
In this absurd expanse of cruel happiness
We are the future freshness
The first night of rest

Gentille and Valcourt lay under the great fig tree that
shaded both terrace and pool. The magic tree, Valcourt
called it; it must have been shaped by the gods because
it was a perfect sphere. He had been gazing at it since
he first arrived at the hotel, appealing to it at times, as

we do when we stand before a painting that makes us feel bigger than life size, or a religious picture that reduces us to our puny, real dimensions. This enormous fig tree stood four storeys tall, so that even from the dining room on the fourth floor you couldn't see the top of it. To Valcourt it was fascinating, reassuring and exotic. In Quebec they sold tiny fig trees as decorative plants. They weren't trees, they were small shrubs. The only reminder of African luxuriance was the dark, lustrous green of their leaves. Here, this giant tamed the wind, organized the landscape. Not a day went by when Valcourt failed to go to the tree, and sit or lie briefly under it. He loved its beauty, its smooth roundness bristling with irregular little spikes, and the vibrant colour of its leaves, which the sun's bright rays and the moon's soft caresses alike would explode into a thousand fireflies. During the great rains that washed all the lands of the country, he would settle himself under this gigantic living umbrella. Not a drop would reach him. At such moments, he had feelings of immortality. This tree was a friend, a protector and a refuge. When he was drunk, he even found himself talking to it and was surprised not to hear it answer.

When she came into the room, Gentille had said, "Make me come again with words." Valcourt had picked up his copy of Paul Éluard's *Oeuvres complètes* and led her under the fig tree. She had lain on the warm grass like a woman waiting to be possessed. Though he had never desired a woman so much, Valcourt hung back. He was still afraid of becoming immersed in the necessity of living. He was making one last stand. Reading would be easier than talking, so that is what he would do.

He read in a gentle, serious voice, unpretentiously but with feeling. He did not really differentiate the lines. He heard the sounds they made as his brain grouped the letters that formed the words that created the sentences. He was speaking to Gentille and living what he was saying more than reciting.

At first the young woman was more charmed by the voice of the man she loved than by the words. At school she had been used to reading Lamartine, Hugo and Musset to a rhythm that made a poem more like a cradle song or ballad, and she felt jostled by this cascade of images and the complicated allegories. But when she heard, "I speak from the depth of the chasm," she asked Valcourt to repeat it, then took his hand.

"It's you, it's me, here. We're speaking from the depth of the chasm." And to herself she repeated, "'I am not afraid, all doors are open,'" for this was how she had been coping these past few days. And Valcourt had to repeat three times, "'this absurd expanse of cruel happiness.'" Gentille was discovering that poetry speaks about life at its worst and its most magnificent. This man, this Paul Éluard, whose name she had never even heard before, was becoming a trusted friend, a kind of guardian angel. He had such a way with all the words of love and all the words of death. And she was at home with these words.

A smile challenged
The gathering night for each star
A single smile for us two

"I want to read everything your Monsieur Éluard has written."

Valcourt lay back on the grass beside her. He did not close his eyes because the fig tree was protecting him from whatever light and reflection there was.

"I didn't know a woman could come with so much gentleness and so little caressing," Gentille said.

Had she come? Valcourt hoped so. He had made love to her delicately, shyly and with restraint, as if not to crush a costly fabric. She had said "yes" a hundred times, never closing her eyes, quivering slightly, until her back arched and then subsided.

"Thank you for being so gentle."

She had fallen asleep the way small children do, with their little fists clenched, thinking they're going to heaven and they're floating on clouds. Valcourt watched her until the first barkings of dogs rose from the valleys and the first curls of smoke penetrated the pockets of morning fog lying like fleecy lakes between Kigali's still-dark hills. All this time, he was haunted by something Gérard Depardieu had said to Catherine Deneuve in Truffaut's film *Le Dernier Métro:* "Yes, I love you. And you're so beautiful it hurts to look at you." Valcourt had slept for an hour perhaps.

The gardener appeared and waved nonchalantly when he saw the half-naked couple lying under the tree, as though all things were normal in this chaotic world. He was not wrong.

The canine cacophony yielded progressively to the human cacophony. The buzzards took flight in search of the fresh refuse produced by the night. When the buzzards had flown over the city at length and staked out their territory, the jackdaws left the lower branches of the eucalyptus trees around the hotel garden to go and make do, humbly as befits an inferior and obedient race, with places the buzzards had scorned. The croaking of all the city's ravens was drowned out by horrid clumpings of French boots as a squad of presidential guardsmen jogged around the hotel, as they did every morning. The noise had wakened Gentille.

"You don't know what they're singing as they run. They're singing that they're going to kill them all. Your friends, they mean."

"They mean you too, Gentille."

They had breakfast on the terrace, in the protective shade of the fig tree. Gentille was still in her very rumpled waitress's uniform with the golden badge bearing her name. The waiters avoided Valcourt's eye and his signals, but Zozo, who was delighted with their happiness, came quickly to end the discrimination.

"You have chosen well, Monsieur Bernard, she is the most beautiful, and without wishing to make a pun, the most *gentille*, the nicest young lady I know, and all those waiters are only jealous or afraid." Zozo even went to the kitchen himself to make sure Monsieur Bernard and Madame Gentille's fried eggs would not be overcooked. They were perfect.

Valcourt and Gentille went back to the marketplace. It was after seven o'clock but Cyprien was not in his usual place and no one had seen him. They drove up to the hill where the tobacco seller lived. The remains of a fire still smouldered in one of the two metal barrels that had lit up the militiamen's night. Beside the highway, a flock of ferocious, squawking birds were fighting over the mutilated and disjointed bodies of a man and a woman, which appeared to have been thrown one on top of the other. Valcourt recognized Cyprien's red shirt, then the long rugged face with the narrow moustache that he used to trim with such care. A few metres to the right, a dead-drunk militiaman lay snoring on a filthy mattress, clutching a bloodstained machete.

We can all turn into killers, Valcourt had often maintained, even the most peaceful and generous of us. All it takes is a certain circumstance, something that clicks, a failing, a patient conditioning, rage, disappointment. The prehistoric predator and the primitive warrior are still alive beneath the successive varnishings that civilization has applied to mankind. All the Good and Evil of humanity is in our genes. Either one can emerge at any moment, as abruptly as a tornado can appear and destroy everything where minutes before only soft, warm breezes blew.

For several seconds, a killer's genes rose up in Valcourt's blood and a flood of proteins invaded and jangled his brain. Only a firm "No, Bernard!" from Gentille prevented Valcourt from becoming a killer. He had seized the machete from the militiaman's hands and brandished it over his head as the young man woke and with haggard eyes perceived his own imminent death. Flinging the weapon into the ditch, Valcourt returned to the car, appalled to think that if it had not been for Gentille he would have butchered the fellow remorselessly, the way Cyprien and Georgina had been butchered.

At the police station a few hundred yards from the roadblock, the police officer and militia leader in charge of operations recounted that Cyprien had fallen blind drunk on the road in front of a passing unidentified vehicle. Cyprien's wife, after being advised of the accident, had been knocked down by another unidentified vehicle. Marinating in the banana beer he was drinking, and belching between sentences, the police sergeant added that the bodies had been left in the road to allow relatives to come and take them and give them a decent burial, and if no one came today he would take care of it himself because he was a good Christian.

"And the children?"

The sergeant continued to lie with an assurance and contempt for veracity that reminded Valcourt of his spells in Communist countries. He did not know where the children were, perhaps with relatives or friends.

What about the machete wounds on Cyprien's skull, and his wife's belly slashed open, and her right breast cut off, and Cyprien's arm that several ravens were feasting on two or three metres from the tree trunk? The unidentified vehicles did all that? Was it reckless drivers coming home from a wedding, in vehicles with machete-clad tires?

The sergeant kept drinking imperturbably. Perhaps maniacs had cut up the bodies. He asked Valcourt if he wished to lodge a complaint and took a yellowed form out of a drawer.

"You were at the roadblock when we passed it last night. You were in charge of what went on and you were the one checking identities."

The sergeant poured himself another glass of beer, picked up a pencil and sharpened it slowly with a hunting knife. He licked the point and with a smirk, almost laughing out loud, began.

"Name, address, profession, nationality and civil status, please."

Valcourt stood up without another word.

"Goodbye, Monsieur Bernard Valcourt, of room 312, Hôtel des Mille-Collines, journalist, expatriate

Canadian and protector of the Tutsi hooker Gentille Sibomana. Goodbye, I have taken careful note of your complaint and will forward it to the prosecutor at the earliest opportunity."

Unable to contain himself any longer, the sergeant now guffawed. Wasn't he funny, this little White walking around with his hooker, talking about justice and rights and all those things preventing the Hutus, to whom the country belonged, from governing these Tutsi foreigners from faraway Ethiopia as they pleased.

On the door of the little dried-mud house someone had scrawled in red, "Death to the cockroaches." A small child was crying. On a mat covering the red earth floor lay the headless bodies of Cyprien's two boys in a huge pool of blood, on which hundreds of mosquitoes and other insects were feeding. The girl had been spared, a typical practice with the Hutu extremists. When they did not kill the boys, they would cut off their feet so they could not become soldiers when they were older. The girls could always be raped and give pleasure a few years later.

At the orphanage, which was run by Belgian nuns and sponsored by the president's wife, Madame Agathe, they were received coldly. The mother superior informed them that hers was an establishment of excellent reputation on which hundreds of future Belgian parents were depending for the adoption of children that were sound in body and mind. These good, charitable people were investing a great deal of money, and their requirements, rightly, were substantial. The little girl sleeping in Gentille's arms did not appear to have the necessary endowments. If her parents were killed at a roadblock it was no doubt because they were doing something wrong. "And when there's something criminal in the parents, there's often some in the children." Besides, this child could have AIDS. No one would want to pay to adopt her and the orphanage could not pursue its charitable and essential work without the income derived from adoption.

Valcourt never raised his voice when he was angry.

"If I understand correctly, you and Madame la Présidente specialize in the export of fresh young flesh. You are trying to reduce Rwanda's trade deficit by selling babies. How are the profits split between La Présidente and you? Perhaps you have a price list, depending on whether it's a boy or a girl. Do skinny Tutsis sell for less than sturdy Hutus? And do the prices vary according to the children's ages, the colour of their eyes and their social class?"

Valcourt and Gentille went back to the hotel with Cyprien and Georgina's little girl, having decided to keep her themselves for the moment, buying diapers and baby food on the way.

Raphaël was already sitting by the pool. Valcourt told him what had happened.

"Valcourt, sometimes your naivety astonishes me. You showed up at La Présidente's orphanage with the little girl of parents killed at a roadblock. You didn't know the good sisters are more into international trade than charity?"

Valcourt had heard talk of it of course, but once again he hadn't wanted to believe the worst.

"And all Cyprien's neighbours, all his friends and relatives are terrified today, because here, killers talk.

In the bars in the morning they talk about their exploits of the night before. It's their way of sowing terror in people's minds. Listen to me, Valcourt, I'm talking about people I know. I'm talking about my own neighbours, who burned down my house, and buddies I play football with every Sunday, who'll kill me when the section head says it's Raphaël's turn. I know them because, in a way, I'm just like them."

"You've got nothing in common with that bunch."

"On the contrary. We're all Rwandans, all prisoners of the same twisted history that has made us paranoid and schizophrenic at the same time. And like them I was born filled with hate and prejudice. D'you understand? What I'm saying is, if the Tutsis controlled the army here the way they do in Burundi, we'd kill them all, those Hutus. And I'd be right up there. Then I'd go and confess. Buy me a beer. I'm broke."

Valcourt ordered two big bottles of Primus.

"Take this killing of Cyprien and his wife. In each of their wounds, in the killing of the boys, in the way it was done and the weapons used, there are messages. Each atrocity is a symbol and an example. It's supposed to serve as a model for the future. You've seen a small rehearsal for a genocide. But today they've killed Cypriens at roadblocks everywhere in the country. Are you doing anything to stop that?"

Valcourt had no words, no argument to advance in reply. Everything his friend had said was true except for one thing. Valcourt's powerlessness did not make him an accomplice; his presence here did not indicate his approval or even his indifference. Much as he might like to be a general, he was only a solitary onlooker, and he could act only as such, a man alone.

Before leaving, he said to the Tutsi Raphaël, "Gentille is Hutu, Raphaël. You talk, you denounce, but like all those guys who want to kill you, you decide her origin and her future by the colour of her skin and how slim she is. You're right, the Whites have started a kind of Nazism here. You're indignant about any kind of discrimination, but they've succeeded so well that even you turn Hutus into Tutsis just because of narrow noses. When the apocalypse comes, as you rightly say it will, and you're holding a machete only to defend yourself, a short, squat man will walk toward you. He'll tell you he's lost his papers. And it will be true. But you won't believe him because the man will be short and squat. And thinking to defend or avenge your own, with a clear conscience and sure of your patriotism and democratic ideals, you'll kill a Tutsi who's unfortunately been born with the body of a Hutu. Raphaël, Gentille is a Hutu, but the same night you kill that Tutsi with a Hutu's body, you'll save Gentille because her body looks like yours. You're rationalizing just the way they do. It's a prison, that kind of thinking, and death too."

At the office of the assistant chief prosecutor—who didn't wish to meet with him—Valcourt's denunciation and request for an inquiry had been carefully registered by underlings. To show him clearly with what scorn they regarded this false accusation against the forces of order of a sovereign state by a foreigner who was merely tolerated in the country, they assigned his case to the lowest deputy prosecutor. The young man was suffocating in his too-tight suit, and his hard collar made the veins of his neck bulge. He was sweating profusely. In his buttonhole he was wearing the insignia of the president's party. He questioned Valcourt aggressively, as if he were a criminal. Like a hyena, viciously. Valcourt replied patiently and politely to the most ridiculous questions, never once pointing out contradictions or objecting to veiled insults or perfidious allusions. With these people it was best to bend like a reed.

"You have already made us waste our time over that story of the prostitute whose body was supposed to have disappeared. Why should we take you seriously this time?"

"Monsieur, I saw the dead bodies, the wounds, the two murdered children. That ought to be cause enough to open an inquiry."

"Do you drink a lot, Monsieur Valcourt? Or like many aid workers, do you smoke a little hashish perhaps?"

"I like beer, but I only smoke Marlboros."

With each question, he wondered why he was wasting his time trying to obey the rules of the game when he was only bringing trouble on himself.

Before leaving the hotel, Gentille had admired his bravery and he had told her, "I'm not brave, not a bit. I'm actually rather yellow by nature. But I can't behave any other way. I don't even feel I'm doing my duty. I act by reflex, because that's the way one ought to in a civilized society. I'm like a child who follows a book of rules. You excuse yourself when you bump someone by mistake, you say thank you and goodbye to the shopkeeper, you open the door for women, you help the blind across the street, you say hello before ordering a beer, you get up on the bus and give your seat to an old lady, you vote even if you don't like any of the candidates, and when you witness a crime you go to the police so the crime will be solved and in due course justice will be done. No, my darling, I'm not brave, I'm just trying to do things right, and here, that's not easy."

"You accuse the police sergeant of complicity in the murder of two adult persons and two children," the deputy prosecutor resumed. "You are aware of the gravity of these accusations, especially since they originate with an expatriate working for the progress of the Rwandan state and who is paid by the republic?"

Yes, indeed, Valcourt was perfectly aware of it.

"We have here a report from the same police sergeant who declares that he was attacked by a gang of RPF rebels and that during the fighting he lost two patriots. A Hutu traitor was guiding these rebels, who are not Rwandans, you know, but Ugandans claiming to be Tutsis in exile. This person, a tobacco vendor in the marketplace, was called Cyprien. Are we speaking of the same individual? His wife attempted to come to her husband's defence and she also was killed during the skirmish. These are the facts as they have been reported to us. Do you still wish to lay a complaint and contest the version of all the patriots manning the roadblock?"

"There has to be a choice, Monsieur Deputy Prosecutor. The officer spoke to me of unidentified vehicles and to you of a murderous attack by the RPF. Tell me, Monsieur Deputy, where did you do your law studies?"

"In Canada, Monsieur Valcourt, in your own city of Montreal, on a scholarship from the Canadian government. I lived near Lafontaine Park. Perhaps you know it?"

Valcourt had been born at 3211 Mentana Street, very near the big park. Suddenly, all he could think of was getting some sleep. But he insisted that his complaint not be set aside. And yes, he would go and testify before the court and remained ready to serve justice, "if ever justice exists here as it does in the vicinity of Lafontaine Park, Monsieur Deputy."

"Are you not afraid of the consequences, Monsieur Valcourt? I mean, afraid that what you are doing could be interpreted in various ways by the authorities?"

Valcourt raised his hand slowly as if in a sign of peace, indicating that he'd had enough, he was going, this play-acting was wearing him out. Of course, he thought as he stood on the steps a moment later, looking at the marketplace where Cyprien was no longer selling his tobacco, of course he was afraid of the consequences of his denunciations. But every step, every act, he realized fully, imprisoned him, prevented him from turning back. How could he hold his tongue and just look on? And then, a little girl was asleep with Gentille in his room. If her loneliness was not to kill her, someone, someday, would have to find a way to tell her how her parents died, tell her about the killers and the senseless hatred driving them.

He couldn't see anyone but himself and Gentille doing this for her. An article, an in-depth report might perhaps stir public opinion and influence his government which in turn would talk about it to another, he told himself as he passed the Kigali Night, into which exuberant French paras were trooping noisily. But what a fool I am! he thought. It takes ten thousand dead Africans to furrow the brow of even one left-leaning White. Even ten thousand's not enough. And they aren't noble deaths, either—they make humanity blush. The media don't show dead bodies cut up by men and shredded by vultures and wild dogs. They show the pitiful victims of drought, swollen little bellies, eyes bigger than TV screens, the tragic children of famine and the elements—that's what moves people. Then committees get set up and humanitarian souls get busy and mobilize. Contributions flow. Encouraged by their parents, rich kids break open their piggy banks. Governments, feeling a warm wind of popular solidarity blowing, push and shove at the humanitarian aid wicket. But when it's men like us killing other men like us, and doing it brutally with whatever's handy, people cover their faces. And when they're expendable men, like these in this country . . .

Valcourt didn't really know why he was going once again to pester the Canadian general. He had no hope of being able to influence the course of things, but insisted on seeing him anyway.

The general listened politely, sometimes scribbling a few words on a yellow notepad. Valcourt was telling him nothing, or almost nothing, that he did not know. He had already asked the UN for permission to intervene and seize the deposits of arms that the extremists were planning to distribute among the populace. Another Canadian general and UN functionary had turned him down.

Valcourt said he did not understand why the general needed approval and more soldiers in order to intervene—his commission stated that he should ensure the protection of the civilian population of the capital. A few dozen Belgian paras could dispense with all the roadblocks in the city in a single night. And he knew there were killings every day and every night in Kigali. And they weren't isolated incidents, not anymore. They couldn't be shrugged off as the work of a few extremists. Even the police were now into extortion.

"Yes, if I interpreted my commission proactively, I'd have enough evidence to intervene, but the commission wasn't entrusted to me alone. I'm a soldier who refers the matter to his superiors when in doubt. Politically, Monsieur, things are not simple. I would like to protect civilians, but I do not want to risk losing soldiers, even one, without written authorization. I am not here to save Rwandans, I am here to ensure respect of the Arusha accord. As for the police, I work in complete cooperation with Colonel Théoneste, the chief of police. He is a man of his word, a professional, and he swears to me that he punishes outbursts and misconduct."

There it was. In UN eyes, the massacre of Cyprien and his wife and children was mere "misconduct."

"And if the great cleansing of Tutsis and their supporters that the extremist radio and publications are calling for began, what would you do?"

"Nothing, Monsieur, nothing. I don't have the necessary number of troops to intervene. They will not give them to me. We will protect the United Nations buildings and personnel and perhaps the expatriates, if that doesn't place the lives of our soldiers in danger. For the rest, that's a problem between Rwandans."

"You know there'll be massacres."

"There have already been in Bugesera. They're talking about thousands dead."

"And you do nothing."

The general seemed out of patience. He had done his duty. He had sent several informants to the site, who had confirmed the rumours and gathered eyewitness reports. He repeated that he had sent this information to New York, and that his superiors had asked him to continue to monitor the situation and warn them if ever these outbursts came to endanger the lives of members of the various UN organizations at work in the country. He was preparing a plan of evacuation for the multi-lateral force and expatriates, and he thanked Valcourt for coming but could not give him any more time.

On his way back to the hotel, Valcourt ran into Raphaël and told him, "Forget the Blue Berets, they won't lift a finger. You guys are on your own."

And he explained. The general had done everything to justify his present passivity and future impotence. Had asked another of his own kind, a public servant, for permission he did not need and knew would be refused. Had written reports asking for more troops, knowing that no country wanted to send more troops to Rwanda, but knowing also, which was more serious, that with the several thousand soldiers he already had he could neutralize the extremists of the presidential guard and their principal accomplices in a few hours. Like the general, Valcourt had watched the Rwandan army's manoeuvres and exercises and had barely managed to keep himself from laughing out loud and offending his hosts as well as the French military instructors, who looked the other way while their pupils floundered like Boy Scouts on their first outing in the woods. A few hundred professional soldiers could take control of the capital in a matter of hours. The UN didn't need reinforcements, just a bold leader on the spot. All the Western military experts knew it, and in particular the UN general himself.

"Raphaël, I can't do any more. It's all too enormous. I've tried, what little I could. First it was the television

station, you remember. I thought I'd be giving democ-
racy a boost with that. Then I thought I could fight
AIDS by making a film. There's still no TV station and
I probably won't get to finish the film. I still have
Gentille and the child. I can save maybe two people."

Although more and more profoundly convinced of
his own helplessness, Valcourt wrote a long article on
the murder of his friends, on the looming genocide and
the studied composure of the commander of the United
Nations force. He sent it off to a dozen publications with
which he maintained contact, most of them in Canada.
Only a small Catholic weekly in Belgium accepted it for
publication. He was not much surprised. In 1983, like
hundreds of other journalists, he had received press
releases from humanitarian groups working in Ethiopia. They were predicting an unprecedented famine,
which could kill a million people. The print and elec-
tronic media and UN agencies had all received the
same press releases and detailed reports of rainfall statistics, climatic forecasts, grain reserve figures, soil
humidity indices, and seed shortages after the year-
long drought. Like all the others, Valcourt had paid
little attention to these cries of alarm. Only after seeing
skeletal children collapsing in the dirt roads before the
cameras of the BBC did he go to Ethiopia, just in time
to film the famine's triumph.

Valcourt felt like someone aboard one of those mon-
strous amusement park rides that inspire terror and
exhilaration, both the fear of dying and an immeasura-
ble rush of life, the one emotion impossible to separate
from the other. In this room, only days ago, Méthode
had lain dying. Today, a little girl was laughing to see
the shadow pictures Gentille was making on the wall

with her fingers. Tonight, a few hundred metres away, other little girls would lose their parents amid the whistle of machetes and the thudding of *masus*. All of this seemed linked and inevitable, written into the order of life here.

But the child's laughter and Gentille's motherly joy were speaking to Valcourt of hope again. An hour ago when he left the general's office he wanted to get away. Now he was writing feverishly in his notebook:

"The pitfall . . . thinking it's inevitable, that it's in the nature of the society or the country or humanity, not seeing that a few men make the decisions about all the violence—and if they don't plan it in detail they create the conditions that send it over the top . . . Work up the example of AIDS, the outcast women forced to be part-time prostitutes in order to feed their children because they're denied access to land or property . . . it's not only African sexual behaviour that's at the root of it, though that's a factor . . . Write this country's story through the story of Gentille and her family . . . describe the complacency of international institutions over corruption . . ."

Gentille asked him what he was writing.

"I'm starting to ply my trade again. Trying to say what's hidden behind the bogeymen, the monsters, the caricatures, the symbols, the flags, the uniforms, the grand declarations that lull us to sleep with their good intentions. Trying to put names to the real killers sitting in offices at the presidential palace and the French embassy. They're the ones who draw up lists and give orders, and the ones who finance the operations and distribute the weapons."

"Can't we do anything?" Gentille asked timidly.

"Yes, but it isn't much. Stay as long as possible, observe, denounce, report what we see. Keep the memory of Méthode and Cyprien alive—their examples, pictures, words—for those who'll follow."

He would write for those willing to read, speak to those willing to lend an ear, even half an ear, but that was all. He would knock at no more embassy and legation doors, bring no more denunciations before the representatives of justice and established powers. These things had only been futile agitation, which had soothed his conscience perhaps but was now endangering the only country he was in any position to save: his two women.

Someone knocked at the door just as Gentille was saying with a smile:

"And you'll write about love too, so I'll learn . . ."

"About love, you know as much as I do."

The young man, sweating in his blue suit, starched shirt and nylon tie from another era could only be a newcomer to the Kigali circus ring, probably a Canadian who had been packed off to his posting before anyone remembered to tell him that Rwanda was a hot country.

Jean Lamarre apologized for inconveniencing Valcourt this way. He had tried to telephone but the phone was always busy. He needed Valcourt's help, and urgently. Jean Lamarre, in his dark horn-rimmed glasses that were too big for his small head, and too grand for his position as novice Canadian consular official (though he seemed about ready to request an immediate recall), was faced with an insoluble problem. He rambled on apologetically about his arrival the day before yesterday, about his baggage being misdirected to Mombasa, about the Canadian embassy having abandoned him because it was tournament day at the golf club. He was sorry not to have come yesterday to pay his respects to so eminent a member of the Canadian community in Rwanda as Monsieur Valcourt, all the more since he, Jean Lamarre, was to be in charge of press relations and Monsieur Valcourt was a distinguished journalist whose televised reports he had seen and whose articles he had read.

The child, who had begun to whimper shortly before the young diplomat's appearance, was by now howling determinedly. Her language was simple and direct. "I'm hungry," she howled, "I'm very hungry." She had no name because Cyprien had not bothered to introduce her to the couple who were to become her parents.

"She's your daughter?" enquired Jean Lamarre, who could hardly ignore the source of the cries penetrating the walls and disturbing the idlers swimming about in the pool below with lazy strokes.

"Yes, she's my daughter . . . and I'd like you to meet my wife, Gentille."

Gentille almost fainted when she learned that she was henceforth Valcourt's wife and they were a family.

"I received a call from the KHC morgue. I don't know what this KHC is. They want me to come and identify the body of a Canadian citizen, a Brother François Cardinal, who was murdered by thieves according to the police. I'm asking you to come with me to do the identification. I contacted the police and they tell me that you knew him very well."

No, Valcourt did not know him very well, but well enough to identify his body. "The KHC, by the way, is

the Kigali Hospital Centre." Valcourt left the only domain
he had sworn to save for the one he had made up his
mind to abandon to its fate. The child (we must give a
name to her, Valcourt thought as he left) was howling
harder than ever in Gentille's arms, who was not at all
sure what to do about it, having so recently become a
wife and mother, having made love with her husband
only once, and having known the father of her daughter
for barely a few minutes.

She offered one of her firm, pointed breasts, hoping some liquid might come out of it. Here, children
were nursed at the breast until two or three years old.
The child's lips and budding teeth instantly recognized
the nipple and the howling ceased. But to her immense
distress, not a drop of milk emerged from this breast,
which hardened and tingled to the immense pleasure of
Gentille, who was newly discovering this kind of caress
and would tell Valcourt about it when he returned. And
there must be other secrets in this body of hers whose
subtleties she was unaware of and which no one had
ever before explored with such urgent need. The child
let go of the useless nipple and began to yell again.
Gentille opened a little pot of puréed baby food for her
but she turned up her nose at it. All she knew as yet
were her mother's breasts. Gentille went downstairs
to Agathe's. Among Agathe's girls she would surely
find a milk-filled breast, or a baby bottle if not. At the
hairdressing salon, all the girls who were overflowing
with milk volunteered. So as not to make any of them
jealous, Gentille suggested they take turns nursing the
baby, which they accepted with great enthusiasm, clap-
ping and laughing triumphantly. For nighttime, a bottle
would serve nicely.

The young diplomat, who was on his first posting and should have been paying social calls that day with his seven-months-pregnant wife, admitted that this unforeseen visit to the morgue was not much fun.

"That's what you get, Monsieur," Valcourt said, "for being a diplomat in Rwanda and not playing golf. Get with it, first chance you have. Otherwise you'll find all the chores being dumped in your lap. After the morgue, the burials, then laying the first brick for Canadian-subsidized houses they'll tear down before they've finished putting them up, French lessons in a school Canada has just paid to renovate. Then confabulations around the pool so your Rwandan friends can figure out which Canadian purse strings you hold."

"You paint a very black picture of a country that considers Canada a friend."

"When one is a small country, Monsieur Lamarre, one takes the friends one can get."

"In that I recognize a cynicism typical of you journalists who are Third World specialists."

They were walking alongside a red brick wall against which whole families seemed to be living in a variety of makeshift constructions, mingled with a few street stalls selling food, soaps and pilfered medicines. They overtook three patients being carried laboriously on rough stretchers by their families.

"No, Monsieur Lamarre, there aren't any ambulances, except for soldiers or Whites, and Whites don't come to the KHC. They take a plane. A death can always wait, especially if a body less allows someone to discover life."

Valcourt knew his way around the hospital blind-folded. He had filmed here several times and had met almost all the medical and nursing staff for his film on AIDS.

"The morgue is right at the back. On the way, I'll give you a tour of the property. A little visit to darkest Rwanda."

To the left of the main gate, guarded by a dozen nonchalant soldiers, a small bungalow with dung-coloured stucco walls was slowly but surely crumbling in the shade of some eucalyptus trees. "Welcome to Emergency," read the sign. Three beds with soiled sheets, a photograph of the president centred on the wall, bloodstains on the concrete floor, a bedpan full of urine and a few dressings. On the bed at the back, a young man with machete wounds was voicing all the pain of this earth. An old woman as wizened as a dried-up orange and a little boy holding both hands over his ears sat in a corner, waiting. What was going on? Perhaps the young man was yelling him-self to death. Valcourt and Lamarre went through to a waiting room. Around a table covered with dress-ings, small bottles and ashtrays, male and female nurses were having coffee. An espresso machine was quaintly enthroned on a gurney doing duty as a sideboard.

"Coffee, Monsieur Bernard? We're waiting for the doctor on duty, who had an important lunch date with the deputy minister of health. There's a chance he'll be appointed to the Ministry."

Lamarre whispered with some disgust that they might at least have given the wounded man some painkillers. Valcourt took him by the arm.

"Next visit: Kigali Hospital Centre's Central Pharmacy."

Side by side on straight chairs, patiently working at embroidery, three women sat in silence in an ill-lit grotto. Rats as big as beavers scurried hither and thither. When they saw Valcourt the women put aside their work.

"What a lovely surprise!" said Josephine, the head stockkeeper of the central pharmacy. "Have you come to show how badly off we are?"

Dozens of racks of shelves, three-quarters empty, made a kind of enormous grillework in the semi-darkness. Nothing had changed since Valcourt's last visit. There were still no antibiotics. The next delivery was expected in a month. The last aspirins had been distributed three days ago. An enormous quantity of antifungal ointment had been received from a generous donor country, but people here didn't come to the hospital for skin ailments. There was a little morphine left and a lot of cough syrup, as well as a potion no one knew quite what to do with called Geritol, which, it seemed, could relieve certain ills related to old age. "But you know, Monsieur Bernard, there aren't many old people in the hospital. They stay at home." So not really knowing what to do with this syrup, the pharmacists were giving it to anyone insisting on medicine.

"Would you like to take a picture for your scrapbook?"

In his sweating hand, Lamarre was clutching an old-model Polaroid, marked with a Canadian flag and an inventory number. He was supposed to take pictures of François Cardinal's dead body for the embassy's file.

"I'll spare you the maternity ward, it's too noisy, but on the way to the morgue we should drop by the internal medicine buildings. They're fascinating, you'll see."

The KHC consisted of some thirty low buildings separated by grassed spaces and asphalt paths. If it were not for the long white coats walking hurriedly, pushing gurneys at breakneck speeds, one could have supposed this to be a refugee camp. Everywhere, on the smallest patch of shaded earth or grass, families were cooking, children were playing, young men were ogling young girls. Old people were sleeping, one on a mat, another on a big piece of corrugated cardboard, their heads covered with towels or squares of cheap cotton.

"Monsieur Lamarre, Structural Adjustment 101. Structural adjustment, which you've certainly heard has helped a number of poor countries stabilize their public expenditures, has in a way invented this hospital, which must look rather surreal to a Canadian like you. A gentleman from Washington tells the Rwandan government that it spends too much on public services, that its debt is too high, but it will be helped to repay that debt if—"

"Monsieur Valcourt, I did an internship with the International Monetary Fund. Spare me your leftist demagogy. The public finances of several African countries have been successfully stabilized this way."

"Of course. When you're discussing these things in an office in Washington or drawing econometric curves on a computer, it all seems logical. In a hospital, it doesn't hold up at all. You begin by charging admission fees. Half the patients stop coming to the hospital and go back to the leaf-doctors—that's what they call the witch doctors or charlatans. The cost of medications goes up because they're imported and structural adjustment devalues the local currency. This is how the pharmacy here has turned into an embroidery room. Staff reductions come next. Then you charge for meals, medications, dressings and so on. That's why all these people are swarming and finagling inside and around the hospital walls. Little restaurants selling food for patients, vendors of expired medicines, snake oil, filched antibiotics and various toiletries, and everywhere around you, these families too poor to pay for it all who've come to stay and prepare food for their patient and wash him, watch over him and comfort him. A structural adjustment hospital is a place where one pays for one's death . . . because by the time patients come their condition is such that it would take a miracle or an accident for a cure to happen. Perhaps you'd like me to tell you about a structural adjustment school . . . no? I insist. When I was visiting the Ivory Coast, I discovered that since they'd introduced fees for high-school-level education, more and more young girls were taking to occasional prostitution, and since, like typical Africans, Ivory Coast males detest condoms, this new supply of fresh pussy on the market caused the AIDS propagation rate to skyrocket in the principal cities of the country.

"I'm telling you all this rather like a tourist guide trying to familiarize a newcomer with the country's curiosities. I'm not cynical, Monsieur. I know my country well and assure you that the maps and guides your department has given you are all wrong. Well! Off now to the main internal medicine building, the kingdom of slow decay and transformation of the human being into an oozing, dying spectre."

"You're exaggerating, Monsieur Valcourt."

"I wish you were right, Monsieur Lamarre."

Valcourt pushed open the swinging door of Pavilion B. In a tiny office on the left, a nurse was filling out a form. Jars filled with cotton batting, test tubes, and orange peels littered the small table she was writing on.

"Bonjour, Monsieur Bernard. If it's for Célestine, it's too late. She died yesterday morning."

He had known Célestine at the Cosmos. She had asked him to help her pay for her studies in international secretarial work, just a little loan that she would pay back in a few weeks. She had persisted, putting her hand on his thigh: "Even if you don't give me the loan, I want to go with you tonight, just for the pleasure." She came to try again at the hotel at two in the morning. He had let her sleep on the deckchair on the balcony. He had woken with a start. Célestine was sitting on the edge of the bed, masturbating him studiously. He couldn't come, and gave her the loan. She had been coming back regularly for a bed when she had no john. Then she had disappeared. He had seen her again in Pavilion B, lying head to foot beside an old tubercular patient. She had asked him for another little loan for food.

No, he had not come for Célestine, he said, he had brought a visitor.

"Bernadette, how many do we have today? Monsieur Lamarre, who works for the Canadian government, is doing a study on the financing of health services in Rwanda."

The nurse moved several small bottles and took out a big blue book with gold lettering on its spine, like those old registers that accounts used to be kept in before computers emptied offices of their clumsy files. She slowly scanned the columns with the point of a chewed Bic pen and wrote the figure on a paper hand-kerchief that she took out of her sleeve. Though Pavilion B was holding to about average, she had lost two beds this week; they had collapsed under the weight of the patients lying in them.

"That makes sixty-eight beds and one hundred fifty-three patients. A bit better than last month—seventy beds when we had one hundred eighty patients."

Ridiculous and unbelievable arithmetic for Lamarre, who had spent only five days in a hospital, in a private room, with a big bed and a television set, a desk and several comfortable chairs, not to mention a shower and the small refrigerator that his wife had filled with pâtés and cheeses and several bottles of wine so as to make his stay in such a depressing place more enjoyable. Marie-Ange, his wife, had even spent a night with him. All excited by this audacity and violation of taboo, she had held back several cries she didn't even recognize as her own while he was on top of her, screwing quickly for fear a nurse would open the door and discover them. She had come, already imagining other taboo places as original as the elevator, the airplane toilet, the car in a shopping mall parking lot on a Friday night, and espe-cially, especially, her small office at the Department of External Affairs. Jean Lamarre had turned down all her persistent and increasingly incomprehensible pro-posals, suggesting instead that she go and consult a psychiatrist. The baby to be born in a little less than two months was the product of this penchant for the taboo. It had been conceived in five minutes with a stranger in the parking lot of a chic restaurant where Marie-Ange had gone to eat when her model-employe husband was working late, voluntarily, at the office.

This time she had not held back her cries. The man took fright and fled with his fly open and penis dangling in the cold. Today, sitting under the hotel's great fig tree, all she was thinking about was soon being rid of this enormous belly that was keeping all men at a distance, except for her over-modest husband who always came to bed clothed in pyjamas and never took them off, even when laboriously making love to her.

"How many with AIDS, Bernadette?"

"About a hundred."

They entered a scene of chaos. In each small bed lay two patients, many holding children in their arms. Under many beds lay other patients, sometimes on mats, sometimes on the concrete floor. There were children, some crawling, some running about. Some older children were feeding a greyish gruel to their mothers who were too weak to hold a spoon. In the room beyond, several volunteers, all HIV positive, were trundling an enormous pot with a stew of some kind from bed to bed. They were enrolled in one of Father Louis's programs and came every day to distribute a free meal to AIDS patients who had no family to feed them or were too poor to pay for food. Today the volunteers had more than seventy mouths to feed and were afraid of running short.

"Take some pictures, Monsieur Lamarre. Don't be shy. They'll like it. Every time someone takes pictures or movies of them, a little hope of help to come is born. Anyway, they'll die before they realize that no capital city in the world cares about them."

The young diplomat was sweating more than his clothes could take. He had an irresistible urge to vomit, which, mortified, he did in full view of a flock of laughing children as soon as he emerged from Pavilion B. His visit to the morgue, whose air-conditioning system was not working, did nothing to calm his gut. It was not so much the smell of death issuing from the dozen bodies there, as the odour of life beginning to rot. He asked Valcourt to take the pictures for him and left to vomit again.

Brother Cardinal was reposing on a gurney completely naked. A bullet had pierced his forehead and two others had lodged near his heart. The killers, who knew how to shoot, had murdered him calmly, without wasting their ammunition. The man bore no other sign of violence. Petty thieves or discontented workers were supposed to have killed him. Valcourt took three pictures as Lamarre had asked: one for the embassy, one for the Rwandan police and another for the French secret service, which was what Madame the Consul, informed of Cardinal's death on the tenth hole at the Kigali Golf Club, had ordered Lamarre to produce. The inquiry would be put in the hands of the French because the Rwandan police could not be trusted. And above all, she made it clear, if the embassy said nothing to anyone, the news might spread fastest and farthest through undesirable rumours.

Valcourt found Madame Lamarre under the fig tree while her husband changed his clothes. Gentille was swimming with their new daughter. The diplomat's wife seemed particularly interested in the sexual customs of Africans as she had heard them reported. Valcourt reassured her. She was in no danger, especially in her condition. But yes, White women were attractive to Black men, just as, he had been told, the reverse was true. If he himself had a Black wife, that was a matter of chance rather than a passion for the other colour. As for knowing whether these Blacks with their asses so firm and their breasts so pointed were "better" (this was the term she used) than Whites, he couldn't say. And the prostitutes? He explained that here, if you valued life, masturbation was better. And the child?

"Do you believe in the Immaculate Conception?"

Valcourt called Justin, the pool attendant, who wore his young Apollo anatomy and his glistening skin gloriously, the way others wear their clothes. This young lady, Valcourt told him, in her delicate condition was in need of special attention, not only company, for her husband was working long hours, but also physical relaxation, perhaps even some vigorous massages of which Justin had the secret, he'd heard. Justin declared himself at Madame's service and Madame felt a great shiver sweep through her. She hated the enormous belly separating her from the supple, muscular body parading before her. A river of perspiration wet her thighs. Her already heavy breasts quivered, tingled and hardened till they hurt. Valcourt took his leave. He had agreed to meet Lamarre in the hotel lobby. They were going to François Cardinal's village.

Justin, whose stiffened penis was almost popping through his tiny bathing suit, was already tasting his vengeance. One day, a little drunk with sunshine and beer, he had confided in Valcourt. Every time he fucked a White—and there were so many of them walking around with their uncertain bodies and their hidden lusts, their fascination with the barbarous, powerful negro—every time, he was getting even for being a pool attendant and mere lust object for the boss ladies. He was getting even, too, for being Black. He behaved with the White women the way they hoped and dreamed he would, like a brutish animal, as if he were not really human. They screamed like animals, reduced to his level at last, and begged for more, as if they wanted him to humiliate them even further, turn them into pure unsated flesh, emptied of all mind and all dignity. And it was then, when they were begging for a second humiliation, that real vengeance came. He said no. They could try all they liked, come to his shack at the pool, pester him at his room, promise him money or visas for all the havens of the West, he would turn them down. Around his pool they would lie on their plastic deckchairs, frustrated, jumpy, unsatisfied and bad-tempered because for a few minutes they had known the power of a dark force that now, always smiling, carried on with his humble pool attendant's work, respectfully attending them. Compared to this country's violence, Justin's vengeance was rather gentle, although Valcourt was impressed by its refinement and psychological cruelty. He never lost an opportunity to contribute to the young man's war effort. However, Justin had concealed the real measure of his hatred. He had AIDS. When worried ladies demanded that he put on a condom, he would brandish a forged HIV negative certificate.

Justin did massage her—for he did know something about massage—after sitting her down on a small stool because it was unwise, in her condition, for her to lie on her stomach on the massage table. He began with her neck, shoulders and shoulder blades, on which he worked effectively and conscientiously, with each movement of his fingers pushing aside the shoulder straps of her voluminous dress and ample bra, which slipped down to her waist. She rose several centimetres and let her clothes fall to the floor. The man pressed against her back and just above her nape she felt an enormous penis thrusting into her hair. Two big hands were kneading her breasts so vigorously they began to squirt milk. She wanted to speak but couldn't, except to say, "Take me," in a hoarse, animal voice that was shaped also by sharp, shooting pains from inside her sweat-bathed belly. Justin picked her up by the armpits, lifted her and pushed her to the wall, against which she leaned with her hands and head. With a single brusque, violent movement he entered her the back way. Never had anyone touched or caressed this part of her body, even by accident. Muscles exploded, cried out. Her belly struck the wall. The greater the pain or the pleasure, for they were one and the same, the faster and more often she repeated, "Deeper, deeper." After long minutes when she expected to faint a hundred times over, she screamed as one does only before death, paralyzing the young man, who had never heard such a rending cry. He sat her on the little stool. She was seized with cramps, daggers driving through her belly. A stream of viscous fluid started to flow from her vagina and the contractions began. Marie-Ange gave birth in the shack, attended by a Médecins Sans Frontières doctor who came every day to do his hundred lengths in the pool. He cut the umbilical cord with a Swiss Army knife that a major benefactress of the Red Cross had left with Justin to remember her by.

When Jean Lamarre returned from Mugina with Valcourt around eleven that night, he was a father and cuckold, both for the rest of his days. But the worst was not having even settled in his first posting abroad before fearing he'd be recalled to Ottawa and confined to consular information or the Mongolia section before he could enjoy his first villa, his first gardener or his first cook, which are today—short of being able to influence the course of history—the foremost pleasures for a diplomat representing a country like Canada in Rwanda.

François Cardinal had not been murdered by ordinary petty thieves, or by Tutsi rebels—another version suggested to Lamarre by Lisette, the consul, when he went to see her on the way back to the hotel. Along with Valcourt he had tried to reason with her but she was not in the mood to listen to anyone bringing her disagreeable facts. Her golf tournament had been a disaster. She had been humiliated even by the consul of Tanzania and a secretary at the embassy in Kenya. It was really not the time to bring up the possibility of a diplomatic incident, or worse, a review of the long-standing friendship between Canada and Rwanda. In any event, the inquiry had been entrusted to the special services of the presidency, meaning the French secret service, competent people who would be sure to get at the truth. For the moment, if anyone in Canada asked who had killed Brother Cardinal, the authorities would reply, "Thieves or rebels."

By telephone, Valcourt told a friend in Canadian television that they were very strange thieves because they had left over 150,000 Rwandan francs on the mantelpiece, the pay that the brother was going to distribute to

the members of the egg producers' co-operative that he
ran. As for the Tutsi rebel hypothesis, that was completely hare-brained. The brother was taking in Tutsi
refugees fleeing from the North (the president's region),
where they were terrorized by massacres. No, Cardinal
had been killed by soldiers, in broad daylight, because
his co-operative was a threat to the near-monopoly of a
nephew of the president over the egg trade in the capital, or because he was taking in Tutsis, or both. Valcourt
knew why he had been killed, but it was not the stuff
of news bulletins. Cardinal was working for the dignity of
men, for sharing of the land's riches, for tolerance. In
the eyes of the law governing this country, these were
three offences deserving of the death penalty.

Canadian television simply announced the brother's
death, and noted that while the murder was difficult to
explain it had probably been committed by thieves. Thus
is life recounted, compressed into capsules and composed
by people far away, ignorant but without ill will, who,
sitting at their computers, do not differentiate between
a settling of accounts among bikers and a political
assassination in Rwanda. A dead man is a dead man.

Since the coming of Gentille, in the manner of all
historical watersheds, Valcourt had passed in a matter of
seconds from a world of doom and gloom to a universe
of beauty without the slightest trouble, as if he had
learned to navigate among all the countries of man.
He took no pride in it, only felt that he was luckier
than others.

In his notebook he wrote, "I'm emerging from
another horror. It's not this death that's horrible but
the deceit constructed around it, a way of officially
denying Cardinal. This man is a hero, and his country

is going to treat him purely as a wretched victim of a barbarous, anonymous act. And I come in here where Gentille is sleeping with Cyprien's daughter. I'll lie down beside her in a few minutes. She'll wake up, I know. And we'll make love, quietly so as not to wake the little girl. And after, I'll sleep, like all happy men. But in my sleep there'll be as many nightmares as ecstasies." And that night, for the second time in his life, he made love with Gentille.

The next morning Lamarre brought a long face and a dragging step to the breakfast buffet. It was not being cuckolded that was getting him down; he didn't know about that yet. Or his new fatherhood, which he was quite indifferent to, except for thinking its timing pretty bad. He'd never wanted to be a father and couldn't understand how, in spite of all the precautions they'd taken, Marie-Ange had got pregnant. Probably a forgotten pill. Women are so absentminded.

A patient and methodical civil servant, Jean Lamarre was at thirty following a precise, realistic career plan, because his modest ambition more or less matched his capacity to rise through the ranks. A few years in Africa in a country that caused no problems, like Rwanda. Return to Ottawa as section head. Then consul in a small Asiatic country (he loved Chinese food) and finally cultural attaché in Paris, having to choose among all those invitations to cocktail parties, book launches, exhibition openings and first nights.

But sitting across from Valcourt, who was talking happily about his new daughter while swilling a big Primus and putting away three fried eggs with bacon and sausage as if he hadn't eaten for days, Lamarre knew his still non-existent career was hanging by a thread. Lisette, the skilled tactician, pleading her absence and lack of knowledge of the case, had wakened him at six in the morning to place a great responsibility in his hands, an indication of her confidence in him: he was to write the report on Brother Cardinal's death. The minister, who had heard worrisome rumours about the identity of the murderers and hoped they were untrue, was waiting for his report.

Lamarre sat staring at the scrambled eggs congealed on his plate, saying nothing. He pushed a nervous fork around in the yellow mash.

"You see, I have to write the report on Brother Cardinal's death. And I'd like to know..."

"No, you wouldn't really like to know that Cardinal was fighting with what little he had against great injustices. You don't want to know, and even less write, that members of the president's entourage probably ordered his death. You don't want to know, you want to get out of this looking good. I understand and I feel for you. But you won't get away with it. The dead we hide away turn into ghosts and come back to haunt us. You're screwed. Another victim of this shitty country. If you tell the truth, your career's down the drain. If you back the version the minister wants so his chummy relations with Rwanda can carry on as before, I'll get after you. All we both know will be published one of these days in a Canadian or Belgian or French publication. I swear it. I'll be after you. I'll be a thorn in your side. You'll be my enemy number one. About the murderers I can't do anything, I have no weapons, I'm hopeless on that score, but little accomplices like you

I can fight with words. Monsieur Lamarre, you're an enemy I can handle."

Lamarre pleaded. He didn't deserve to be harassed. Valcourt, full now, shook his head as he sipped a strong espresso. He understood Lamarre's distress. He was even sorry for him. Choosing between the rigours of truth and the shame of mendacity is not easy. He was sorry to have to threaten him but could not do otherwise. The young diplomat had not touched his scrambled eggs. When he got up to go to his room and write his report, he walked with heavy steps and his back bowed as though he had aged thirty years in two days.

The report he wrote conformed to the preliminary conclusions drawn by the French secret service: Brother François Cardinal had been murdered by thieves who were perhaps Tutsi rebels. The embassy and also the Department of External Affairs endorsed this version, which was circulated throughout Canada. Valcourt succeeded in having an article about it published in Belgium. This did nothing to affect Lamarre's career. Three days after their conversation, Lamarre left the hotel for his villa, his houseboy, his cook and his gardener.

Even emptied of her baby, Marie-Ange definitely did not attract him anymore, which was not of too much concern to her, for she was now trying out the gardener, thinking all the while of Justin. The young couple were not seen again in diplomatic circles or restaurants. Lamarre watched kung fu videos and his wife fucked the staff, striving to attain the ecstasy and abandon to which Justin had transported her. She had

pursued the young man, who rejected her scornfully
every time.

Five weeks after the couple's arrival in Rwanda, she
was taken to the Belgian physician who had been following her since the childbirth. She was HIV positive.
She began to scream. When she stopped screaming,
after clawing the doctor in the face, she hissed, "I'll kill
him!" She did nothing of the kind, of course. Justin kept
on transferring his country's death to White women
until his own death. Lamarre, with an eye still on his
career, and perhaps compassionately, organized Marie-
Ange's return to Canada mere days after the inevitable
announcement. Nadine, she who was conceived in a
parking lot and ejected in a tiny shack, he kept with
him. He became a father by obligation, and then for
pleasure. Through the child, who became the only object
of his attention, he discovered a side of life that he had
totally denied himself: silly, spontaneous laughter,
funny faces, nursery rhymes, anxiety over the first
fever when a child turns as red as a glowing ember. To
redeem himself in his own eyes, he wrote a second
report, more hypothetical than the first, in which he
spoke of rumours going round in Cardinal's village that
pointed at soldiers or presidential henchmen as the
killers. He sent this report directly to the minister's
office, saying nothing to his superior, who had sent a
fax praising the work of her French colleagues over
this distressing incident and was patting herself on the
back for having closed the case so quickly, with good
relations between the countries involved kept intact.
Lamarre was no longer interested in playing politics or
planning a career. He would be satisfied to be a good
father, a dull one perhaps but a present and respectful

one. And when he lay on the hard, damp grass in front of his little villa above the Kigali Night and gazed at the stars, this uncontemplative man felt light as he had never done before, certain of having found an occupation that was right for him, and he kissed his sleeping daughter and went to bed with a modicum of self-esteem.

When Valcourt learned of Marie-Ange's illness and departure, he realized how little he still understood about this country he had thought he could explain to people, or about the contagion at work here. Justin, the pool boy, had infected Marie-Ange. And it was he, Valcourt, who had thrust her into Justin's arms. Around the pool, sex was just a game. As if unconsciously he had led Marie-Ange to sex with Justin, who admitted without shame or remorse that he was giving White women back an illness that had been inflicted on Black men. Valcourt didn't spend even a second trying to convince the young man of his error and idiocy. He simply told him that if he saw him lure another woman to his shack he would tell the whole truth to the hotel manager who, with all his contacts in the government, would certainly succeed in having him clapped in prison.

He told the entire story to Gentille, who was less shocked than he feared she would be. She reproached him only (was it really a reproach?) for having hastened a meeting that would have happened anyway, since this woman was "a gift woman," to use her expression. Feeling responsible nevertheless, he had to make his thinking clear to her.

"You see, each country has a colour, a smell, and also a contagious sickness. In my country the sickness is complacency. In France it's arrogance, and in the United States it's ignorance."

"What about Rwanda?"

"Easy power and impunity. Here, there's total disorder. To someone who has a little money or power, everything that seems forbidden elsewhere looks permissible and possible. All it takes is to dare it. Someone who's simply a liar in my country can be a fraud artist here, and the fraud artist gets to be a big-time thief. Chaos and most of all poverty give him powers he wouldn't have elsewhere."

"You're talking about Whites who think all they need do is lift a finger and I'll go up to their room even if they're ugly, and rich Rwandans who tell me I'll lose my job if I don't sleep with them. You're not like that."

"But that's what I did with Madame Lamarre. I used my power to play with her life. When people come here, they catch the power disease. I'm a bit like them. Look at them, all the small-time embassy advisers, the brawny or pimply paratroopers, the dull plodders of the international community, the two-bit consultants who don't spend a single evening without the city's most beautiful women on their arms, and later in bed. All of us turn into little chiefs when we get here."

Gentille smiled. A little chief maybe, but a rather nice, respectful one. She didn't try to reassure him about himself.

"Keep talking," she said, "even if I don't like what I hear sometimes. All those people you mention aren't as bad as you say. I have trouble explaining things in detail the way you do. But keep talking, I like it when you talk to me, I like it when anybody talks to me. Apart from my grandfather, and my father too sometimes, nobody ever talked to me more than a few minutes. My whole life, all I've ever heard is orders, advice, forbiddings, litanies, hymns and sermons. I've never been part of a conversation. I've also heard insults and roars from men showing they were pleased or frustrated, but the only long sentences meant just for me are the ones you've said. So talk. I need to know I can be an ear as well as a . . ."

There are words a Rwandan woman does not pronounce even though the things they represent are common in her life: *ass, fuck, penis,* any word for the female sexual anatomy, or anything physically intimate. Nor do prostitutes use these terms. It's as if saying the word sanctions the sin or humiliation.

"You could have said 'body,' Gentille," Valcourt said softly. "That's not too hard to say. Or 'thing,' or 'object.' Or maybe 'ass'. . ."

Gentille bent her head and closed her eyes.

"You like them, don't you, my . . ."

She hesitated, then whispered: ". . . ass, and my breasts and my sex parts? D'you like talking to me as much?"

"Yes, Gentille, just as much."

"Talk some more, then. Talk to me about you, about home, tell me why you're staying here, and please, please don't tell me it's because of me. That would be kind but too easy. Talk to me, it's so good, so sweet."

There are people like Gentille to whom you must never tell the truth. It would be so simple it would look more like a lie, because life is supposed to be complicated. Nothing now justified Valcourt's staying in Rwanda except Gentille. It was all so simple to him, but he sensed that she wanted him to stay also for her country, and his friends, and the steep hills, and above all for himself.

"Why are you still here?"

"Because I'm kind of slothful and life here makes me get off my butt. My country is naturally slothful and uncourageous too. It only gets off its butt when catastrophes and horrors get beyond the bounds of understanding. But to be honest, I have to say that both of us, my country and I, behave relatively well once the sloth is beaten out of us."

"No, talk to me about your country the way I talk to you about the hills. Tell me about the snow."

"I don't like the snow, or the cold or the winter. I hate winter. But there's one day in the year, a magic moment that even a movie can't reproduce. You wake up one morning and the light in your house is blinding. Outside, the sun is shining twice as bright as at the height of summer, and everything that for weeks has been dirty, grey, brown, dead leaves, mud mixed with faded flowers, everything that autumn has enveloped in gloom, all of it that morning is whiter than your whitest shirt-dress. What's more, this whiteness sparkles with billions of stars that make you think someone has scattered diamond dust over the white earth. It lasts a few hours, sometimes a day. Then this fragile purity is soiled by the dirt that cities give off like sweat from bodies. But in our wide open spaces far from the cities, on our hills that are only little bumps compared to yours, the whiteness of the snow makes a bed that lasts for months. And silence settles in this bed. You don't know what silence is. You can't imagine how it wraps around you and clothes you. Silence dictates the beating of your heart and the pace of your steps.

Here, everything talks. Everything chatters and howls and sighs and shouts. There's not a second that isn't punctuated with a sound, a noise, a bark. Every tree is a loudspeaker, every house a sounding box. So there's this mystery in my hills, and it's silence. You're afraid of silence, I know, you've told me. But it's not empty the way you think. It's heavy and oppressive, because there's not a birdsong, not a footstep, not a note of music or a word to distract us from ourselves. You're right, silence is frightening, because you can't say untruths in silence."

Gentille would never hear silence. Paradoxically, real silence exists only in the torrid heat of the desert and the glacial cold of the far north. Try as he might, Valcourt could not imagine Gentille in the Sahara or the tundra. Why not remove Gentille from the hell of her life here and transplant her into his winter, which would be a lot more comfortable than the benign, permanent summer of the land of a thousand hills? He could do it, today, tomorrow, with no trouble. But far from home in a strange place, with no money of her own and no skill except at serving and being admired, without either of them wanting it she would soon be merely a slave. Being with him would no longer be the fruit of a delicious and lasting conquest but a case of dependence, no matter how tolerable and accepted it might be. Here in this room she might be living in a gilded, comfortable cage, but the door was always open. She knew the roads and pathways around the hotel, as well as ten or twenty refuges that would take her in if ever she decided she had had enough and must return to the pleasures and ambitions natural to someone her age. And this she would do one day. Valcourt had been resigned to it since that first leap of his heart. To think he could hold such beauty prisoner was more than he could bear. He must not steal life from life.

When he tried to explain why he would never take her to Canada, she didn't believe a word of his noble speech. Another woman would have wept, screamed, hurled insults, kicked and pummelled. Not Gentille. It was much worse. She said in a voice worthy of judges and hangmen, "You lied to me!" And went and lay in the other bed. In their whole short life together, ninety-seven nights, this was the only one when Valcourt did not know "the ecstasy of Gentille." This was the name he gave to the blending of their bodies.

Chapter Seven

The morning after this conjugal spat, the only one they ever had, Valcourt got up very early, with the mists and the ravens, before the dogs and the children. Sitting on the balcony which gave him a view of the city, dazzled by the fig tree shining as though a fairy gardener had waxed each of its leaves during the night, he wrote in a careful hand on hotel letter paper:

"Gentille, if I go back to Canada and you want to come, I'll take you with me. But I don't want to go back there. My real country is the country of the people I love. And I love you more than anything in the world. My country is here. We're father and mother now but we must make this adoption official. It would be easier if we were husband and wife. We must also find a name for our daughter. I don't really know what order we should do these things in. So as a start, I'm asking you to marry me. And if ever we had to leave this country, it would be for some place neither of us knows. Then each of us would be as lost as the other, each as poor and dependent."

He crossed the room on tiptoe and put the letter, folded in three, on Gentille's hip. She was not asleep.

"Wait." She read it and wept softly.

Ten years earlier he had been playing the tourist in Paris with his sixteen-year-old daughter. At the Musée de l'Orangerie, they gazed at Monet's *Waterlilies* unbelievingly, they were so astonished, so overcome by the beauty, nuances and subtleties of the painting. "Oh my, papa, it's so lovely," said a choked little voice. Anne-Marie had wept with tenderness at the beauty of life, as Gentille was weeping now. The way a woman weeps, with torn, exhausted muscles and hurting belly, when a red, wrinkled newborn is placed in her arms. For a fleeting moment, Valcourt wanted to tear up the already rumpled sheet of paper, erase the words, go back in time, turn back the clock, start again without yet having succumbed to Gentille's beauty. Her happiness terrified him. He was no match for this young woman's passion for life. He was so much older, inevitably he would be the first to die if life unfolded in the normal way. He could only promise her a tiny window of happiness, he knew, he was now convinced, then a plunge into a horrible, lonely void filled with the emptiness he would leave behind, an emptiness crammed only with memories impossible for her to re-create alone. Men who feel loved to distraction are easy prey to complacency, forgetting how much strength and patience women put into forging happiness. In this, Valcourt was a very ordinary man.

And there was something else. The killers were becoming less inhibited, less cautious and less anonymous every day. They proclaimed their extermination plans on the radio. They laughed about them in the bars. Their ideologues, like Léon Mugasera, were inflaming whole regions with their speeches. After every rally, militiamen hurled themselves like Huns onto the hills, burning, raping, crippling, killing with their Chinese machetes and their French grenades. International commissions came to take note of the damage, dug up bodies from common graves, gathered eyewitness testimony from survivors of the pogroms.

Valcourt would have a drink in the fourth-floor bar with the eminent jurists and experts while they told him ten times more than they would put in their reports. He took notes as he listened, discouraged and each time a little more terrified by the enormity of the revelations, but it was the pepper-and-nutmeg taste of Gentille's sex, the sharp points of her nipples and the trembling of her buttocks at his least caress that really occupied his mind at these times. And he didn't forgive himself for it. For any left-leaning Christian like himself, even if he didn't believe in God, happiness was a kind of sin. How can we be happy when the earth is falling apart before our eyes and humans are turning into demons, and extortions and unspeakable abominations are all that come of it?

One night when he was ruminating this way, alternating between thoughts of Gentille's breasts and what Raphaël was saying about the terrifying death threats he had just received at work, Gentille appeared with the sleeping child in her arms. Raphaël said:

"Happiness has come looking for you, my friend. Gentille, your future husband is an imbecile. You should dump him. He won't make the most of his happiness. He listens to me, pities me, racks his brain to find a way to help me, even though he knows he can't do anything. Tell him. No, I'll tell him, this fool of a White, but not before we've drunk a little champagne. Like Méthode, I want to die happy and in luxury."

Raphaël invited the maître d'hôtel to come and drink with them. The Belgian cook also came to join them, along with a second bottle, and Zozo who was passing by to check on something. Then Émérita, the taxi driver, who was coming to sleep on a banquette in the bar because militiamen were prowling round near her sister's house where she was living. A third bottle arrived with the barman. He had closed up his cash register and had hopes of getting into the buxom Émérita, who had eyes only for Valcourt who had always talked to her like one of the guys at work and never looked at her the way a man looks at a woman.

Raphaël talked without stopping, about AIDS, about corruption and about massacres. He repeated what he had said a thousand times before. Valcourt didn't need to listen closely. He knew what every sentence was going to be before it passed Raphaël's lips. But can you blame people threatened with death for talking about it and repeating themselves? With his naive, permanent smile, Zozo was agreeing: "Yes, Monsieur Raphaël, yes, you're right." Approval and the art of flunkydom were synonymous in Zozo's mind. One never knew if it was the friend or the flunky who was nodding approval.

Then Raphaël said, "Let's talk about more cheerful things." He began telling his raunchy stories, each more far-fetched than the last—he was a bit of a braggart, and quite convinced of his irresistible charm. The tales of his adventures brought knowing laughs, especially when he talked about White women. Then he described being locked up in the soccer stadium in 1990 with eight thousand other rebellion suspects. He didn't remember so much the hunger and the beatings on the soles of his feet, he remembered all the friends he made, and the women who were sweet and obliging so the men would forget their misery.

There were bellows of laughter and conspiratorial looks in the half-darkness of the bar. Faces wore luminous smiles. The little girl slept through all the racket. Gentille squeezed Valcourt's hand. Since the beginning, Valcourt had only smiled occasionally, not laughing, and not joining in with his own stories. Zozo, who turned into a gleeful clown with a single glass of alcohol, was in rapture over all the tales of resilience and survival, for, as at late-night gatherings of war correspondents, there was always a story following hard on the heels of the last. An exploit by one, embellished of course, would make way for another's mortification, promptly to be buried under an even spicier anecdote. Epics were swapped the way children swap marbles or Nintendo cassettes. Incredible deaths, asses rounder and smoother than a full moon, eyes deeper than the ocean, soldiers more barbaric than the Huns and Nazis put together, all vied mightily for listeners' attention. These minutes of intense life shared among friends were all saying the same thing in the same language, using doom and horror to reaffirm life.

Valcourt was not saying anything, guilty once again of being happy in the midst of barbarity, but feeling lighter, as if freed of a dark mass by Gentille's index finger delicately and patiently, as soft as down, stroking its way along the paths of life traced in his hand. Now it was she who was urging him:

"Tell a story, a good one. It's your turn."

He told of a morning in November 1984 at Bati, in the desert of the Tigris in Ethiopia. The great famine, which later aroused all the singers on the planet and left the West the memory of "We Are the World" rather than of its hundreds of thousands of victims, had descended on the north of the country with a gigantic sandstorm that buried everything and turned the desert into a common grave. He had heard tell of the early mornings when the rising sun is preceded by a pink and violet glow along the horizon. Over a pizza in the Addis-Ababa Hilton, a French doctor had told him how there came a moment in this dreamy tableau when groanings began at the same time as long, mysterious incantations intended to keep death at bay, punctuated by strident little cries and the barking of stray dogs. Then, when the pink and violet turned to orange, when the orange was pierced by the sun's first rays and the cadavers on reprieve were waking, you would begin to hear all the sounds of death to come. Lungs exploding, mothers crying, infants wailing, air passages struggling to clear. "A mortuary symphony against a picture-postcard background." That's what the doctor had said.

Valcourt, with Michel, his cameraman, a Vietnam survivor, set up near a small hole in which three or four people seemed to be sleeping, wrapped in goatskins, to watch this Wagnerian sunrise. It was bitter cold. Six hours later, the stony soil would burn any feet laid bare on it. Twenty-five thousand living skeletons, half naked, already broken by hunger, illness and exhaustion, each day endured the shock of heat and cold. And, as the doctor had told him, the full light of day and the doleful symphony began together, for these people of the heat and the desert discovered their dead or their new afflictions in the minutes that followed the cold of the night.

The woman who was waking in her hole while Valcourt recited his introduction to the camera thought perhaps that he was a doctor, nurse or priest. He had a knee on the ground and she laid before him a tiny body wrapped in a goatskin. The baby no longer had enough breath to move a blade of grass, only a whisper, a soft, slow death rattle that Valcourt could hear better than his own words describing the death all around him. He was tempted to finish by saying he had just seen a baby die there by his knees, then to pick it up and hold it for the camera. What a great piece of television it would have made, for Michel, hearing these words, would have slowly turned the lens down to the tiny, emaciated head and closed in to focus on the huge, deep, dark eyes, staring, accusing humanity. Then he would have followed Valcourt's motion, lengthening the focus and stepping slightly to the right. The baby would have been in the foreground, with Valcourt saying, "This is Bernard Valcourt in hell at Bati." To his left, the haggard but dignified eyes of the mother would have been clearly seen, and, in the background, the high clouds streaked with orange and purple heralding the morning and the start of a gruesome accounting.

This accounting at the morgue, a round shed of roughly assembled eucalyptus logs, was the exercise of most concern to Valcourt. He could not show all the little bodies, of course, but for six hours he filmed each of them, noting their names and ages, while they were washed before being laid on beds of eucalyptus branches. They would enter paradise clean and sweet-smelling.

Back in Montreal, nothing was the way it had been before. He began by trying, when he talked, not to use the coded language and objective distancing that stifle and falsify reality. A small, thinking mine exploded in his brain, muddling the right and left hemispheres, scattering the neurons of reason and feeling, transforming an efficient old order into a kind of boiling magma that mixed up everything—smells, memories, things he had read, ideas, principles, desires. He had thought about nothing but work before, and now his thoughts were occupied only with love, abandon in love, and anger. He wanted to shout out loud all he had seen, experienced, discovered, but had only half said because he'd been sticking to the cautious language of journalism that turns a lying prime minister into a man making progress and a slimy financier into an astute business-man. He tried to make a few people uncomfortable and had some success. Without realizing, and especially without wishing to, he'd fixed himself on the fringe of society that matters and does not forgive those that leave it. He discovered this little by little, one disappointment after another, one rebuff after another, then, what was worse, one evidence of indifference after another. And now on this night of dire happenings turned to laughter, Gentille's finger as soft as down was tracing life in the palm of his hand, and the little girl's head was warming his thigh, and Raphaël said to him:

"It's fascinating. It follows, there's a kind of justice. You find happiness with the derelicts of the earth. So make us feel good, there isn't much that does. Tell us you like the happiness you've found here. Make us feel good, tell us that for all the machetes and cut-off arms and raped women we can give beauty and gentleness too. And your own happiness, Bernard, stop hiding it, live it with us. It'll reassure us about ourselves."

Valcourt, a little drunk, but as emotional as when his daughter was born, stood up with his glass in his hand.

"I, Bernard Valcourt, expatriate tolerated in your country, have the honour of asking you for the hand of the most beautiful woman in Rwanda."

His friends exploded. The maître d'hôtel hugged him. Raphaël climbed up on the stainless steel bar and began to dance. Gentille let a few salty little pearls run down her satiny cheeks. Zozo tripped over an empty bottle left lying on the floor. The child began to howl, frightened by the din. Émérita, a member of a fundamentalist Baptist church, dropped to her knees and intoned several verses from the Bible. The barman leaned down and passed his hand over her buttocks, sure of getting his usual slap since he had already had five. She interrupted her prayer.

"Célestin, God has brought us a great blessing tonight. He'll surely forgive us all the sins you and I will commit later."

Célestin, who had been waiting three years for this moment, was seized with great anxiety. Would he be able to honour the woman of his dreams? He rushed behind the bar, broke six eggs into a shaker, added beer and a whole bottle of pepper sauce, and drank it all down at one go. Émérita drank alcohol for the first time in her life that night, and the champagne's effect sent wayward, wandering little ants through her head and bosom, making her tingle and tremble. This was her first real sin after twenty-seven years of shunning the pleasures that her mother sold in her Sodoma brothel. Célestin's huge hands took possession of her breasts.

"Émérita's becoming a woman!" cried Zozo, observing as always. Then, with a loud laugh that everyone heard, he added, "Let's hope Célestin's a man."

Normally Célestin, who had no sense of humour at all, would have strangled the little gnome publicly daring to cast doubt on his virility, but Émérita laughed harder than all the others while groping him clumsily, not really knowing how to show and act out this desire to be a woman that Valcourt had unconsciously aroused in her. For she would never cease to be in love with the crusty older man who was doing less and less to hide his smiles. But it was God's will to make her fat, round and heavy, and Valcourt would have needed both hands to caress a single breast, and then some. It was also in the mysterious ways of the Creator that she would be giving herself up to sin in the arms of a man who could lift her and surround her with his giant's body. Nothing escapes the Almighty, she thought, nearing ecstasy, with a hand feeling its way between her thighs. She was ready, in spite of all these friends around her. But the big moist hand paused just before touching her privates and withdrew slowly.

"Wait a while longer," said Célestin. "It will be better."

This was how, even before discovering pleasure, Émérita discovered the torture and impatience and finally the dream of desire which leads to total abandon.

"Look," Célestin continued emotionally, "for people who're going to be dead soon, we're not doing too badly."

The taxiwoman cast a long look around the rollicking bar. The children of God could be magnificent, she thought. All her friends, threatened, frightened, ruined, sick, all her friends were celebrating life. In this racket where tears were being shed amid the laughter, and as many bad jokes as gentle words were being exchanged, no one was drowning in alcohol. They were all drunk but perfectly lucid. No one was dancing any wild, theatrical fandango to exorcise the abomination spreading outside, that clings to bodies and souls like a second skin.

Gentille was trying to put the child back to sleep. Valcourt stopped looking at her and he too turned to watch his friends in admiration. In one of those surges of humanity that seem to grasp people when the only way out seems to be flight or death, they were betting on life.

And at last Valcourt was able to say, without ifs, ands or buts, "I'm happy."

And Émérita found pleasure, after everyone had left the bar.

Chapter Eight

Normally, Émérita avoided the potholes of Kigali's streets with a skill that made all the other taxi drivers jealous. Not this morning, while she was driving Valcourt to arrange the wedding and baptism with Father Louis. The rusted, ramshackle Honda took the full brunt of every hole and fissure. Émérita whistled tunes, jeered at men for driving like women, blew her horn needlessly, and shouted greetings at people she knew, which meant almost all the working adults. There was no holding her. For an evangelical churchwoman, the jokes she was cracking were in questionable taste.

"I committed my first real sin by having a glass of champagne last night, Valcourt, and I won't tell you what others I committed with Célestin after you left. I've made up for lost time. You know, I found out why making love's a sin, so it's forbidden. Making love's dangerous, it gets you wanting more, it gets you wanting to live forever. Making love blows your mind. I found out why my mother's so rich and why the truck drivers love her so. She provides them with beautiful girls, delicious, spicy brochettes (the best in town after Lando's), cold beer and comfortable beds. Freedom, that's what making love is. And last night, with my legs wrapped around Célestin's body, nearly squeezing the breath out of him, and with his sweat on my breasts, I felt freedom. And I thanked God for letting me sin. I told him I loved him even more than before, but I'd keep my distance from his pastors who tell us all our troubles are part of the divine Order. I told God—I was talking to him while Célestin was tearing my little veil and torturing me, before giving me pleasure like I'd never had before—I told him his churches were using his divine Word to make us accept the injustices being done to us and the death being planned for us. But you know, Valcourt, I found out too that I didn't want to die. Before, dying meant going to paradise. Now, it means the end of life. And life, Valcourt, it's life that's paradise."

There was a mixture of sadness and tenderness in Valcourt's smile. His friend's abundance of energy worried him, in fact. For weeks, she had been accusing friends and relatives of taking everything lying down, simply watching the great black night approach. They knew the people who were planning it, had contact with them, sometimes even had a beer with them, but never spoke out. Stoically, they would predict each other's death, then in a swell of ultimate confidence in humanity, in the international community, in life and in God, they would demolish their own ironclad and inarguable analyses. And before turning in to sleep off their last beer, they would conclude that the Hutu extremists, who were human like themselves, would never go beyond the point of no return; nobody wanted to believe what a familiar hand was writing on the wall.

The opposition must be more visible and more active, Émérita told Valcourt. All opposition supporters must speak up loudly and clearly—individually, in their families, in their sections—and denounce every violent act. The guilty were known, she said. They must be identified, isolated, expelled from their neighbourhoods; they must be barred from the churches unless they confessed their crimes; their names must be published in the newspapers.

The taxiwoman's first night of love had turned her into a *pasionaria*. It was awesome, but suicidal. Valcourt knew she would do exactly what she preached once she got home to her neighbourhood that night. She would plant her massive body resolutely before a militiaman and order him to go home, lecturing him and quoting several verses from the Bible, convinced that the Word of God would edify the most dull-witted and convert them, the way Paul was converted on the road to Damascus.

Valcourt briefly considered pointing out to her that the tissue-thin pages of the Scriptures would do little to protect bodies, even saintly bodies, from the steel of machetes. But to what end? The words of mere men are as naught against the Word of God. He decided to hold his tongue. He was ill placed to be giving advice to this happy woman considering he was getting himself into all kinds of trouble for more or less the same reasons, out of a pure, overwhelming passion for life as it is, instead of talking about life as it might be. Each moment stolen from fear is a paradise.

Father Louis pulled several times on his pipe before reacting. His position was never easy. In this country, even the most normal of things, like a marriage or baptism, could without apparent reason become a calamity or a provocation. As the head of Caritas, a major French Catholic aid organization, he was also administrator of the World Food Program in Rwanda. Caritas had established a pharmacy for the benefit of the poor, which was in competition with the regime's favourites who held medication import licences. And the Caritas crafts shop sold handmade goods at a fifth of the prices charged in the tourist traps but paid their peasant suppliers five times better than the gangster friends of the government. The women who served as his social assistants did more than set a good example and distribute powdered milk. They taught self-sufficiency to abandoned women. They distributed condoms, organized community kitchens. With thousands of little everyday acts they challenged ethnic discrimination, the exploitation of women and profiteering in essential goods. They knit small community loyalties that were noticed in high places and found suspect if not subversive.

In his meetings with ministers, Father Louis kept urging tolerance, moderation and equality. He did it discreetly and politely, for he was convinced that whatever disaster occurred, whichever side won, he must stay, not to save souls (souls save themselves), but to help.

Father Louis was not taken in by his own argument. For nearly forty years he had chosen to consort with bandits and murderers, some of whom had had the gall to come and confess to him. He kept walking a fragile tightrope, alone, protecting the dissenters as best he could and keeping company with their stalkers because he had to. Each side wanted to appropriate him and kept insisting he had to choose. He had chosen long since but could not carry on the work he considered essential without denying himself the luxury, or conceit, of giving voice to the growing horror he had been feeling since coming to Rwanda. God knew it—that was enough. Sometimes, lying awake, he did some figuring, adding up the number of lives he was probably saving by keeping silent. He didn't know how many exactly, but some. If he had talked, would he have saved more?

One night he had confided in Valcourt, who was writing an article on the rumours of massacres in the South. The two of them had been drinking all evening and with champagne bubbles going to his head the old priest revealed some appalling facts. Yes, he could prove that over several days ten thousand Tutsis had been massacred in Bugesera. A kind of dress rehearsal for the genocide the Hutu extremists were lusting after. At six in the morning he had knocked at Valcourt's door and Valcourt had agreed not to publish what he had told him.

Now he put the old briar pipe he had owned for forty years in the ashtray and bowed his head with a sigh.

"Monsieur Valcourt, you know the friendship I feel for you, and also how highly I think of Gentille. I can't deny your love. The word around Kigali is turning you into Romeo and Juliet. Have you thought about the difference in your ages, however, and the enormous cultural gap between you? To be frank, I don't want to see this marriage happen. And if I had the power, I'd even force you to leave, for your own good and Gentille's too."

He picked up the pipe and took a long draw on it.

"I've got an old-fashioned streak, you know, Valcourt," he said. "The priest's turns of phrase come to me easily, the clichés that the Church and its blind followers feed on because they live in the Scriptures, not in real life. What I've said to you I've said with the voice of reason, you'll admit. It's a perverse trap I've been thrashing around in for years. What does reasonable reason say? That the young don't go with the old. That misfortune is part of life. That where there are men you'll have all the faults of men. It also says there must be obedience. To parents, to bosses, to governments. It adds that rebellion is an adolescent thing and acceptance of order marks the passage to adulthood. It tells us too that war is inevitable and massacres are part of the nature of things. Reason tells us to accept the world around us. I have never been reasonable. I've always thought I could fight the world around me. How? By saving a hungry child, washing a patient with AIDS, distributing medicines, preaching what is called the Good Word, saying mass, which is the completely unreasonable sacrifice of the Son of God. Yes, I believe in him, don't frown your atheist's frown. And then I think of what all those reasonable people have accomplished. They got us into two world wars. They organized the Holocaust, the way economists and businessmen plan regional economic development or the expansion of a multinational corporation. They were also responsible for Vietnam, Nicaragua, apartheid in South Africa, and the hundred or more wars that have ravaged this continent since the colonizers left. Those killers weren't out of their minds. There were a few neurotics, like Hitler, but without reasonable people, without hundreds of thousands of believers, good, reasonable Christians, none of these sores of humanity would have worsened to the point they did. People who butcher human beings by spearing and slashing with bayonets are all upright, respectable folk. And when circumstances don't lead them to war they close their eyes to injustice—no, they organize injustice. And when they don't organize it, they tolerate it, encourage it, abet and finance it.

"Valcourt, ever since I asked you not to publish what I told you about last year's massacre, I haven't felt like a Christian anymore. I've had enough of being reasonable. Forget what I just said about your marriage. I don't know if that was a bad joke at my own expense or just the knee-jerk of a priest. Of course I'll marry you and Gentille, and I've forgotten you told me you were divorced. You don't know what a pleasure it's going to be to bless the union of two people who really love each other, even if Gentille *is* much too young for you. I won't change my mind about that. We'll celebrate the marriage Sunday of next week, April the ninth. The baptism too."

Valcourt was about to rise when the old priest put his hand on his and squeezed it and asked him to stay. He relit his pipe, then opened a small sideboard and took out a bottle and two tiny, finely cut glasses.

"A brandy from Champagne, my home turf." He drank his in one draft and poured himself another. "The glasses are too small.

"I can't keep quiet any longer. There are thousands of us missionaries in Africa who have chosen the path of silence, staking our faith on our presence and endurance. We maintain that God is above the struggles between men. In these confrontations we almost always opt for the perpetuity of the Church. We're not the only ones who think this way. Your humanitarian organizations would rather collaborate with a dictator than denounce him. Us too. We do it for the same reasons, essentially. If we speak out—because that's the issue—we'll have to leave and the poor people will be worse off than ever. It's often true. Not all this continent's keepers of souls, the missionaries and humanitarians, should be dumped in the same trash can for complicitous silence. But we of the Church of Christ have less reason to be excused, precisely because our teaching and our faith speak of the dignity of man, of respect, justice and charity. Magnificent preaching, which is empty of meaning and reality because for decades we have been condoning the worst imaginable crimes, in the name of an improbable future and an abstract eternity. If I could testify before a court, I would have all the members of this government put in prison, plus at least half the international experts from the International Monetary Fund and the World Bank who, without the slightest scruple, feed the insatiable appetites of all the dictators of Africa. Valcourt, I'm about to commit the most dreadful sacrilege."

The old priest bent his head until it was almost resting on his knees. Then abruptly raised it again.

"For nearly thirty years, Colonel Théoneste—you know him—has been coming to confession once a week. He's a good father and a good Christian. He came yesterday and his first words were: 'Father, I admit to preparing a great massacre, the final massacre.' It was not God's representative he was speaking to, it was a man he was confiding a secret to. No, not a secret—information, tons of information. It wasn't a confession, Valcourt, it was a tipoff. I did not give him absolution. Take notes."

Valcourt took out his notebook.

"Elimination of the president, who has decided to accept free elections . . . List of fifteen hundred names . . . all the leaders of the Liberal Party and the Social Democratic Party . . . priorities: Lando, Faustin, the prime minister's wife, Agathe . . . the moderate Hutu civil servants and professionals . . . all Tutsis in important positions. Work to be carried out by the presidential guard . . . then mobilization of the militias in all neighbourhoods of the capital, set-up of roadblocks . . . checking of identities . . . all Tutsis identified at checkpoints to be eliminated by the militias, supported by police elements . . . Systematic combing of the city by soldiers and militiamen, street by street . . . each section head will give them a list of persons to be eliminated and houses to be destroyed . . . no women or male children to be spared . . . once Kigali is cleansed, the presidential guard will start organizing the cleansing in Gitarama, then Butare . . . not one Tutsi must survive."

Studiously, methodically, coolly, a few hundred men were planning the elimination of a segment of humanity. In the initial phase, it would be relatively easy to do away with their political enemies, the important people, but after that? How could they believe, as did the Nazi leaders, that the majority of the population would follow and join this small number, and agree not only to point the finger at suspect houses but also incite the rabble to kill their neighbours and comrades at work? How could they seriously believe that the people would agree to turn into killers by the thousands? Most of all, how could they have been so sure of it?

"Tell me it's not possible, Gentille."

"No, now you know anything's possible here."

They were lying under the great fig tree. A gentle, warm wind rustled the tree, bringing the barking of stray dogs and raucous music from the discotheque on Republic Square. Some reckless drivers were defying the curfew with squealing tires and blaring horns. Gentille stoically rocked the child and hummed a ballad from her hill. Valcourt was feeling very low and deriving more pain than pleasure from Gentille's hand lightly caressing his arm. She was right. He had known it for a long time but had been refusing to admit it. And now he must live with the certainty and Théoneste's revelations. Even Gentille's presence under this too-perfect tree, her existence, her futile beauty in the face of the horror to come were sinking a hole in his chest. There was nothing he could do, except kiss his wife the better to cling to life's straw.

But old reflexes rarely vanish. Bright and early the next morning, Valcourt showed up at the UN head office with his notes and lists of names and of places where the extremists were hiding arms—with the plan of a genocide. The major general refused to see him and sent word that if he had important information, he could entrust it to his liaison officer, a notorious extremist.

Valcourt rushed out onto the road leading to Kazenze, where Émérita lived. He wanted to warn her, but also ask her advice.

A hundred metres beyond the crossroads, policemen had set up a roadblock and were stopping all passage. Valcourt went through on foot, waving his press card. There were several dozen people around the taxi-woman's house. A real rumpus. People were shouting and crying. Others were brandishing machetes and clubs. Émérita's brothel-keeper mother lay prostrate on the red earth, her body enormous and flabby. Josephine, Émérita's sister, took Valcourt's hand.

"Come and see what they've done to my little sister."

Valcourt shook his head.

"You have to," said Josephine. "She really loved you."

A trickle of water was still running in the shower, tracing red, winding paths like patient snakes. On the walls and floor, mementos, evocations of what once had been arms, a face, breasts. In this small space, the grenade slipped through the window had pulverized the body into a hundred little pieces of flesh. Valcourt began to vomit. He wanted to cry but in his despair could only hiccup to the epileptic rhythm of the emptying of his stomach.

Just below the house, at the crossing of the Kazenze road and the boulevard that leads downtown, some *interahamwes* were partying. They could be heard bellowing the song about eliminating the cockroaches. They were cavorting around outside a small bar that served as their headquarters, from which they habitually harassed all the Tutsis passing by.

After leaving Valcourt at Caritas to see Father

Louis, this was where Émérita had gone, along with several friends and a police sergeant who was posted at the crossroads. Josephine had tried to dissuade her.

"The more we tuck our heads down between our shoulders, the faster we walk by pretending we don't see them, the surer they'll be they can exterminate us. Our silence and docility give them courage and strength," Émérita had replied.

To the police sergeant she had described the threats, the incidents of young girls being dragged behind the shanty at nightfall, the bodies that were found along the road every morning and the burning of houses. It was known who was doing these things. Many witnesses had seen them at it. They must be arrested.

The policeman, embarrassed, said he could not request an official investigation on such insubstantial proof, and the complainant and her witnesses would have to appear before the prosecutor and lay a formal complaint. To show diligence, he asked the militiamen to disperse and put away their arms. They withdrew to a distance of about a hundred metres, laughing lewdly and shouting insults. Émérita was savouring her small victory. She gave them the finger. They would be back of course, but she and her friends would do it all over again. Walking to the little house, she had told her sister and the several friends with her how some villagers in Bugesera, with bows and arrows, clubs and stones, had defended themselves against the soldiers and escaped the massacres of the year before.

"Of course they think they're all-powerful. We never lift a finger, we walk like lambs and let ourselves die bleating."

The friends nodded, more to be polite than enthusi-

astically, some already convinced that she had just
signed their death warrant. She left them to take a
shower. She would rather not have washed away the
sweet, sharp scent of love from her body, it had been
affording her such voluptuous pleasure since leaving
the hotel, but business is business, and a businesswoman, as she was described on her card, must be
irreproachably clean. She was singing, or rather bellowing, "Parlez-moi d'amour" when through the tiny
window someone had let drop a French grenade that
had travelled via Cairo through Zaïre before landing in
Émérita's shower. Josephine, who was peeling potatoes
when the explosion happened, told the whole story to
Valcourt. She also told him never to come and visit her
and not to show up at the funeral. No, it wasn't that she
felt any bitterness toward him. She was only thinking
of his safety.

"Go back to Canada, it'll be better for you."

And she held him tight in her arms, not the distant
embrace that Rwandans give, with the hands, keeping a
space between the bodies, but the embrace one gives
a very dear friend.

When he went back to the taxi waiting for him near
the roadblock, a policeman called to him.

"You know that terrorist Émérita? Did she have
friends you can identify?"

"Yes, me."

Chapter Nine

A big Primus, another big Primus, a dip in the pool, a
little hot sun, a third big Primus, another dip, then to
sleep until the next morning without a word to anyone,
even Gentille, till the ravens and buzzards took off
noisily for the dumps freshly filled with garbage
overnight and for the roadsides and streets littered
with new corpses no one dared gather up. This was
what Valcourt wanted when he entered the hotel lobby
to be greeted by Zozo, as always nicer than necessary.

"A lot of messages for you, Monsieur Bernard, and a
lot of Canadians at the hotel."

It looked like a Sunday at the pool in Kigali.
Rwanda's entire Canadian colony was in a state of excite-

ment. There were a few shy, reserved aid workers and a few nuns who were wondering why they had been asked to come to the hotel, but most of them were living a life of great adventure here, with perks of prestige, power and freedom they had never known before. Their subordinates called them "chief" and they behaved accordingly. All the professors at the University of Butare had been summoned, as well as the Quebec government officials loaned to ministries where they were trying to instill a minimum of discipline in ill-paid counterparts whose bosses were openly robbing the till. There was even the forestry engineer in charge of protecting the great natural forest of Nyungwe, where thousands of marijuana plants were growing as though in a large, well-ordered farm. His salary, those of several other foresters and the cost of their studies on tree species were paid by the Canadian government. He knew the trade, this bald, obsequious little man who was so ugly the hotel prostitutes accepted his clumsy advances with unconcealed distaste.

Every one of these good people gathered around the pool had seen a Rwandan colleague disappear mysteriously, or funds evaporate as if by magic. They talked about it among themselves, almost always jokingly, as if they were swapping sex or fishing stories in a tavern. They were totally powerless in any case, they would explain whenever cornered into talking about it. If they spoke out, they wouldn't be believed. Worse, if they were believed their programs would be cancelled and they would go back to being anonymous civil servants.

Under the big awning, embassy staff members were handing out walkie-talkies and an evacuation plan covering all the Canadians. Madame the Consul explained that the Tutsi terrorism was growing—there was talk of an RPF army breakthrough toward the capital from the region of Byumba. Administrative measures were being introduced as a precaution, because Ottawa was worried by rumours it was hearing through the media. There was no reason to panic, however. The Rwandan army, with excellent support from its French advisers, who were very active, was in control of the situation.

Valcourt asked for news of the inquiry into the murder of Brother François. The Rwandan police report was final, Lisette told him. The little brother who organized co-operatives and gathered up displaced persons had been killed by people he was protecting. Displaced Tutsis or labourers disguised as soldiers. The motive was theft. The consul made these pronouncements in the peremptory tone of a teacher addressing a pupil with learning problems.

"You're trying to make a fool of me," Valcourt said to her, while she wondered whether she'd at least have time for nine holes before sundown.

"Monsieur Valcourt, there are some things intellectuals like you won't ever understand. Minor crises over individuals must never destabilize relations between states. You're too sentimental to live in this country."

Élise was there too, obedient to the orders of her boss, who was nicknamed "the Countess" and was making a career out of aid work the way others do out of diplomacy or fraud, which in this country made her an honest-to-goodness professional. Élise seemed mightily amused by this sudden uproar. Too amused by half, mocking the student trainees who were as edgy as the veterans—and too caustic with her comments, too ironical with her humour for the Countess who told her off, reminding her that the whole program of AIDS detection was financed by the government she was ridiculing. Élise yelled in reply that all the killers in this country loved Canada, such a worthy country in its silence, its refusal to take sides. And because she could not separate her motions from her emotions, or her thoughts from her words, she shoved the Countess into the chlorine-reeking pool. There were a few bursts of laughter but mostly a shocked silence filled with reproof and scorn for this angry outburst that was so un-Canadian. Each expatriate community maintained a surface unanimity. Its members could tear one another apart ferociously over the telephone or at meetings behind closed doors but, in public, solidarity was the watchword and anyone who broke it was soon *persona non grata*—his or her projects had trouble getting financed and contracts evaporated.

Élise refused to comply with these rules. She went through life like a born guerrilla fighter. This front-line nurse hadn't been through the abortion battle in Quebec in the 1970s only to come to Rwanda and keep a register of AIDS cases. She hadn't lived and worked with the Salvadorean rebellion only to wither away in silence in this stinking dung-heap. As the Countess clumsily hauled herself out of the pool, dripping and mortified and missing a high-heeled shoe and a large part of her dignity, Élise watched, smiling. Then she went and joined Valcourt.

"Next time I'll whack her."

A big flock of jackdaws made a thousand little shadows on the surface of the pool. From a distance, very high in the sky, the buzzards observed, turning in wide circles. Around the pool, order reigned once again. The

Tutsis of the People's Bank took their places. Léo, who was making a film on the great Rwandan democracy, financed jointly by Canada and the president's party, was moving about from table to table distributing smiles and lies like a negro Maurice Chevalier in a bad musical comedy. The Kigali Canadians left with their walkie-talkies and their plan of evacuation. The rest of the aid workers who were staying at the hotel were already drunk and vying in noisiness with the Belgians. In a corner of the bar, Madame Agathe's girls giggled as they sipped their Pepsis. The evening was going to be profitable. They just wished the Belgians would go someplace else. They were coarse and brutal. The Canadians, now, were a bit nerdy. They courted the girls at the bar as if they weren't hookers. They told them stories, held their hands, whispered soft words, offered them wine and whisky before daring, almost apologetically, to invite them to their rooms, without ever asking the price of the ride. And when they learned it, even if the girl had doubled the normal price, they would tut-tut over the sorry lot that fate had dealt her. And fork out a nice fat tip besides, the big-hearted humanists. The French, the girls said, rape and take. They don't talk, and when they pay they fling the money on the bed contemptuously.

"The Belgians insult us while they shoot their wad and tell us we don't deserve any better, that we're all sluts, then after they've put their pants back on they haggle over the price. The Canadians are nice. They tend to tell us what's good for us. They seem to worry about our future as they fondle our breasts. They insist on a lot of kissing before they get inside us. When they pay, they're always embarrassed. They try to disguise a fuck as a love story. Probably because they're as afraid of losing themselves in the fuck as in love. The Canadians are okay—even drunk, they're reasonable."

Bernadette, who was telling Gentille all this, would have liked all her clientele to vanish into thin air. She didn't want to work anymore, but what else was she going to do? In the beginning, even when she was exhausted, she never refused a john. Not for the money, just for the pleasure and chance of fulfilling her dream. The pleasure of surprising caresses and kisses. A tongue playing in her ear while a deft finger set a nipple quivering. Well, yes, the johns were all in a hurry and got into her faster than she would have liked, generally dispensed with amorous demonstrations and cut short their tenderness. But she was getting more pleasure here than when she was working at Sodoma, and then at the Hôtel des Diplomates.

And she still had her dream. A hundred, two hundred johns had had relations with her. There were some who were regulars and wanted to pay less or else get her into sexual activities that Rwandan tradition forbade, or would show affection by bringing her little gifts that she knew were inexpensive and insignificant. Tiny bottles of alcohol and sets of toiletries given away on airplanes, old magazines (she couldn't read, or barely anyhow). The most generous went so far as to offer a few cheap bits of jewellery from the Nairobi airport duty-free shop. But all her sexual prowess, her beauty, her total availability and her vigour (she was a good lay, she wanted no doubt about that) were not enough for them. They were not content with her body, which she gave without reserve (except for tradition's requirement), and all her caresses, which she'd learned to refine and adapt to the various tastes of Whites—no, besides all this, and for the same price, she had to admire and love them, transform johns into heroes, into supermen, and most of all into men amorously desired. And they would tell her a girl as intelligent as she was (funny, they never said "woman," though she was nearly thirty), a girl as beautiful as she was, could remake her life with a little help. Bernadette, who was sterile, dreamed of owning a children's clothing shop and had asked one of her first rich johns to lend her a small sum of money. The rotund and paunchy German almost died laughing his deep, coarse laugh. He hadn't been talking about that kind of help, which she would squander in any event, knowing nothing about business, but a recommendation or sponsorship for the kind of employment she was capable of, such as cleaner at the embassy, or maid in a family of aid workers, and later, perhaps, a recommendation for a visa. Others, even more impatient to take her love as a trophy, went further still with the rape of her soul. After the trinkets might come a little cotton dress worth less than the price of the fuck, and only occasionally flowers worth half the price of the dress but demonstrating depth of feeling and perhaps even commitment. She would find herself someone, even if he was ugly, bald and adipose with one foot in the grave, who would get her out of here and take her to Belgium or Australia, Canada or Italy. Anywhere.

To that nice, shy French accountant who in just a few days had progressed from nylon stockings to a bouquet of irises, from talk about her intelligence to the new life she could make for herself with his help if he could swing it, and finally how happy it would make him to spend a lot of time with her, to this nice

gentleman—who set the alarm so he'd be back in his
room by four o'clock—she had suggested going to spend
the weekend in Kagera Park to see the giraffes and
lions and zebras roaming free. The man's skinny limbs
had stiffened, and his complacent smile, the smile of a
male who's just ejaculated, became an accountant's or
diplomat's smile held at the corners with paper clips.

"I could never explain to the embassy my being
away."

The hungriest for love, she continued, was a
Lebanese businessman who controlled several interests
in the Ruhengeri district and who came to Kigali on
business every Monday. In four Mondays he went
straight from caresses to sudden declarations of love.
Not a single gift, not a single flower, nothing. But he
could not, he realized, live without her. He hadn't made
love to his wife for as long as he'd known Bernadette.
And Bernadette was fond of him, enough anyway to
marry twice, as she put it. He made her laugh all the
time and caressed her the way she imagined it was done
in Europe, where Lebanon was located. He spent the
night with her, encircling her with his arms, engulfing
her with his huge, hairy torso and—ah, supreme proof
of devotion—having Tuesday morning breakfast with
her in public on the main terrace, being bold and open
enough to touch her hand between two mouthfuls of
bacon. This was a real lover.

On the fifth Monday morning, she left Kigali with
him. At first she would be a nursemaid looking after the
children and would have her own room in the main
house. They mustn't rush things. His wife was the official owner of a large share in his companies, but in a
few months, with his lawyers, he would manage to

change the situation. She understood and squeezed his hand. He smiled at her. When they came to the cross-roads at Base, the three great volcanoes, Muhabura dominating, appeared on the horizon, each with its coronet of milk-white clouds turned rosy by the sun. At last she'd be able to visit the National Volcano Park, to see and almost touch the famous gorillas that she knew only from photographs. The Lebanese businessman's Mercedes cruised as if on a carpet along the highway financed by the Chinese so that the president might return in all comfort to his native region. Bernadette smiled. This was what happiness must be.

Unfortunately, a cousin of the Lebanese man was occupying her room. She slept in a former pigsty converted to a dormitory for domestics. Her lover's wife, an enormous, faded woman whose oily skin was perpetually stained by the kohl carried down from her watery eyes, terrorized her relentlessly. Selim, after a week, forgot about the tender words. He no longer caressed her and took just a few minutes to have her wherever he came across her in the house or garden, without even a kiss or a fondle for her breasts. He had asked her never to wear panties so as not to delay things in case his wife might be nearby. When Mourad, his twenty-year-old son, woke her to say his father wanted to speak to her, she got up without a word. On the muddy path leading to the garden, the boy, who was walking behind her, pushed her into the red clay.

"My father doesn't want you anymore. He's given you to me." He lay on her and held her hard by the wrists. "If you fight me, I'll kill you. So many bodies are found along the roads first thing in the morning that nobody'll ask any questions, you dirty whore!"

He was right and she didn't want to be hurt. Slowly, she spread her legs and tried to turn over. This wouldn't be her first rape. A hand shoved her head into the mud, which filled her mouth when she opened it wide to scream in pain. A hard penis pierced her in that dirty, secret, forbidden place. It was as if a single knife thrust had severed her muscles. This penis was raping the last part of her body that belonged to her. Dirty perhaps, impure, forbidden as tradition maintained, but intact. One day, a man she loved might perhaps have asked her to yield this secret place to him, and she would have done it with joy. Now she no longer had anything pure to offer.

At long last, with no tears left to shed, she fell asleep in a ditch beside the Chinese highway. In the morning she walked several hundred metres, but the pain was paralyzing. She sat on a big stone and waited to die, for she would not stir from that stone unless someone came and took her from it. A truck stopped and a young man gestured to her to get in. He was wearing the militia cap and was bouncing on his seat to a Michael Jackson cassette.

"You're going back to Kigali at the right time," he said. "In time for the great day. I've got a truck full of tools for the work, for the job to be done. In a few weeks the Tutsis won't be stopping us from living anymore."

The truck driver's hand came to rest on her thigh. Again she knew she was trapped, that it would do no good to resist. If she said no he would beat her, or worse, leave her by the road and another truck driver would come along, or a soldier.

"D'you want me by the front or the back door?"

He braked so hard the truck skidded several metres before coming to a stop almost against the mountain.

"You're a White's whore, talking like that. You're not going to give me Whites' sicknesses in your ass, like AIDS and all the rest. I'm a Rwandan, a real one. We don't do things like that."

Then he climbed on top of her, cigarette butt between his lips. It only lasted a few short minutes. Bernadette closed her eyes, relieved not to have suffered more, and slept all the way to Kigali.

Since she'd been back at the hotel, all the girls were jealous of her. She was beautiful, of course, with her great firm breasts and thighs as sturdy and round as pillars. The first night, an Italian from the World Bank, discouraged by the effects of politics on his organization, was dancing the tarantella in the fourth-floor bar. He was singing horribly off-key, with a bottle of whisky in his hand. He tripped and crashed laughing to the floor at the feet of Bernadette, who was still feeling desolate.

"What's your act?" demanded the laughing Italian.

Bernadette ran her hand through her hair and replied that her act was anything men wanted, stressing, "Anything the other girls here don't want to do."

It was true. Very soon a large segment of the White city knew it and from then on Bernadette had only steady johns. They came alone or in pairs. Others brought their wives. These johns respected her. They paid without argument. They didn't suggest she change her life—on the contrary. They praised her competence and generosity. Now that she no longer belonged to herself, she was able to give herself to all, men and women both. She no longer even dreamed of getting away and accumulated money without knowing exactly what she would do with it. And if by mischance a john talked to her of love, she would say:

"For that, it will cost you double."

Élise, who was in the habit of interrupting conversations, had listened to Bernadette without a word. She was holding an envelope bearing Bernadette's name and a five-digit number. Bernadette had not kept her appointment at the Detection Centre and Élise had been hunting all over for her since she had gone to Ruhengeri. Now Élise held out the envelope, whose contents she did not know. Bernadette froze. What did the number mean, she wondered. Nothing, it didn't mean anything. And no, Élise didn't know the result of her test. Bernadette looked a long time at the envelope before speaking again.

"Let's say I've got AIDS. I'll have to make my johns put on condoms, won't I? Let's say they all put on condoms, I'll get sick soon anyway, won't I? And I'll start getting thin, like you've told me. I'll have diarrhea and fever, then maybe TB and sores in my mouth. Well, the TB I can take care of, the medicines are free. The sores too, with Nizoral that'll cost me fifteen johns' worth. But even then I won't be cured. The sores will be back and the fever too, and my breasts will start to droop like wilting leaves. I'm right, Élise, aren't I? And there are medicines to control the sickness that the rich people in your country can afford. You've told me about them. So I need two or three thousand johns a year to buy me your medicines. Can you imagine two or three thousand sicknesses a year to cure only one? Not to cure, just to take longer to die, die with dignity, as you say. But dying's dying. You're all here like immortal angels to hold our hands till we're in our coffins. I don't need you to help me die. I took the test because I was in love, Élise. A dream. A man and children. In my dream the woman couldn't have the sickness. A dream, Élise, to leave, just leave. For anywhere, your icy cold, your snow that blocks the streets, the poor district of Brussels or the sidewalks of Paris. Anywhere except here. Élise, Valcourt, you're nice but useless. I don't want to know what the envelope says. HIV positive, I'll die. HIV negative, I'll die. You watch us, you take notes, you write reports, you write articles. While we die with you watching us all the time, you live, you thrive. I like you both, but don't you get a feeling, sometimes, that you're living off our death?"

Bernadette tore the envelope into tiny pieces and scattered them to the wind, then spat on the ground. She went and took her place at the big table at the far end of the pool bar.

Night fell as always here, by surprise, an enfolding wave of darkness that melted over the red earth. And in perfect synchrony, the buzzards and ravens hushed their clamour, the johns began to whisper, the girls prepared themselves. Upstairs on the fourth floor, the dining room was filling with experts and wise consultants, meticulous, exemplary recorders of all woes and all impoverishments.

Zozo had set up a table under the fig tree with a starched white tablecloth from the dining room. "Émérita would have liked that," he said, letting a big tear roll down his full-moon face. Tomato salad, fillets of tilapia in lemon butter, overripe Camembert, overpriced and slightly corked Côtes du Rhône. Émérita, thought Valcourt, to sustain her corpulence would rather have had steak and french fries, or some chicken legs. Élise, who was normally a real chatterbox, had not yet said a word. Valcourt and Gentille were half-heartedly talking about preparations for their wedding.

"Bernadette's right," said Élise, poking her tilapia fillet with a restless fork. "We save one but watch ten more die. When I arrived here three years ago, only ten per cent of the tests were positive. But even if Bernadette's right, even if we're just powerless voyeurs, even if we're kind of living off their deaths as she says, she hasn't convinced me I should leave. I'm going to stay, I'm going to carry on. With my little lectures and my condoms, maybe I'll persuade only one per cent, but that one per cent won't die. That's enough for me. And then hope, goddammit, what about hope! Christ, that counts!"

Well, La Québecoise was coming back to life, it appeared.

"To Émérita, who believed in hope!" They drank to Émérita. "But seriously, Valcourt, you must leave with Gentille and the child. For now, this isn't a country for lovers, it's a country of madmen and fighters. Get away from here. Give the little girl a nice place to grow up in, you two. A normal place."

Softly, Gentille asked Valcourt if he wanted to leave; nothing was keeping her here.

"What about the morning mist in all the valleys of Kigali, Gentille, and the sun lifting those fluffy mushroom-like clouds, and the concert from the children running down the hills to school? And the slow pace of Sunday morning, when you walk almost ceremonially in your blue dress to the Church of the Holy Family. And the songs and dances of the mass, which are more easygoing folk songs than canticles, more love songs than hymns of adoration. Then the goat's-meat brochettes at Lando's and the fresh tilapia from Lake Kivu. The lean dry chicken that's had the run of the hills. The tomato display in Kigali market, with thirty women back of it arguing and chuckling and hiding their poverty behind picture-postcard smiles. The Ruhengeri highway, with those Cinemascope volcanoes. The steep flanks of the hills that your ancestors tamed and turned into thousands of fertile little terraces, which millions of people are still cultivating like quiet, efficient ants. The rainy season's midday storms that are wiped away in minutes by the sun. The cool of the breeze in the hills when God rests, because, as the saying goes, it's to Rwanda that he comes to sleep. You want to leave all that?"

For over twenty years Valcourt had earned his bread and butter from wars, massacres and famines. For all this time, he had had a house but no country. Now he had a country to defend and it was Gentille's, Méthode's, Cyprien's and Zozo's. He had come to the end of a long road and could say at last, "Here is where I want to live." This is what he was explaining to Gentille, purposely avoiding her eyes, weighing each word, keeping his own eyes fixed on his empty plate so that hers would not distract him further, so that each sentence would describe as precisely as possible the monumental discovery he had made—the discovery of a woman he wanted to die with, and of a country. What is a country for someone who is neither a soldier nor a rabid patriot? A place of subtle affinities, an implicit understanding between the land and the foot that treads it. A familiarity, an agreement, a secret sharing with the colours and smells of it. The impression that the wind is with us and is sometimes carrying us.

A renunciation that does not imply acceptance of the idiocy and inhumanity that the country nurtures.

Leaving, even temporarily, did not appeal to him at all. He knew by now that once you've found the place that makes you feel at peace, you can't leave it without ceasing to live, becoming a zombie, an empty body walking around in the barren space of a dreary diaspora. He had walked so far and hesitated, faltered and backtracked so many times before finding his own hill.

"If you asked me to leave I'd do it reluctantly, knowing that one grey autumn day we'd miss the sweet, warm breath of the eucalyptus so much that each of us would be blaming the other for the choice. Gentille, we're not leaving here unless you really want to go, or unless they throw us out."

Élise, who, for all her recriminations, threats and anger, had decided long ago that she too was going to stay, stood up and declared:

"Valcourt, you're crazier than I thought."

Gentille wanted to kiss him but instead, under cover of the table, put a toe on her future husband's foot.

Élise kissed and hugged them both harder than usual, then left carrying away what remained of the Côtes du Rhône, "for the road."

That night, Valcourt woke with a start, covered in sweat. Gentille was not there. The child was asleep in the other bed. He turned on the bedside lamp, then saw the young woman on the deckchair on the balcony, her nakedness outlined by the twofold reflection of moonlight and a candle. A yellow light on her delicate shoulder, a whitish touch on her angular hip. She was reading. She turned when she heard his step.

"I was worried when I didn't see you."

"Next time I want to read then, I'll turn on the light even if it wakes you," she said teasingly.

She was reading Éluard.

"You don't know how much I'm discovering reading this book, Bernard. You talk so well, as if you were born knowing how to talk. You find words for all your emotions and people can understand you. I was taught not to talk about all the commotion inside of me. I'm not used to it and can't find the words. So sometimes at night when you're fast asleep and I'm lying awake, I come here and learn to give words to my love and my life. Even if they're someone else's words, they're mine too. Listen: 'We are the first cloud we two / In this absurd expanse of cruel happiness.' That's just like us, don't you think?"

They didn't sleep. They lay quietly on their backs, breathing calmly and steadily, content with the peacefulness and serenity in them.

When the first pink glow touched Gentille's slender foot, Valcourt whispered, "What are we going to call the child?"

She murmured, "Émérita."

Chapter Ten

Some stony land on the heights above Nyamirambo had been cleared for a new cemetery. There were as many militiamen and uniformed and plainclothes policemen in attendance as family and friends of Émérita. Lando had not come. He had spent the last few days shut in at home and the evenings at his restaurant, surrounded by a dozen armed men. Monsieur Faustin rather nervously delivered a short speech to fit the occasion. When he spoke the word "democracy," he dropped the volume of his voice so far that only his immediate neighbours heard it. Then it was Émérita's mother's turn. Before speaking, she walked slowly round the hole, kicking angrily at pebbles.

Then she turned to the whole gaggle of cops standing ten or so metres off.

"Look at me, you little shit-ass murderers, scum of the hills. Look at my wide face and flat nose, my deep-set eyes, my broad hips and big behind. There's no mistaking me, I'm a real Hutu. Not a single Tutsi in my family to slim us down or lighten our skin. Émérita had my nose, my face and my butt. Like me, she was a real Hutu. More real than any of you. I'm telling you, when a Hutu chops his sister up in little pieces that won't even fill a coffin, I'm telling you, that Hutu's sick. You killed her because she was a friend to Tutsis. You didn't understand what that meant. She just wanted to be a Rwandan, to have friends on all the hills. And you, Gaspard, playing with your machete and looking stuck-up, you ought to understand because you've been coming to my brothel twice a week for Jasmine, who's more Tutsi than I am Hutu, Jasmine from Butare, who's been getting lots of beer and flowers from you, and who you keep proposing to and who keeps turning you down because you don't give her any pleasure. Émérita's losing nothing losing you. She's with the angels."

Gaspard had taken to his heels but he knew they would find him and kill him for having loved and courted a Tutsi prostitute. Émérita's mother knew it too. She came back to the grave and threw in a small bouquet of roses.

"I've killed one, my darling. I'm going to kill some more."

Gentille and Bernard had sent their regrets because they were leaving that day to announce their marriage to Gentille's family, especially her father, Jean-Damascène, who was living in Butare. They joked together that this would be their honeymoon trip, 175 kilometres of peaceful roads and contrasting landscapes, sharp rises and sometimes giddying descents. They would stop to visit her friend Marie at Rundo, just outside Kigali, and at Mugina thirty kilometres farther on where Gentille's cousin Stratton was living now.

Just before the modern brick factory, which wasn't working because the minister had sold the German machines to a Zimbabwean colleague, they came to the usual roadblock but had no trouble passing through. After crossing the placid Nyabarongo River, the road began to twist and turn and climbed steeply all the way to Rundo.

Gentille wanted Valcourt to meet Marie, who had been her teacher. Marie was thirty-five and had nine children. She was a teacher at Rundo's elementary school and had married the assistant burgomaster. With their two incomes they were able to afford the family that their religious convictions dictated. But Marie had not been paid for six months and her husband Charles had lost his job several weeks before because he had refused to draw up a list of all the Tutsi families in the commune. Since then he had been in hiding with Hutu friends. Charles didn't know if he was really a Tutsi although he had the Tutsi physique and a Tutsi identity card, and yes, although his grandfather had been a dignitary at the mwami's court. With her head bowed and her eyes almost closed, Marie apologized for Charles's not being there, as if the man's absence was an affront to her guests.

It was noon and the children were declaring their hunger. Marie shooed them away, scolding them. She had guests she hadn't seen for a long time. The children would eat later. Here, when friends turn up at midday they're taken straight to table, and when they're great friends the family kills the goat that's kept tied by a foot in the yard. Playing with the children, Gentille took a discreet look about the house. There was no goat in the yard or the kitchen, not a single chicken either, only a bag of rice and a few dry beans. Not even a withered tomato or some bruised bananas. She called Valcourt, who offered the children a ride in the car. They piled happily into the capacious Land Rover, the eldest standing on the rear bumper. They came back twenty minutes later with thirty brochettes, two fat roast chickens and several kilos of tomatoes.

Meanwhile Marie had told the whole story to Gentille, who probably knew it already. Marie wondered if she shouldn't leave with the children for Butare. For several days the strangest rumours had been going round. A group of militiamen from the North were camping at the crossroads. Others were living in a warehouse that belonged to the commune. She couldn't bring herself to abandon Charles, whom she was visiting under cover of night, or her forty pupils who were making such progress in French.

Valcourt opened one of the bottles of Côtes du Rhône he had brought in order to celebrate with the Butare in-laws. Marie drank the first two glasses of alcohol she had ever had in her life, and when she was thoroughly tipsy Gentille told her she was getting married. At the news, Marie clapped excitedly, thanking God for her young friend's liberation. This was the word she used before asking if she wasn't afraid of the cold in Canada. She would never understand why the two lovers (who could leave whenever they wanted) had decided to stay in this country but was overcome to learn that they had, and shyly gave Valcourt a brief kiss on the forehead that felt to him like a warm, gentle breath or the touch of a passing swallow.

The Land Rover had almost reached the crossroads and was about to turn right toward Gitarama. Marie was still waving goodbye with both hands, making a windmill in the air as the vehicle disappeared behind the dark mass of the service station, which had had no gasoline for three months. Like small pennants of living flesh, her hands stayed held in the air. Marie would not leave either. She would remain on Charles and the children's hill. These steep cliffs were perhaps worth clinging to after all, worth defending against the gravediggers.

Before the turn onto the dirt road leading to Mugina there were two roadblocks manned by militiamen who were making many passengers get out of their cars and sending them back on foot the way they had come, without their baggage. Sometimes a car or truck simply had to turn around and go back. The militiamen were young and obviously drunk. Not a single policeman, not a single soldier. Ten metres from the second roadblock, Valcourt saw the body of a woman lying in the long grass beside the red dirt road. He stopped. Her orange scarf, bright red pullover and green skirt, the colours of the Rwandan flag, might have looked like a fine primitive painting if she had only been sleeping, exhausted by digging in the fields. Her long legs were spread, her knees covered by her bloodstained underpants. Her green skirt was pulled up to her hips and a broad flow of coagulated blood issued from her vagina. An accurate machete had sliced her throat, where hundreds of red ants were already making a nest. In the trampled grass was a small piece of worn cardboard bearing the seal of the republic and a badly taken photograph. Alice Byumiraga, age twenty-seven, Mugina Commune, Tutsi.

In this region, the hills are close and watch one another. The valleys lie long and sinuous, and are so deep and steep-sided that to cross a distance of only one kilometre one must suffer twenty-five on ill-kept dirt roads.

Stratton was Gentille's favourite cousin. On a long thin neck, he bore like a toy the head of a little learned mouse with eyes that sparkled, especially when telling the local legends and the tall tales he had learned watching European television, which had made Gentille laugh a lot when she was a child.

From his father's house, where Stratton had been living since he fled the Bugesera region two years earlier, he pointed a long, slightly crooked finger at each thatched house clinging to the flanks of the hills across the valley. Hills so close you might think you could reach out and touch them, but at the same time so far away that each was like an independent little country jealous of its neighbours.

"*Ma petite* Gentille, half your family lives over there. See that big house opposite, beside the banana grove? Georges lives there, he's one of your uncles. You don't know him and it's best that way. He bought a Hutu identity card twenty years ago and eats pig meat and spaghetti every day so as not to be thin like a Tutsi. He's been a success and has become head of the *interahamwes* of the commune. He's the one in charge of the new roadblock they've set up just before the dirt road. Farther down, the five small houses, those are his sons'. To the left, a bit higher, that's Simone's house—she's his sister who refuses to become a Hutu. Simone has five daughters, all as beautiful as can be, but she's only been able to marry off one, to a cousin of mine from Butare. Below Simone's house (see it, near the clump of eucalyptus?), that big bungalow, that's another cousin's. He's a friend of Lando's, the Tutsi minister, perhaps you know him. But he's put his house up for sale and wants to go and live in Belgium. Then there are all the others I won't name for you, the families are so big. But from our common ancestor who one day wanted to turn us all into Tutsis to save our lives and open the doors of the Belgian schools to us, we're over six hundred descendants on three hills here. A little over half are officially Tutsis, and some, like you, have the physical appearance. The ones our ancestor's clever plan didn't succeed in changing, the ones he failed, are getting ready to kill us as soon as they get the word."

Valcourt put the yellow card on the table littered with empty Primus bottles. Stratton looked at the picture.

"That's one of Simone's daughters, the most beautiful of Simone's daughters. Georges has killed his niece."

As in all the country's major and lesser principalities, the centre of the town was dominated by an imposing church. Mugina's was one of those contrived modern horrors with a sloping roof and a bell tower on the side, vaguely inspired by Le Corbusier. Several thousand people were camping on the broad expanse of vacant land around it. Stratton guided Gentille and Valcourt through the crowd, stopping sometimes to talk to a man, who would invariably nod respectfully and then turn and give orders.

Along the dirt road a wide trench was being dug, and with the earth dug out of it an embankment was being built, spiked with pieces of wood. Children were bringing stones and making piles of them at regular intervals. The inside of the church had been turned into a workshop and child-care centre. Dozens of children were running about in the aisles, women were sleeping on the hard pews of blond wood, groups of men were holding confabulations all over the place, others were coming in carrying big pieces of wood and stacking them in a corner. At the rood screen, some thirty young men were making bows and arrows. On the altar devoid of any religious symbol were a few hunting rifles and a hundred or so cartridges.

These several thousand people had fled from Sake, Gashora and Kazenze, which could all be seen to the east. It hadn't been a collective flight or in response to anyone's signal. Seeing the increasing numbers of Tutsis being murdered, families and individuals were fleeing toward Butare, then perhaps Burundi. By day they would sleep in swamps and ditches. When night fell they would move slowly, avoiding the paved or dirt roads and built-up areas. Mugina had a large Tutsi population and many of the fugitives had close or distant relatives here. Stratton and several others had persuaded the first arrivals to stay and regroup. They had requisitioned the church, whereupon the Belgian priest had left because he did not want to get involved in politics. So had his Hutu assistant, who went and set himself up at the roadblock where Simone's daughter was killed. Since there were more and more rumours of

killings and the refugees were more and more numerous, it was decided, after much discussion and with
encouragement from Stratton and a number of local
sages, to turn the Mugina plateau into a Tutsi fortress.
"Alone, one dies without dignity," said Stratton to
Valcourt and Gentille as he thanked them for their
visit. But they must leave while it was still daylight,
because once night fell militiamen controlled the dirt
road leading to the highway.

"*Ma petite*, you are your great-great-grandfather's
finest achievement. We should set you up in a museum
and invite the population to come and admire you, and
find out that a Hutu woman can be more beautiful than
the most magnificent of Tutsis. . ."

His laughter came to an abrupt end.

"A few years ago I didn't really know what I was
and it wasn't so bad," he continued. "I wasn't Tutsi or
Hutu, just Rwandan, and that suited me, because what
I was was all right, a mixture made of a combination of
random couplings and great-great-grandfather's plan.
But today they don't leave me any choice. They're
forcing me to become a Tutsi again, even though I
don't want to. I don't want to die by mistake, you
understand."

Gentille kissed him the way Whites do, with her
arms around him, then pinched his nose the way she
used to when she was little.

Driving down to the Butare highway, they passed
dozens of young men coming the other way armed with
machetes and *masus*. Some of them were carrying cases
of Primus on their shoulders. There were two more
roadblocks to be passed, watched sullenly by militiamen. After glancing at Valcourt's papers they clustered

about Gentille, who refused each time to translate what they were saying.

Butare was living as if in a bubble. This former capital of Rwanda—it was then called Astrida, from the name of a Belgian queen—still had the air of a peaceful and indolent colonial city. At the Hôtel Ibis, Monsieur Robert, the Belgian proprietor of forty years' standing, was observing the day's happenings as usual from the big round table in the perpetually shaded corner of the terrace. He and his wife and son spent a good eight hours a day here, joined from time to time by all the university town's decrepit expatriates and all its Rwandan professors dreaming of going to teach in a Canadian university. The rest of the tables were occupied by a constantly replenished tide of foreign aid workers and their Rwandan counterparts. On the surface, none of the demons and madness that were tearing the other regions of the country to pieces were at work here. A few militiamen had in fact turned up to see the burgomaster not long before, armed with papers signed by a colonel from headquarters, but the burgomaster had had them escorted to the border of the commune without even receiving them.

Monsieur Robert was disappointed when he saw Gentille and Valcourt, who was carrying a suitcase, coming toward the big round table. If Gentille, the most beautiful woman in Butare, was arriving like this, holding Valcourt's hand, it was pretty serious. He had never had any illusions, but there was nothing to stop a big-bellied Belgian from dreaming, especially if he was rich and lived in Africa. As for Valcourt, he was shaking a little as he greeted all these people he knew at least by sight. And Gentille was now breaking, one by one, all the rules governing Rwandan behaviour between man and woman. She was speaking up, asserting herself. For the last few days she had been going ahead of him when they entered a shop or restaurant. When Valcourt spoke about her, their relationship or their plans, she did not bow her head and look at the ground, she sat or stood even straighter, like an alluring statue, with her back arched and her eyes bright. He remembered how timidly she used to walk, her shoulders hunched, eyes cast down and hidden by lids half closed. Her voice was then only a murmur, and her laugh a thin, shy smile that she covered with an embarrassed hand. Today, Valcourt told himself, she would not hesitate to kiss him in public if she felt like it.

Two chairs were brought, and two bottles of Primus. It was Gentille who announced their coming marriage. The news was greeted with smiles but no real emotion. These old colonial hands and veteran aid workers had seen marriages between expatriates and star-struck or ambitious young things before. The couple's decision to live in Rwanda didn't surprise them either. At the beginning, this was always the way. But wishes were expressed for much happiness.

Valcourt raised the deteriorating situation in Kigali and around the capital. A red-haired Belgian, who had been teaching philosophy since the university's foundation in 1963, laughed and said, "They have to kill each other at regular intervals. It's like the menstrual cycle: a lot of blood flows, then everything returns to normal."

Gentille stood up and put her hand on Valcourt's shoulder.

"We won't sleep here tonight after all, Bernard. We'll go to papa's."

When they arrived at the big brick house surrounded by its impenetrable rugo hedge, Gentille asked Valcourt to wait outside while she announced the news to her father.

Valcourt sat down on a rock several metres from the house. In the distance he could see the twinkling lights of the old capital as it dozed off insouciantly, then, between this canvas of flickering candles and himself, an immense hole, both black and silent. But after a few seconds, as his eyes adapted to the darkness, he detected a thread of smoke. Then another, then ten, a hundred, a thousand. A thousand, ten thousand little pinpoints of light were piercing the cover of night and letting as many tiny white ribbons escape. And from this cover pierced with ten thousand stars, like a sky inverted, there rose ten thousand gentle breathings, gasps, muffled barkings, shy tears, restrained laughter, together composing a warm, murmuring sound. The hush spoken by the silence was the language of the hills. And depending on whether he was thinking of the men clinging to the flanks of the hills or the peacefulness flooding through him, Valcourt could choose to listen to the murmuring of humanity or the wondrous hush of silence.

He had not heard Jean-Damascène approaching.

"Monsieur, I am honoured by the honour you are paying our family and our hill."

The moon highlighted an angular face. The deep voice spoke of a stern teacher, and the eyes . . . the eyes were Gentille's, dark and silky, burning and exciting. The man spoke like a master from another era, which he was. He prolonged his sentences as if watching them unfold while formulating them. Gentille's father, Valcourt thought, must surely have decided one day that he was going to speak French better than those he had learned it from.

"I'm going to call you 'son,' even though I think— you'll forgive me—that you're older than I. It will be strange, but it's a term I like. It's what I call all my sons-in-law. And my daughters-in-law I call 'daughter.'"

He beckoned to Valcourt to follow him. He set off along the path Gentille and Valcourt had come by after leaving the Jeep at the end of the dirt road. His long, bent frame was outlined against a sky glittering with a hundred thousand stars. Valcourt was following a spectre, a living dead man humming a languorous melody. Jean-Damascène stopped by a tree that had been twisted by the winds, with branches thrust down toward the valley, forming a kind of elongated parasol whose far end was protecting only a void.

"It was under this fig tree that my great-grandfather Kawa died. In a way we are sitting on his grave, because no cemetery wanted to have him. Gentille told me that you knew our family secret, the pact that Kawa made with the devil so that we would cease to be what we were and his descendants would become members of a superior race. Monsieur Valcourt, my son, there is still time not to join this family and not to belong to this hill. No one will hold it against you, least of all Gentille, if you decide against an accursed destiny that can lead only to death. Kawa succeeded beyond all his dreams. Half his descendants are officially Tutsis and the other half have the physical characteristics to varying degrees, even though their identity cards show that they are Hutus. You could say that Kawa invented the Rwanda of today and his family is the horrible summation of it. A man alone on a hill, manipulating the ingredients of life, condemns those he creates to all sicknesses and all dangers.

"Until 1959, this pact with the devil brought us only pleasure and prosperity. Then the Belgians, who were a bit lost in an Africa that was shaking free of the colonial mould, and probably a bit tired of this unprofitable country, discovered as if by magic the virtues of democracy and the law of majority rule. Overnight, the shiftless Hutu became an incarnation of modern progress, and the shapeless mass of ignorant peasants a legitimate democratic majority. Even God complied, and his Gospel became a promise of justice and equality. The parish priests, who had had only Tutsi altar boys and seminarists, began to sing hallelujahs to the majority from the pulpit. The shepherds sent out calls to forgotten flocks and exhorted their members to take the pews closest to the altar. Kawa had to die a second time. People's souls are mysteriously capable sometimes of taking on the folds of the skin they're covered with. From all corners of the hill, Hutu sons and daughters of Kawa, who until then had been disappointed only to be tall like a Tutsi or have a Tutsi nose, were shouting loud and clear that they belonged to a new race that democracy made superior and dominant. Not many short, dark Hutus believed these turncoats, these mutants of history. But some of the turncoats were so convincing, making themselves the worst enemies of their brothers and cousins, that the new masters of the country decided to trust them and took them into their circles, their businesses and their families.

"This hill is still today Kawa's family's hill. See how peaceful and fixed in time it is. That is the landscape's lie, telling you that all the ferocity of Nature, every steep slope, has been tamed by man's patient toil, humanity's exemplary conquest of the unconquerable. What delusion! While we were clearing each square centimetre of these precipitous slopes, planting beans where nothing was growing but stones and brambles, and bananas where there had been only thistles, a cousin was hiding behind a rugo hedge, waiting for his cousin so he could kill him and thus prove his own Hutu identity. Our big, fine family, neither Hutu nor Tutsi, began to tear itself apart like a pack of mad, hungry dogs. Part of the hill scattered, some to Burundi, where the Tutsis dominate, some to Zaïre, most to Uganda.

"My son, today we have closed the circle of history and absurdity. The head of the *interahamwes*, who have sworn to cut the throats of all the Tutsis and send them all the way to Egypt by the Kagera River, is a Tutsi. He's an uncle of Gentille's. The number two of the RPF, the Tutsi army that's preparing vengeance from Uganda, is a Hutu, and he's also an uncle of Gentille's. Both of them—they don't know this, but either one will do it—both want to kill Gentille, who doesn't belong to either side. Gentille is like the fruit of the red earth of this hill, a mysterious mix of all the seeds and all the toil of this country. Son, you're going to marry a country they want to kill, one that could be simply Rwandan if it had the chance, the country of a thousand hills, which all of us, nameless and heedless of origin, have built like patient, obstinate fools. Son, we must flee the madness that invents peoples and tribes. It respects neither the country's sons nor its daughters. It creates demons and spells, lies that become truth and rumours that are claimed as historical fact. But if you are crazy enough to embrace this hill, its consuming madness and its most beautiful daughter, I shall love you more than my own sons."

"Monsieur, I ask you for the hand of your daughter Gentille and the hospitality of this hill, because here is where I want to live."

Jean-Damascène knelt, scratched at the earth with his long fingers, and placed in Valcourt's hands a few pebbles, a little rich red soil, some blades of grass and a leafy twig fallen from the fig tree.

"I give you my daughter and Kawa's hill."

When her father had gone back into the house, Gentille came and joined Valcourt.

With the lightest touch of her lips, she kissed his forehead, his nose, placed barely a breath on his lips, then with featherlight finger traced all the roads on his lined face. "Teach me desire," she had said to him one night. He had replied that he didn't know how, but together they would learn the secret. All she had known before about the pleasure of sex was the furious fumbling of hands and a penis taking what they wanted. Now with her own body, which she was discovering through Valcourt's caresses, with her own body that she was finding as beautiful as the pleasure he was bringing her, she was beginning to discover the body of the man. Patiently, she explored the territory, with only the man's breathing and the contraction of his muscles to guide her. She resisted the urgency to be caressed herself, the too pressing desire to be entered. She had learned to calm the man as he prepared to die with ecstasy so that he, and she too, came to be a parcel of flesh so sensitive that each new caress became an unbearable torture that only mutual suicide could release. And each time they died together, like tonight on Kawa's grave, they told each other, without saying so, that this was their last death.

Neither the first rooster, nor the first dog, nor the sun, nor Jean-Damascène, who left a big pot of coffee, a little bread, some tomatoes and hard-cooked eggs beside their naked bodies, wakened them. When she opened her eyes, Gentille saw her father watching them from a distance, sitting by the house. She covered herself modestly but was surprised to feel no shame or embarrassment. She waved happily, inviting him to come. With a little smile he shook his head. He would have liked to come to them walking with his wife, Jeanne, but when he learned he had AIDS he had sent her to live with her parents. "You have the right to live," he had told her. She too would have rejoiced to see these birds take flight.

"Come, papa, come and eat."

He joined them, his heart light finally. There was only one cup for the coffee and they passed it around, laughing at nothing. Gentille and Valcourt would be married in three days, on April the ninth. Then they would come back to the hill and live with Jean-Damascène.

"But I'll be dead soon, *ma fille*."

No, there were medicines that could be got in Europe. Valcourt would surely find work at the university or with one of the humanitarian organizations swarming in the area. Yes, they told each other, wanting to believe it, we can still dream, who says we can't?

But Valcourt would also work with his father-in-law, who with help from Sister Franca had founded the first association of HIV patients in Rwanda. There were only a dozen members but they had great plans, the first of which was to break the customary silence and combat the shame. To the Western reader, all this seems very simple and ordinary. To a lower-middle-class Rwandan, it is a major achievement. But Jean-Damascène was not a man to varnish a situation to protect his own fortunes. As much as his great-grandfather Kawa had built his lineage on untruth and deceit, Jean-Damascène had raised his own children in truth and honesty, even at the cost of darkening the dreams of those he loved. This hill, so peaceful in appearance, was a minefield. He explained this to Valcourt, for Gentille had known it since childhood. His hill, like all the others, could have no peace unless the mines exploded, unmasking in the horror of twisted flesh and shattered families the madness of those who had planted them. But everything would have to explode before the blind and the deaf would finally see and hear the fire and screams rising from the hell they had created.

The three stayed sitting under the fig tree. Relatives and friends arrived, some bringing flowers, others beer. They would stay a few minutes after bowing almost formally to Valcourt, whose hand they would shake gingerly, then they would go back to their plot of land or behind their rugo hedge to watch time go by. While their old-fashioned courtesy and reserve delighted Valcourt, Gentille was disappointed, for against all expectations she had hoped that her happiness would be noted and celebrated by some outbursts of joy or transgressions of the cold hill etiquette. She tried to encourage conversation, would recount an anecdote about a neighbour who would just bow his head shyly; she tried a few jokes, which met with nothing more than polite smiles. Valcourt whispered in her ear that he much preferred the silence of the hill to the hotel's noisiness.

People, he told her, are shaped somehow by their climate and the land they live in. Those who live by the sea are like the currents and tides; they go and come, and discover many shores. Their words and loves are like water that slips between one's fingers and is never still. Mountain people have fought the mountain to win their place. Once they have conquered it they protect their mountain, and others coming from far below in the valley risk being seen as enemies. Hill people take time before greeting each other. They study one another and only slowly accept one another, but once their guard is lowered or their word is given, they will be as firm as their hill in their commitment.

Gentille understood at last that Valcourt did not want to stay here only to please her. He felt good here.

Chapter Eleven

In Kigali on this sixth of April, 1994, a dozen men met in an office at the barracks of the presidential guard, opposite the United Nations Building on Revolution Boulevard. They had completed the lists and each name had been approved. One thousand five hundred names: politicians of the opposition, both Hutus and Tutsis, moderate businessmen hoping for a sharing of power between the two ethnic groups with democracy as an added bonus, activist priests, members of human rights associations, journalists. The presidential guard, the Zero networks* and certain soldiers and policemen

* The secret high command of the genocide and its lieutenants.

would eliminate them as soon as the president had been assassinated. Then the police force, section heads and militias would throw up the roadblocks. Colonel Théoneste undertook to hoodwink and neutralize the UN forces. Every Tutsi house in Kigali had been identified. No one must leave the city, or even a section. Each group of *interahamwes* would be accompanied by a policeman or a soldier.

"And don't trust identity papers, use your heads," snapped Colonel Athanase.* "If they're tall, if they're thin, if they're pale, they're Tutsis, cockroaches we must wipe off the face of the earth."

Valcourt and Gentille had decided to leave at sundown so as to be in Kigali around ten that night, given the increasing number of military roadblocks. While Jean-Damascène was stirring up the fire, the parade of neighbours and relatives continued. They had all been invited to Kigali for the wedding, but only Gentille's father had said he might come.

More and more gifts were accumulating in front of Gentille, who expressed her thanks humbly to each donor while Valcourt hid his surprise at so much generosity. A few chickens, goats, bags of rice, some baskets of tomatoes, a lance—a traditional weapon because Whites like old things—several woven baskets and trays decorated with enigmatic geometrical motifs, and a big earthenware urn.

Since the visitors seemed to want to stay, the wedding-gift goats had to be killed. When the relatives

---

* Colonel Athanase was a member of the High Command.

saw that two goats were cooking over the big fire, and chickens too, they dispatched some young messengers who returned with hands laden with tomatoes, lettuces, onions, eggs and cheese to round out the feast. No one guffawed or spoke loudly, but the voices were no longer murmuring.

The women formed a big circle around Gentille after shooing the children away from her. Gentille was laughing, bubbling with talk. It took only a look, a laugh, a sigh to set her off again. The men stood in little groups, often in silence, observing the valley and the hill opposite. From time to time one of them would go and ask Jean-Damascène to interpret for him, since none of them spoke anything but Kinyarwanda, and in their language Valcourt could only say *yégo, oya* and *inzoga,* meaning "yes," "no" and "beer." The man (for it was always a man, this cousin or friend) would bow his head slightly to Valcourt and then wait while Jean-Damascène repeated what had been confided to him. All spoke words of welcome and praised the beauty of the future bride who, said one, would bear beautiful children despite being so thin, but would not be able to work in the fields. And all of them, through Jean-Damascène, told Valcourt to take Gentille to another country. When silence indicated that the translation had ended, each would take a step back and extend a hand to Valcourt while almost turning away, as if the skins of these two hands touching would be performing a culpable indecency. The last of the men—a pure Tutsi the anthropologists would say, slender, bony and gentle all at once, with high cheekbones and shining eyes—did not extend his hand when silence came. He looked Valcourt straight in the eye, spat on the ground and put his foot on the white liquid and crushed it, as if he wanted his saliva to sully the ground.

"He says he respects you but you must not keep Gentille on rotten land."

From the circle of women the laughter and chuckles were becoming louder. The circle had drawn closer and Gentille, while still the centre of attention, was now just an opportunity for countless confidences. There were bursts of laughter but the words that provoked them were whispered. And each woman telling of her pleasure did it with her head bowed. The men drifted imperturbably around the fire, prodding at goat or chicken, scolding a child who went too close to the cliff. The men were not interested in women's pleasure, which seemed too much like children's, women being children.

They had been driving in silence for thirty minutes. Somewhere in the vast shambles of neighbouring Zaïre, the sun had disappeared like a gold piece from the hand of a magician. They had passed the military roadblock on the way out of Butare without a hitch.

"You laughed a lot."

Gentille exploded with laughter as though she were still with her circle of women. Yes, they had laughed a lot because they were talking about men, but more precisely about men in bed.

"When we were teenagers we would meet in a round house, five or six girls with an older woman, a woman who knew men. We would sit on a mat with our legs stretched out. We would put a hand inside our underpants. The woman told us to rub and caress our privates to make them wet, then open them and find a little thing that would make us tremble when we touched it, like a little tongue hidden between the lips. I know now that that's called lips and a clitoris. The woman who initiated us talked of 'the woman's hiding place.' Then we would caress ourselves. It was also a kind of game, a contest to see who would have the most pleasure, the longest possible. This afternoon, my friends asked me if our teenage discoveries were helping me today and if the White was getting the benefit. I told them about all your caresses and all mine. Then they exchanged all their secrets and longings, and especially their desires, because they don't have many secrets."

"And why all that little-girl laughter?"

"Embarrassment, shyness, modesty. They still have teenage dreams and can only talk about their longings and secret thoughts if they're laughing at them."

An unusual number of vehicles were heading toward Butare. During the descent toward Nyabisindu, lightning tore through the night as in a Goya painting. Figures appeared, silhouetted briefly between vehicles that seemed to be turning or backing up without reason. Macabre confusion. On the side of the road a minibus was disgorging its passengers. Keeping his hand on the horn, Valcourt wove a course through the turmoil. A hundred metres farther on, a dozen soldiers were guarding a roadblock lit by a few torches in the hands of militiamen. Kigali-bound minibuses and taxis could continue but without their passengers who were returning to Butare, carrying their suitcases on their heads. Private vehicles had to turn around and go back. The soldier Valcourt showed his papers to couldn't read. A non-commissioned officer of some kind appeared, revolver in hand, shouting and slobbering.

He looked at Valcourt's press pass for a bare fraction of a second.

"The Tutsis are attacking Kigali and a government collaborator's riding round with a cockroach girl."

Valcourt handed him Gentille's identity card. The soldier became even more incensed.

"False papers, false papers! Whores, just whores seducing even our friends. Go, go, but that one, we'll get her when you're not there to protect her."

Valcourt turned on the radio. On Radio Rwanda, a commentator was listing the economic achievements of 1993. Radio Mille-Collines, the extremist Hutu station, was playing classical music, which was surprising. Usually it played American pop music to attract the young, and interlarded it with calls to violence and angry speeches about Hutu traitors trucking with the *inkotanyis*. For months the journalists at Radio Mille-Collines had been naming traitors, enemies, plotters. When one of these was mysteriously murdered, a commentator would say that the victim had asked for his own death, that he had been the scum of the earth and while he, the commentator, did not approve of the murder, he understood that Hutus threatened in their very existence might think that only the disappearance of the Tutsis and their allies would guarantee their existence.

At Ruhango another roadblock barred the way. While Valcourt was showing his and Gentille's papers, the music, Mozart's *Requiem*, was interrupted.

"The President of the Republic of Rwanda, Juvénal Habyarimana, died when his plane exploded above the air base at Kanombé. The plane, which was preparing to land, was hit by a missile fired by Tutsi rebels. The government has declared a curfew and asks all the loyal population of the republic to take up arms to confront the invasion of the cockroaches. Your neighbours could be murderers. Be vigilant."

It was half past nine on Thursday the sixth of April, 1994, and Gentille was returning to Kigali to be married the following Sunday. Valcourt had been telling her about Cyprien's confidences, Colonel Théoneste's confession to Father Louis and his own fruitless meetings with the United Nations general. Whenever Raphaël had given his great oration on Rwandan Nazism and compared the Tutsis to the Jews, and in Gentille's presence talked about the "final solution," Valcourt had always tried to tone down the problem. Without conviction, he raised the presence of the United Nations and above all the fact that the international community would not tolerate the elimination of an entire people from the face of the earth. He did believe that there would be horrible massacres. He could imagine tens of thousands of deaths, because this much had already happened. As things were now going it seemed logical, or at least not inexplicable. By the time they passed the roadblock at Gitarama, he had lost his last illusions. In excellent French the sergeant told him:

"You're returning to Kigali just in time to see the triumph of the Hutu people."

Gentille seemed to be asleep, curled up in her seat like a little girl exhausted by a long journey. On the uphill climb toward Rundo, Valcourt took a dirt road leading to a small valley from where one could see both Stratton's hill and the first lights of the outskirts of

Kigali. He was reassured by the silence, the scent of eucalyptus, even more by the scent of Gentille, and most of all by her tranquil breathing. All this wove together in a kind of murmur, a barely perceptible pulsation giving his life rhythm and meaning. A few weeks earlier, Václav Havel, president of the Czech Republic, had given a speech to the General Assembly of the United Nations in which he had invoked "the order of life," which for an atheist was intended to replace the sacred. What Valcourt was feeling was the enfolding breath of the order of life. In spite of the gathering signs, in spite of the sergeant's assertions confirming his worst conjectures, he could not lose all hope. No death, no massacre had ever made him lose hope for man. From the napalm in Vietnam, he had come away burned; from the Cambodian holocaust, speechless; from the Ethiopian famine, broken, exhausted, stooped. But in the name of something he had not managed to define, which he himself might well call the order of life, he had to carry on. And carrying on meant looking straight ahead and walking, walking.

"Gentille, you asleep?"

"No, I'm thinking about you. I know exactly why I love you. You live like an animal guided by instinct. As if your eyes are closed and your ears are blocked, but there's a secret compass inside you that always directs you to the small and forgotten, or impossible loves, like ours. You know you can't do anything, that your being here won't change a thing, but you keep going anyway. Bernard, there's still time to turn back to Butare."

"No, no, we have to go back to Kigali, we're getting married on Sunday. Tomorrow you have to pick out your dress."

The official radio station was broadcasting an international news bulletin in French. A release from Quebec announced that the Parti Québécois government would probably hold a referendum on sovereignty within a year. The ethnic cleansing in the former Yugoslavia was continuing and more and more countries were considering a military intervention by NATO. On Radio Mille-Collines, a hollering voice was enumerating the list of Tutsi accomplices who were threatening to take power: Agathe Uwilingiyiamana, who was spitting on her parents, turning her back on them, and who was prime minister of the transitional government; Landouald, who liked to be called "Lando," vice-president of the Liberal Party; Faustin, president of the Social Democratic Party, a Hutu traitor who was fond of Tutsi hookers.

"The work has only begun. This time we mustn't stop before it's finished. We've forgiven them so often. In 1963 they didn't get it, in spite of warnings that cost them a lot. Ten years later we've shown them our power and our right to this country once again, but it's like when you cut up earthworms: machetes have only multiplied them and made them bolder and more perverted. Today they've killed our president and are getting ready to kill you all. You're in a state of legitimate defence. We must eradicate the enemy. A little music and we'll be back with the latest news. This is Radio Mille-Collines, free radio-television, the voice of freedom and democracy. Here is John Lennon's 'Imagine.'"

There was uncustomary commotion at the Rundo crossroads. Shadows were running this way and that. Fires were burning. A minor picture of the apocalypse, thought Valcourt, kissing Gentille on the forehead tenderly. They said nothing but both were thinking of

Marie who lived a hundred metres to the left, and it was left they turned when they came to the roadblock. The Jeep was suddenly surrounded by a dozen militiamen armed with machetes and *masus*. A policeman ordered them to continue on their way to Kigali or go back toward Butare. They must not go into Rundo.

"It's for your own safety. The rebels are infiltrating the hills."

The soldiers manning the last roadblock before Kigali didn't seem worried about the supposed invasion of Tutsi rebels from Uganda. They were more numerous and more talkative than usual. The lieutenant, whom Valcourt knew by sight, made great welcoming signs as he walked toward the Jeep.

"Good evening, Monsieur from the television station. You're arriving just in time for some great shots. We've begun to cleanse the capital."

As soon as they were into the city they could hear the sharp, chilling sounds of gunshots from all around. Valcourt knew war, and the sounds he was hearing were not those of engagements between soldiers. The rebels had not invaded the city. Hundreds of killers were on the prowl, noisily carrying out their work.

It was eleven o'clock when Valcourt and Gentille arrived at the hotel. At the gate, the usual peddlers of smuggled cigarettes and bogus antique carvings were gone and a dozen presidential guardsmen were inspecting every vehicle going in or out. In the background, United Nations soldiers were standing around watching. Some hundred people had invaded the lobby. The men were crowding around the reception desk or talking. The women, sitting on the mosaic floor, were trying to keep children quiet or coax them to sleep. No one had any baggage and a few women were wandering around in bathrobes. Monsieur Georges, the assistant manager, was moving about with dignity amid the confusion, assuring everyone of a room as soon as one of his guests moved out. For the moment, the hotel was glad to have them all, but it would be better if they settled down outside, around the pool. Madame Agathe's girls, who had abandoned the pool and fourth-floor bars, were suggesting rendezvous in the shower stalls near the pool, the hairdressing salon or the women's washroom in the basement. Around the pool, noisiness had given way to muttering. Ensconced on their plastic deckchairs, the consultants and transient expatriates, those great adventurers of international aid who had seen it all before, were feigning indifference, masking the fear that kept them stuck to their seats. From table to table they clustered together, leaving their local counterparts to their anxieties and their rumours, forming little circles of petrified but outwardly unperturbed Whites. As professionals in things African, they anticipated a few excesses in the initial hours, which frightened them, but they also knew that the Belgian, French or American paras would step in promptly to extricate their precious compatriots from the hellfires that the great powers had helped ignite.

Valcourt and Gentille wandered around hand in hand amid the pandemonium for a few minutes. They went to their room and found the child they were going to christen Émérita sound asleep. Alice, the young Muslim girl from Nyamirambo, was watching though not understanding a word of a CNN program on new European fashion trends. She didn't feel like going to work and even less like taking the risk of going home. Gentille bedded her down on the balcony with several pillows and a heavy wool blanket while Valcourt went up to the bar to get something to eat and drink. He came back with a case of mediocre Côtes du Rhône, some cheeses, some bread and three cartons of milk.

"The barman advised me to go easy, especially with the wine. With all these newcomers, the stock's going to run out pretty fast."

He opened a bottle and poured three glasses, but Alice declined because of her religion. She accepted a piece of bread, which she spread with cheese as though it were butter. The Camembert wasn't bad and the wine was less corked than usual. Valcourt and Gentille sat cross-legged, face to face on the bed like two children making up ghost stories when their parents think they're asleep. But they weren't talking. They gazed at each other, their eyes moving only when there were gunshots. They ate hungrily and drank quickly, as if they were devouring chunks of life.

"Gentille, d'you know when I fell in love with you?"

"The night you came and drove me home?"

"No, the first morning. It was six o'clock and you'd just started your internship. I'd asked for eggs turned over, but they weren't. With bacon, but I ended up with ham. But all I could see were your breasts almost cutting through your starched blouse and your behind that must have been shaped by a genius of a sculptor, and I didn't want to say anything that wouldn't be nice to such a beauty. When I got up to go, you whispered, as frightened as a gazelle that scents a lion, 'Monsieur, it's my first day interning. I hope you'll forgive me. I reread my order slips. You asked for bacon and eggs turned over. Why didn't you say anything? Thank you.' You spoke looking at the ground. You were so upset and so embarrassed, so embarrassed. I didn't say anything. I was paralyzed by your beauty and enchanted by your coming to me that way. I watched you from that moment on. I knew when you started and finished work. You'd bring me a Primus and I was the one who was shaking when I thanked you."

"And when did I fall in love with you?"

"After that phony Parisian asked you for a herb tea?"

"No, my first day interning. When I realized I was more important to someone than my mistakes."

"So why did we wait so long?"

"I don't know, but I'm not sorry."

They lay down and in spite of the shouting, loud talk and crying of children coming up from the pool, around midnight fell into a deep and peaceful sleep.

According to eyewitness reports gathered from neighbours, this was the hour when their friend Landouald, his Québécoise wife, Hélène, and their two children were murdered by presidential guardsmen. Raphaël's body was found eight or ten metres from Élise's house, where he was trying to take refuge. Six months after the genocide, Valcourt was present when they exhumed several thousand decomposed bodies from a common grave alongside the hospital wall, a stone's throw from the Detection Centre where André worked, the gentle musician who made his living distributing condoms. Valcourt recognized his guitar case but no one could identify the body. The family decided to give a proper burial to the guitar. Marie's husband succeeded in hiding his wife and six of his nine children in the false ceiling of a Hutu friend's house. They spent nearly two months there. Charles himself was killed while trying to save the three other children; the three boys were also felled by machetes and clubs. With fifteen thousand refugees, Stratton resisted attacks from soldiers and militiamen for a week. Almost all were massacred. Of the 320 members of Stratton's family, seventeen survived. By night, Stratton travelled through fields and swamps, a distance of a hundred kilometres, to Gentille's father's house, to find Jean-Damascène nearing death from the tuberculosis that was destroying his lungs.

The next morning at breakfast, Valcourt and Gentille learned in bits and pieces that their world was collapsing around them. There were now several hundred people camping around the pool, in the parking lot and in the corridors of the hotel. The hotel's water supply and telephone lines had been cut. Victor, the restaurant owner, was hailed as a hero when he showed up with a hundred loaves of bread, bottles of water and all the eggs in his restaurant's refrigerator. He had already made ten trips between his restaurant on Justice Avenue and the hotel. A hundred people had taken refuge in his basement there. In his shiny beige Peugeot, waving handfuls of money at the militiamen and policemen, he was driving them four at a time to the Mille-Collines. The rumour had got around fast: the presence of White aid workers and experts as well as some UN soldiers made the hotel, which belonged to the Belgian airline Sabena, an even safer sanctuary than the churches. Victor asked Valcourt to accompany him on these comings and goings. His presence could be useful.

Valcourt got in the car with Victor, who steered with one hand and counted a rosary with the other. Having the White with his papers from the Ministry of Information in the car with him could only help. At the very first roadblock, Valcourt blanched and thought he'd pass out. A long, wavy line of bodies snaked down one side of Justice Avenue. Beside it, militiamen and policemen were ordering passengers out of their vehicles. A single machete blow was often enough, then teenagers dragged the still-quivering body to the side of the pavement. The men's bodies, clothed, made black and white patches; the women's were exposed, legs spread, breasts bared, pink or red underpants around their knees. Many were still alive. Valcourt could see them tremble and hear them rattle as they breathed and moaned. The men were killed skillfully and accurately with a single shot or machete stroke, but the women didn't have the right to a quick, clean death. They were mutilated, tortured, raped, but not finished off as the killers would have done with wounded animals. They were allowed to bleed to death, to feel death coming rattle by rattle, gob by gob of blood-filled spit, to punish them for having brought so many Tutsis into the world, but also to punish them for their arrogance, for the young killers had been told that Tutsi women considered themselves too good for Hutus.

Victor and Valcourt followed a red pickup truck. Standing in the back of it were three presidential guardsmen and a cameraman who was calmly filming the long multicoloured ribbon. They stopped and got out near a woman all dressed in pink, lying on her back. Two children were kneeling beside her, crying.

One of the soldiers turned the woman's light body over with his foot, and her slender arm extended toward him as though appealing for help. The cameraman kept filming, moving around her to get more angles and close-ups, long shots and medium shots, then put down his camera, unzipped his fly and penetrated her. When he raised his head, probably after ejaculating, Valcourt recognized him. It was Dieudonné, his best student. Victor was muttering, "Hail Mary, full of grace, the Lord is with you . . ." The ravens and buzzards were flying low, circling over the banquet being offered them. Valcourt vomited himself inside out.

They passed the prison and police headquarters, from which group after group of armed militiamen poured forth, each with a policeman, and clambered into vehicles that headed off in the direction of Nyamirambo, Gikondo or Muhima. Victor turned onto Hospital Street, then Revolution Boulevard. The vendors of expired medications and women selling food who usually clustered about the entrance to the Kigali Hospital Centre were gone. There was no doctor doing a triage of the wounded coming to receive treatment. Soldiers were casting a quick eye at the injured. Their method of selection showed incontrovertible logic: someone with a machete wound could only be a rebel and was finished off. The body was tossed onto the piles of other bodies that trucks, buses and cars were unloading. Militiamen were rummaging through the clothes and brandishing their precious finds with whoops and laughter.

Victor had approached the leader at the roadblock near his restaurant and offered to feed his men. He wanted to do his bit for the republic, he said. A handful of militiamen, already dead drunk, were asleep outside the restaurant. Inside, two policemen were guarding some terrified female captives. "Cockroaches, Tutsi cockroaches we're going to find some good Hutus for." Valcourt recognized an employee at the television station to whom he had never spoken and whose name he didn't even know. Instinctively, he moved toward her. She put a hushing finger to her lips and signalled a frantic no with her eyes, then turned her back to him. Victor, who had seen the move, gripped Valcourt by the sleeve, still counting his beads.

Victor was a hard-working man. Aside from being the proprietor of a very popular restaurant, he was also the owner of a number of trucks that transported fish from Lake Kivu. He always took as his cut a good share of the load to recover his incidental expenses, an arrangement that enabled him to serve the best and least expensive fried tilapias in town. In the basement of his restaurant he had set up a machine shop plus the offices of an import company that did business only with South Africa. Victor revered two prophets, Jesus and Nelson Mandela. Jesus held the future of the world in his hands and Nelson Mandela held the future of Africa in his. If the former Robben Island prisoner had freed a country that had belonged to the Whites and given it to the Blacks without much killing while allowing the Whites to exist too, then he might well save Rwanda, where the majority was as black as the minority. All the businesspeople who looked to Europe and the United States for trade laughed at this pious, uneducated man who wanted to do business with Africans. They ignored him so completely that Victor could import Mandela's small electric motors built with Israeli technology, and his light agricultural machinery, without paying any bribes at all to Akazu members or customs agents. Only Victor's workshop, of course, had the necessary parts and expertise to repair what he sold. Victor was rich, but that was not important to him. What he wanted was to live in peace with his wife and six children and, above all, get into heaven.

Two militiamen opened the big black metal doors that gave access to the machine shop. Victor stopped the Peugeot and asked them to close the doors behind him. Ahead on the other side was a lane a hundred metres long that joined a street leading to the Church of the Holy Family. From there they could get back to the hotel without going through the Revolution Square roadblock.

"Victor, I knew one of the prisoners."

"I knew almost all of them."

Victor got three women who were hiding in the shop into the car. At the bottom of the hill he stopped outside his house and came back with a bundle of money and a handgun, which he slipped under his belt. The soldiers guarding the hotel entrance recognized his car and waved him through, but he stopped and gave the lieutenant ten thousand francs for beer and cigarettes for his men. Over the next few days, he brought a hundred people to the hotel in this way. Forty children spent two months in his machine shop and all were saved. One day, while he was bringing food back to the hotel, a policeman refused the money he was proffering and asked him to get out of the car. Victor closed his eyes and stepped on the gas. The Peugeot hit an oil barrel, throwing a militiaman who was sitting on it against the windshield and onto the ground. Victor made it back inside the hotel and there lay low until the extremists were defeated.

Not only Kigali was engulfed by the insanity. Newly arrived refugees at the hotel were bringing terrifying news. Identical operations were going on at Rumagana, Zaza, Kazenze, Nyamata, Rundo and Mugina.

The Canadian general came to reassure the expatriates and the notables who had taken refuge in the hotel. He talked like a press release. The international community would not remain indifferent, but for the moment the UN forces could only intervene peaceably, in the hope that their presence alone would bring those responsible for these excesses back to reason. One of the leaders of the Liberal Party—Lando's party and that of most Tutsis—approached him, looked him in the eyes, which he turned away, and spat on his shiny boots.

"Shut up. You're pathetic. They killed ten of your own soldiers* and even then you didn't react. If you can't defend your own soldiers, you're not going to have us believe you're going to protect us."

The general bowed his head and left the hotel with the round-shouldered, heavy gait of a man condemned.

At Monsieur Georges's request, Gentille had agreed to go back to work. After two days of massacres, there were almost a thousand people at the hotel, including a hundred children. With several of Madame Agathe's girls, she established a small area for chil-

---

* On the morning of April 7, 1994, ten Belgian Blue Berets were taken prisoner by members of the presidential guard and then beaten and murdered. The UN forces made no attempt to free them. The Belgian contingent was recalled by its government. Before leaving, several Belgian soldiers tore up their United Nations badges and spat on the blue flag.

dren in a secluded part of the garden behind the fig tree and the aviary. She organized games and took the children in groups to the pool. Monsieur Georges had also set up a kind of refugee committee, of which Victor and Valcourt were members. The committee talked for hours on end, envisioning the best and worst scenarios, calculating reserves of food, trying to find equitable rationing methods while taking account of the fact that the hotel also had "normal" guests. Gentille and Valcourt shared the strange impression that they themselves were the only ones living normally. The young woman took care of children, comforted worried mothers, prepared bottles, seemingly endowed with such serenity and lightness of touch that she appeared to float above a world she had ceased to be part of. With Victor, Valcourt (who was hardly even-tempered himself) came up with hundreds of soothing arguments to cool the squabbles and innocuous but still disruptive confrontations bred by close quarters and fear, even among the most reasonable of beings.

On Friday, April the seventh, Father Louis arrived at the cocktail hour with a large suitcase. He had come at the request of a messenger paid by Victor. Several hours earlier, an envoy from the French embassy had asked him to get ready to leave the country. French and Belgian troops would be arriving any moment at Kigali airport to evacuate White foreign nationals and their families.*

---

* The first French plane left Kigali with the president's widow, Agathe Habyarimana, and some thirty members of her family, some of whom were among the principal organizers of the genocide. The widow received a sum of 200,000 francs for pocket money on her arrival in Paris. All these murderers are living in freedom in France as these lines are written.

"Make no mistake," the priest added, accepting the whisky that Victor poured into a plastic glass, "they're not coming to stay and save the country. They're giving themselves three days, then they'll be gone again. But I can't go, if only because I've got a wedding and a baptism to celebrate on Sunday, as I told him. He didn't seem to understand."

Then, smiling mischievously as children do, he asked Gentille to close her eyes because he had a surprise for her. He opened the big cardboard suitcase and took out a wedding dress. Valcourt thought it was awful, but it was exactly what every young Rwandan girl dreams of and longs to have. "You didn't know I was in the wedding-dress business." The dresses were made by former prostitutes suffering from AIDS and were rented out by a Caritas boutique. To buy one would sometimes cost a bride's family as much as three years' income.

The dress was pink and blue with epaulettes and lace and sequin-trimmed frills and flounces, an ugly princess-of-the-masked-ball costume, a clumsy imitation of outdated bourgeois finery—Valcourt saw in it all the insidious perversions of colonization that impose even the colonizer's castoffs on the colonized. Gentille was going to be married dressed up as a middle-class, small-town girl from the year 1900 while the world was falling apart in 1994.

Gentille didn't like the dress any better than Valcourt but she was weeping for joy. When she had dreamed of her wedding, she had seen her dark skin made radiant by a dress so white, so diaphanously pure that it turned her into a black-and-white butterfly ready to take flight. She wasn't being offered the wings she had imagined, but then, she was already on wings. Valcourt looked at the absurd creation Gentille was wearing as she skipped in delight around the table, and since we are transformed by the happiness of those we love, even when we don't understand it, all he saw was the rapturousness of her smile.

Nearly a thousand people crowded about the pool that Sunday to attend the mass that Father Louis recited in a monotone. Almost all the Whites had already been evacuated. It was a gathering of Rwandans, and their prayers were neither feigned nor timid. Their voices in chorus filled the air. Their hymns rose like great flights of birds above the belt of eucalyptus trees around the hotel and hovered over the neighbouring hills. Gentille, in her too-big dress, prayed and sang with her eyes closed. Valcourt envied the believers for whom death opens the gates of heaven with all its rewards. But he too was praying in his fashion. He abandoned himself to follow in the footsteps of others, accepting their pace, following whatever tortuous path they showed him. Father Louis raised the Host above his head. Valcourt bowed his head respectfully, as in the days when he served mass at Sainte-Bernadette Church in the north end of Montreal. God didn't exist, but he deserved that we bow down before his Word.

Victor had not only unearthed a cassette of the Wedding March, he had found two beautiful gold wedding rings, which the bride and groom exchanged. He had also had enough beer brought into the hotel that several hundred people felt they were taking part in a real celebration. After then baptizing Cyprien's daughter, who was christened Marie-Ange Émérita,

Father Louis folded up his portable altar and left without telling anyone that he had been ordered to leave for Bangui in a few hours, with all the employees of the French embassy.* Madame Agathe gave the little girl a stuffed chimpanzee and Gentille gave her a silk scarf in Sabena colours, gifts she had bought from the shrewish Belgian who ran the souvenir shop in the hotel lobby.

Monsieur Georges had set up a table under the fig tree in the spot where Father Louis had placed his altar. An appetizer of asparagus, then roast chicken with buttered young beans, a fine salad, an almost ripe round of brie. The new bride and groom shared this sumptuous repast with Victor and Élise. Jean-Damascène had decided finally not to make the trip. Élise had come to say goodbye. She was leaving with the French. A beautiful Sunday at the pool in Kigali, thought Valcourt, relishing the hotel's last bottle of Côtes du Rhône as if it were a truly great wine. A little tipsy, more from fatigue and emotion than wine, he and Gentille went up to their room. From their third-floor balcony they watched wordlessly as several hotel employees forming a chain passed water along from the pool in kitchen pots. The hotel was beginning to drink its pool.

That day in its major international bulletin CNN spent twenty seconds on the recurrence of ethnic problems in Rwanda, giving assurances, however, that foreign

---

* The French employees, of course. As in most Western embassies, the majority of local employees were Tutsis. All those who worked for the French and had taken refuge on French embassy property were abandoned by the French and were massacred there within hours of the evacuation of the diplomats and their families.

nationals were safe. Even the perspicacious BBC said little more. Radio-France Internationale talked about recurrent confrontations and ancestral tribalisms, wondering if Africans would ever be able to rid themselves of their ancient demons that kept provoking the most dreadful atrocities.

Gentille opened Éluard and read:

By day the house, by night the street
The street musicians
All play till lost in silence
Under the black sky clearly we see

She read in a voice that was firm yet filled with emotion, because the words were too close to reality, until night fell in a matter of seconds, as if God were placing a cover on a cauldron. Sometimes from very far away came a shrill scream; you'd have thought all the men on earth were after a single animal and disembowelling it.

Tomorrow they would have pain and absurdity back in their lives. Valcourt closed the door to the balcony and drew the curtains. Gentille sang a strange, sad ballad that lulled Émérita to sleep. She and Valcourt undressed, determined to celebrate their wedding night as if the whole world were celebrating their happiness with them.

They loved peacefully and long, without noisy or passionate embrace, like two streams meeting and blending and in the flow of the current losing their original colours. They were not in the time that was, or in the land of a thousand hills. For a few hours they lived elsewhere. And the sleep into which they drifted to the rhythm of their daughter's breathing was simply another place for their radiance.

It was Monsieur Georges, the assistant manager, who awakened them with a big pot of coffee and a triumphant smile that disconcerted them.

"Prepare yourselves for your wedding trip. I've arranged everything. You're leaving in two hours. Destination Nairobi with an English crew. You'll come back when the bad season's over. For now there's nothing more for you to do here. The country doesn't need refugees, it needs soldiers to kill the madmen."

"What about our friends?" Valcourt wanted to know.

"You can't do anything for them by staying here."

Leaving didn't mean betraying their friends any more than their country. They would be back. They had no time to pack, for Victor came to warn them that the UN troops were waiting and were leaving the hotel in fifteen minutes. Valcourt took his computer, his Walkman and several cassettes; Gentille took the chimpanzee, her wedding dress and Éluard. With Émérita, they climbed into a UNAMIR* truck in which eight or ten haggard-looking Whites were already crowded with their suitcases. Four Senegalese soldiers mounted guard with guns in their hands. An armoured car went ahead.

At the foot of Republic Avenue they saw a hundred dead bodies piled up outside the French Cultural Centre. They turned right onto the Boulevard of the Organization of African Unity. Gentille could only look for a moment or two. Valcourt had not told her about the multicoloured ribbon strung out along the streets of Kigali. She bowed her head and asked

* UN Assistance Mission for Rwanda.

Émérita to sit at her feet. At major crossroads, the ribbon stopped and became an enormous mass of flesh heaped up like old clothes.

Just beyond Gikondo, five minutes from the airport, the little convoy stopped at a roadblock manned by a dozen Rwandan soldiers who surrounded the truck. They made the passengers get out to check their papers. They were only interested in Gentille, who explained that she was Valcourt's wife. Five soldiers surrounded her, passing her papers from one to another. The more she protested, the more they laughed. False papers. Her face, her legs told them she was a Tutsi. False marriage. No one had signed marriage papers. Émérita, whom Gentille was holding by the hand, was howling. Oh yes, she was their daughter, but by adoption. The soldiers laughed harder still. The Senegalese sergeant in charge of the small convoy tried to intervene. He was shot dead. Valcourt lunged in Gentille's direction. He was knocked unconscious with a rifle butt.

He came to in the plane. They told him that the sergeant in command of the detachment of presidential guards had prevented the young woman and child from being harmed. He had, it seemed, taken them under his protection.

Chapter Twelve

In Nairobi, Valcourt learned the enormity of the massacres. He had feared there might be as many as a hundred thousand deaths and now he was hearing talk of half a million. Fire and sword ruled the whole country, except for the Butare district. The army of the Rwandan Patriotic Front had left its Ugandan refuge and was rapidly approaching Kigali, meeting little resistance. While the Rwandan forces did not resemble a real army in anything but the name and the uniforms, the Tutsi troops of the RPF were professional, disciplined soldiers, the officers products of English and American military schools. Two days earlier the RPF had liberated the little town of Byumba and many who had succeeded in escaping the pogroms were now taking refuge there.

A week later, Valcourt was walking back and forth on the muddy high plateau of Byumba, where a hundred thousand refugees were already huddled together. With Raïka, a Somalian who was working for African Rights, he was gathering eyewitness reports so that a true history could be written of the genocide that was still raging a hundred kilometres to the south. He was moving in a strange universe here, composed entirely of women, old men and children. Their gaze was not empty but chillingly absent, turned inward, or quite simply dead. Like people who can see but will not. Only a few women would speak, in hushed voices, their eyes fixed on the ground, where they kept them long after they had finished their almost clinical descriptions (for they had only concrete words) of the murders of their husbands and sons. The rapes these shy, prudish women described with a wealth of blood-curdling detail, as if they were dictating the reports of their own autopsies. They spoke of the worst mutilations and most perverse assaults with a composure and detachment that made these acts even more heinous.

And with each story he recorded, Valcourt, of course, was sure he was hearing Gentille's. If he had returned with a grain of hope, the four weeks he spent at Byumba destroyed it. He interviewed about a hundred people who had fled Kigali, four of whom had stayed at the Mille-Collines. There was no trace of Gentille. He would go to Kigali to find out how Gentille and their daughter had died. Then . . . then he . . . He could not finish the sentence his brain was trying to compose. Silence settled in his head the way absence had made its eternal nest in the gaze of those women.

To get from Byumba to the outskirts of Kigali took him and Raïka a week, following a battalion of RPF soldiers. It was a kind of descent into hell. A curious journey, a little like that of a Christian performing the Stations of the Cross on Good Friday, each of the four-teen stations opening the wounds wider and bringing him inescapably closer to death. Rather than avoiding or fleeing horror, the two men were pursuing it, hunt-ing it down in the remotest corners, like pathologists minutely noting the nature of wounds, evaluating how long it took for death to come.

Raïka was stuffing himself with Ativan. Valcourt would fall asleep like a drunken brute. Grotesque forms would wake him, hideous, putrescent bodies, caricatures of humans with arms shaped like machetes. Gentille would appear in the distance in a halo. The closer she came, for she was running toward him, the more she would become a horrible distortion of what she had been. She turned ash-grey and an incandescent river of lava ran from her belly. And when her twisted mouth, her rotted lips, placed themselves on his, he would wake with a loud cry, the smell of his own sweat all around him. The black night would glitter with a thousand stars.

Often he slept for only an hour and then would stay sitting, not thinking anything, his nose catching what-ever whiffs of death wafted from the smallest thicket. Even the invasive eucalyptus that was capable of sucking up all the land's water could not impose its fresh scent. The pungent smell of human death was killing the smell of the trees. Every night Valcourt imagined a different death for Gentille, and the closer he and Raïka came to Kigali the more appalling his wife's murder grew. In the nightmares that peopled every second of his sleep, it was Gentille who received all the tortures and humiliation that the women, their gaze buried in the blood-reddened ground, had confided to him, with shame, the way one admits the basest obscenity to a silent priest.

On the hills, in the little villages, in the squares and places where markets and meetings happen, the same stories were repeated. Neighbours, friends, sometimes relatives had come and had killed. Amid confusion perhaps, but efficiently. The killers were known, they were named. Every dead body had a known killer. In the towns both large and small, the genocide had been more systematic. Meetings had been organized, watchwords and directives had been given, plans had been laid. If the methods seemed so inhuman, if the killers killed with such savagery, it was not because they were improvising or were out of their minds, but simply that they were too poor to build gas chambers.

It was at Nyamata, an indolent, sizeable village whose low houses straggled along one wide, sandy street, that Valcourt and Raïka really understood. They were walking the paths of a second Holocaust.

They were taken to "the parish," which in Rwanda refers to a gathering of buildings—elementary school, secondary school, health care clinic, residence—a veritable fortress of red brick around the church. The soldiers on guard advised them not to go any closer. From the nine or ten buildings a stink arose that was more revolting than liquid pig manure freshly spread on a hot summer day. It was not just the smell of death but of all deaths and all rotting things.

At the beginning of the massacres, almost all Tutsis shared a single reflex: the militiamen would not dare attack the house of God. By the tens of thousands, from all the hills and all the hamlets, they had run, walked and crawled through the night, and with a great sigh of relief had squatted in the choir of a church, or the entrance of a presbytery, or in a classroom with a crucifix looking down from the wall. God, the last rampart against inhumanity. But in this gentle springtime, God and more notably most of his pious vicars had abandoned their flocks. The churches became Rwanda's gas chambers. In each building of the parish of Nyamata were piled hundreds upon hundreds of bodies. Three thousand people had squeezed into the round church, under the gleaming metal roof. They had closed the heavy wrought-iron doors behind them. The killers, frustrated not to be able to enter, finished their business with grenades. A few dozen grenades did the job and blew a thousand little holes in the roof, which on this sunny day made a thousand diamonds of light on the floor of the church. Three diamonds sparkled on what Valcourt thought he recognized as Gentille's neck.

Valcourt and Raïka were no longer taking reports from survivors, or very few. Their guides were efficient and determined, leading them from one common grave to the next, from one church to another.

They had almost reached Kigali but had to make a stop at Ntarama, where the RPF soldiers led them once again to the church. There they found the same formless carpet of bodies, the same stench of putrefaction that enters not through the nose but through the mouth and invades one's guts. It was as if the smell of death was trying to purge everything living from Valcourt's body. His stomach had emptied repeatedly for days. Now only a trickle of bile wet the corners of his mouth.

At a turn in the road he saw the first hill of Kigali. This was Gentille's place. He was coming back to where he would feel he was in his own house.

The city was quiet and empty. Only a few military vehicles were driving sedately on the long Boulevard of the Organization of African Unity. At the major crossroads there were a few disciplined and polite RPF soldiers on watch. The endless ribbon of bodies had disappeared. Where death had put on its most indecent show, long trenches had been dug that made a red ochre hem at the side of the asphalt. Here and there one could make out a splash of colour, a shirt, a dress, a red scarf that the lime had not completely covered.

Valcourt was stopping at each grave, hoping not to recognize anyone. He walked slowly, examining the clothes, studying the shapes of the bodies, trying to figure out the faces. Fear had taken the place of horror. But it was a contradictory, ambiguous fear that he could not pinpoint. His last remaining shred of logic, of analytical capacity, all the evidence he had heard, everything, absolutely everything told him that Gentille was dead. He was afraid in fact not to know for sure that she was dead, because then her disappearance would mean that her death was just one of a hundred thousand other deaths, like a drop of water in a sea of nameless and faceless tragedies. Gentille deserved to live until her own death, and Valcourt knew he would not be able to live unless he could write the story of her death. He wasn't interested in the killers, didn't care much what their names were. Obedient bit-players, ridiculous puppets, poor devils conned by everyone. In his country you couldn't bring them to trial or demand punishment because the courts would declare them insane on account of collective poisoning of their minds.

At the hotel, the only thing left unscathed was the fig tree, whose luxuriant beauty stood like a foil for the idiocy of men. Valcourt came across several soldiers camping in the rubble-strewn lobby. The pool was empty. The hotel's refugees had drunk all the water. They had also eaten the few birds in the aviary, whose door was swinging in the wind, grating on its hinges. Some of the eucalyptus trees around the pool were missing. They had been cut down for boiling water once there was no more wood from tables or bedroom furniture to burn. The ravens and buzzards and jackdaws were making do, perching more numerous than ever on the remaining branches.

Valcourt's eyes roamed over every centimetre of the big, now desolate garden. Well, he was home, he said to himself. He looked around at his empty house like a widower coming home alone after burying his wife. The pain and sadness were numbed. He felt neither anger nor bitterness. Not even despair. Worse, inside himself, dig as he might, he could find only a void. An absolute void. Gentille had given meaning to this landscape. Now it was his turn to try and give it one.

Zozo was looking at him and it was not a dream or a mirage. Only his lips were smiling. His huge black eyes were looking at Valcourt with the desolate sadness of beaten dogs. Why, why had Valcourt come back? To retrace Gentille's steps from the moment a sergeant of the presidential guard had separated her from him.

"Monsieur Bernard, I don't know anything. I only know she's dead."

Valcourt knew that already, he had never been under any illusions. But he explained that he couldn't go back to Canada until he'd found out exactly how she died.

He inquired after friends. He knew the replies but did it out of respect for their memory. He who was alive had to hear each of their names and the word "dead" after it. He would say a name and Zozo would reply "dead." This way they were commemorating the funerals of some thirty people, including all of Madame Agathe's girls. Victor?

"Victor," said Zozo, laughing, "would be pleased to receive customers at his restaurant."

Victor hugged Valcourt, holding him for many seconds on his broad chest, as though Valcourt were the survivor and not himself. Then he put his two hands on his friend's shoulders and squeezed them almost roughly.

"You're a man, Valcourt. There aren't many who'd have the courage to come back and revisit the darkest moments of their life."

"She's dead, isn't she? D'you know how? D'you know who?"

"Yes, she's dead, Émérita's mother told me, but I don't know how."

"And the sergeant?"

"I don't know. Come and eat. You'll forgive me, I don't have fish or beer. But I have eggs, beans, tomatoes and South African champagne."

Victor recounted his life-saving operations the way one recounts camping adventures or fishing trips. He laughed about each of the problems he'd overcome and made fun of his fears. He protested vigorously when Valcourt praised his courage. He'd only done what any man with a little money would have done in his place. To Zozo, who also expressed bountiful admiration, he replied soberly that he was not a hero, he was a Christian.

"Will you help me find out what happened to Gentille?" Valcourt asked. Victor nodded, turning away his eyes.

With a bottle of champagne in his hand, Valcourt went up to room 312. The bed was no longer there. He lay down on the balcony and listened to the silence, which was ruffled just barely once in a while by the barkings of dogs. No shouting, no laughing, no human sound except occasionally a motor. A warm wind and a shower enveloped the city. The birds lowered their heads and wrapped their wings closer. Valcourt huddled against the wall.

In the morning he went up to Rundo, which was already being called the town of widows and orphans. Out of two hundred men, around fifty had survived, most of whom had fled to Zaïre because killers had made all those widows and orphans. Six hundred. The Hutu and Tutsi widows had got together and decided to divide up the homeless children. Marie had taken in three, two of whom were boys she showed to Valcourt. Their father, a neighbour and good friend, had killed her husband. "They were close friends with my eldest . . . and children aren't responsible for our crimes." He gave her a little money. She asked him to find help to rebuild the school. Like Victor and Zozo, she told him that Gentille was dead, but she didn't know where or how. He left to go back to Kigali.

He found a more or less intact mattress and a few bedclothes in the litter scattered through the abandoned hotel and took them out under the fig tree. Lying around on the floor in his old room were some clothes that had been his. He picked them up and discovered *Essais* by Camus, the other book which, along with the Éluard, had been his entire library. The first pages of this La Pléiade edition had been torn out, probably because the fine paper made good toilet paper. He smiled at the thought. The book now began at page 49: "I no longer wish to be happy now, just to be aware."

Zozo arrived while he was reading. He was bringing a small bowl of spicy soup, a roast chicken and two bottles of champagne. He told Valcourt how his whole family had died. He knew each one's wounds and the names of all the killers. A cousin had survived. He had helped her and they were going to be married in his native parish of Nyamata. Another small miracle, said Zozo: he, Béatrice (his future wife), Victor and several others had been saved by Hutus. Valcourt pictured the roof of the church pierced by a thousand killer stars.

"I'll stay till your wedding."

"You mustn't . . . Victor asked me to give you this. Someone turned it over to him the other day, just after you left."

It was a school workbook, like the ones Valcourt used to have in elementary school nearly fifty years before. A blue cover, fifty pages or so lightly lined in blue and with a pink vertical line indicating the margin. On the last three lines of page one, a title: "The Story of Gentille After Her Wedding." The words lined up obediently, like fine lacework made of tall loops and steady, round curves. Valcourt recognized this writing. It was his mother's and his four sisters', the airy, fragile hand that Québécois nuns had taught and that had been learned by all the young Rwandan girls who, like Gentille, had gone to Butare's Social Service School. He could imagine the sparkling red, green or blue stars and the pink and blond cherubs that the sisters affixed to recognize the quality of the work. To write as gracefully as that, one had to do it patiently, with one's head slightly bent, in a kind of meditational state before the words one was writing.

Chapter Thirteen

April 10

*I do not know who I am writing to, but I know why.
Yesterday I married a man whom I love as I never
thought it possible to love. Today I am shut up in a
little room in Sergeant Modeste's house. I am writing to
tell of the death (for I am going to die) of an ordinary
young woman. I do not have political ideas, I do not
belong to any party. I have no enemies that I know of,
except perhaps the many men I have said no to. I have
the long body of a Tutsi and the determination of a
Hutu. I look at myself and know I'm a good mixture.
And if all the bloods mixing in my veins have not made
sicknesses for me, maybe it's because they can get along*

*together. I am not anyone's enemy. I am Gentille,
daughter of Jean-Damascène, a generous, upright man.
I am the wife of Bernard Valcourt, who taught me love
while teaching me the words of love, and I am the
adoptive mother of Émérita. I shall never see my husband again, I know. To support me in what is to come,
what I have left is my daughter's breathing as she
sleeps in my arms, and words I never stop reading,
and transcribe here the better to explain.*

> *I am daughter of a lake
> Which has not dimmed
> . . . At absurd rapes I laugh
> I am still in flower*

April 11
*Yesterday Modeste came after his family was asleep.
His wife is jealous. He wanted to protect me, he said. A
Tutsi woman in his section had been raped by ten of
his soldiers. Then they did even worse. Her anus was
perforated with a big stick, her nipples were cut off.
Modeste doesn't want that to happen to me, that's why
he's keeping me here although his wife is jealous and is
making trouble for him. But to thank him I could be
nice, I could be gentille. He doesn't even know that's my
name. I don't want to be raped, I don't want to be hurt.
I opened my legs. He didn't even want me to undress.
He entered me without a word and did his business. I
know he'll come back tomorrow and I'll open my legs
again without protesting so he won't beat me, so I can
stay here. Because I'm hidden here.*

April 12
He came back before the end of the morning with more
horror stories. He's not bad-looking, he has a fine body.
He always wants to have me right away. It will be
another rape, I know, but why is there never anything
but humiliation and submission? I wanted to caress
him the way Bernard taught me to, not to caress him,
but to close my eyes and bring back memories with the
tips of my fingers. He treated me like a whore and
didn't even look at me although I was all naked.
Someone, someday, reading these lines, if that ever
happens, will surely never understand why a woman
being raped would rather get pleasure from it. I
don't have a choice. Every time he appears, I know.
I don't want to fight, I don't want to defend myself. I
don't want him to be rough with me and tear me. But
I know he's going to plant his penis in me. Since I'm
going to die, I'd rather my rapist remind me of my hus-
band and give me pleasure. I know it's ridiculous. This
time he was in less of a hurry and pawed my breasts
and my buttocks. Not a single memory came back. I'm
ashamed not to want to resist, but I still want to live.

April 13
His wife came. She's even thinner than I am, you'd
think she was a Tutsi. She's very jealous. I want to
steal her husband, she told me, and she won't let me do
it. Her two brothers came with her. They hurt me.
When they had finished with me I was bleeding from
everywhere. Émérita was screaming. Modeste came in
the night to have me. He saw the blood and left without
saying anything. One rape less. He must have thought
I had my period.

A Sunday at the Pool in Kigali

April 14

*Bernard, why did you have me discover what a mys-
terious, secret garden the body is, a garden for explor-
ing endlessly without ever finding the beginning or
the end? Why did you teach me desire, and also the
ecstasy of creating the other's climax? A few days ago
I was a thousand points of pleasure, a thousand
musical notes transformed into a hymn by your fingers,
your lips, your tongue. Today I'm only two dirty,
stinking little holes they keep trying to make bigger.
For them I do not have eyes, or breasts, or thighs. I
do not possess cheeks or ears. And I am certain they
do not even feel pleasure. They empty themselves,
relieve themselves the way one urinates or d . . . (I
can't write that word), sweating because one has held
it in too long. Most of all, why did you teach me pure
pleasure, the kind that takes us to a world owing
nothing to love or desire, a world of pure chemistry,
cells dilating and exploding, a universe of sharp
smells, skins rubbing, hair matting with sweat,
nipples hardening, quivering, the blood boils so hard.
Bernard, to you I'll admit, I like sex, or "fucking" as
you say when you're playing the cold, callous male.
Every time the door opens and Modeste comes in, he
mounts me like I'm a bale of hay. I'm not human anymore. I have no name and even less soul. I'm a thing,
not even a dog that gets stroked or a goat that gets
protected and then eaten with gusto. I'm a vagina.
I'm a hole. Éluard, dear Éluard, I'm glad I have you
so I know I'm not alone and so I can say what I'm
living through.*

April 15
Modeste asked me why all Tutsis thought they were
superior to Hutus and why they wanted to eliminate
them from the earth. No one believes I'm a Hutu. I
don't know what to reply to these stupid questions. He
told me he didn't like killing but had no choice. Either
he killed the enemies and their friends or he'd be
killed. It's as simple as that in his mind. He's afraid of
dying, so he kills, he kills in order to live. Today he did
a lot of killing. He seems pleased with his work. He did
a raid on Holy Family Church with some militiamen.
Although the priests protested, they killed around
thirty cockroaches. That's what he calls them. He
never says "Tutsis." He asked me if I was still bleeding
and I told him yes. He doesn't want a bleeding hole. I
felt like telling him I had breasts, hands and a mouth
that could give him as much pleasure as my bleeding
little hole. I didn't. But I know I will. I have to get some
pleasure out of dying. Later his wife came. She's not so
bad. The child can't live here, she told me. Her sister,
who is sterile and unhappy, will look after Émérita.
Émérita left, but first she kissed me on the cheek. I
touch my cheek to feel her with me still. I have no
husband anymore. I have no child anymore.

Nothing have we sown that is not ravaged

April 16
Sunday. That means I've been married a week. They
don't kill on Sundays, it seems. The house was full of
relatives and friends talking and having fun. I could
hear the neighbours laughing and calling to each other

*from house to house. Modeste came, looking a bit
ashamed. His wife thinks he's in love with me and he has
to prove to her he's not, then as well there are militiamen
who say he's protecting a Tutsi hooker and keeping her
for himself. He has to prove he's not to them too. He
opened the door and they all came in, his wife first, and
she spat in my face. They didn't even ask me to undress.
They know I'm beautiful but they're not interested in that.
They don't want to look, they want to get inside. The first
was enormous and completely drunk. He picked me up
with one arm and laid me on the little table so my legs
dangled and he could stay standing, without ever leaning
on me. "They're dirty, the Tutsis, they have to be washed."
And he stuck his beer bottle in my vagina. That caused a
big burst of laughter. I stopped counting at ten. I watched
Modeste watching. None of them pulled down their pants,
nobody touched me, but all of them looked at me while
they banged away and forced and ejaculated. Modeste
had his turn last. He couldn't get it up. Everyone laughed
at him. I'm tired and now I'm sure I'm going to die.*

April 17
*Modeste came with a cup of coffee and a piece of bread.
He said he was sorry but I had to understand. If he
hadn't given me, worse things could have happened to
me. He saved my life and he wants me to be grateful.
Worse things? Yes, for example, having my breasts cut
off with a machete, my forehead slashed, my hands
split between the fingers, and then being left, as they've
done with all the others. As he has done with all the
others, all the enemies. I'm alive and he wanted me to
say thank you. In a few days all the Tutsis will be*

dead. Then I told him I was even deader than the corpses, I could smell my stinking death coming from my guts through all my pores. I think I raised my voice and he hit me.

> *Sweet future, I am this pierced eye*
> *This open belly and these nerves in tatters*
> *I who am the object of worms and ravens*

April 18

> *I am in earth instead of on earth*

Bernard, I'm speaking to you and I see you listening. I know you don't hold it against me that I've looked for pleasure in my pain. But I haven't been able to guide them to the paths I discovered with you. They don't hear me. I don't speak their language. I don't live on the same planet. I know they'll kill me when I get to stink of all the smells of all their foul penises. If I can't get any pleasure from this slow walk toward death, I might as well run out into the sun and die from one machete slash. In a few minutes I'm going to leave this house with this workbook and Éluard, freer than I ever thought I'd be, because now, Bernard, I'm already dead.

> *We shall not grow old together*
> *This is the day*
> *Too much: time is overfull*
> *My love so light now has the weight of torture*

Gentille left the wretched little room she had been kept in and found the house empty.

After walking for several minutes in the Sodoma district where Modeste lived, she saw a roadblock guarded by some laughing militiamen. She no longer had enough strength to walk. She sat in the middle of the dirt road then lay down, pulling up her dress and spreading her legs, preparing to receive the last indignity. This is where she would die. But Gentille no longer had the beauty that had driven men wild with desire ten days earlier. She was only a mass of bruises and swellings now. The two militiamen who came to look reacted with distaste. The younger, who could not have been more than sixteen, bent down and tore her shirt-dress, then ripped off her bra. Only her breasts had been spared. They stood up, pointed and firm, like an accusation and a contradiction. The boy gave two quick strokes with his machete and Gentille's breasts opened like red pomegranates. The militiamen dragged the young woman to the side of the road and left her there.

Émérita's mother, who had not ceased operating her bordello a few metres away, heard her moaning in the long grass and brought her inside to one of the little green-stuccoed rooms. In another room, the old battle-axe was hiding Doctor Jean-Marie who, with respect and affection, was attending to all the girls in the district. He was a good Tutsi. With a few dressings still left to him and ordinary thread, he tried to repair the damage, but he was giving Gentille only a short time to live. She was shivering with fever and racked by a terrible cough and he had nothing left but aspirins. Émérita's mother read Valcourt's name on the flyleaf of the book of works by Paul Éluard. She tore out the leaf, put it in an envelope and sent one of the young militiamen at the roadblock to find Victor, Valcourt's friend. Gentille and Victor had a long conversation and Gentille gave Victor the blue workbook. Victor knelt and prayed for a long time at her bedside, then left and went back to the Mille-Collines. Gentille was dead.

Chapter Fourteen

Later that evening, Valcourt went down to Victor's with
Zozo. Beer had arrived from Uganda, and beef. The
exiles of 1963 and 1972, or their children, were coming
back in droves. The richest were arriving aboard trucks
filled with produce and setting themselves up in abandoned shops, not worrying about the possible return of
their owners. The peasants, traditional herders, were
returning with their herds which were ravaging the few
fields that had not been harvested. All these people
spoke English and behaved as if they'd never left the
country, which was now theirs again. There was room.
The BBC was saying that nearly two million Hutus had
fled to Zaïre before the lightning-fast advance of the

Tutsi troops, five hundred thousand to Tanzania, and the number of dead was estimated at nearly a million. Half the inhabitants of the country had vanished, either dead or in flight. Two months to empty a country.

Victor had invited all the survivors he knew. They had all been saved by Hutus who had not hesitated to run the direst risks to hide them. He wanted Valcourt to gather the survivors' first-hand stories and make a film or write a book or articles about them. The genocide mustn't be forgotten, he told him, but we mustn't make demons of all the Hutus either. One day we'll have to learn to live together again. The survivors told their stories until the middle of the night, while Valcourt took notes and silent guests tucked into the beef and beer from Uganda.

Then, when they were alone, Valcourt asked Victor if he had seen Gentille's body, if he knew when and how she had died, and who had killed her.

"It was Émérita's mother who saw her body and found the workbook. That's all I know. Why d'you want to know more?"

"Dead people have the right to live, Victor."

He must complete the interrupted story, fill the workbook's empty pages with words, reconstruct the last hours, the last days.

"Victor, I have to find Modeste, his wife, his family, the militiamen at the roadblock. Will you help me? And I have to find Émérita too."

"You want to get even?"

Valcourt raised his shoulders, almost with a smile.

"No, not at all. Get even with who? Modeste? That's for the police and the courts, when there are any. Is he the only one guilty? Get even with History? With Belgian priests who sowed the seeds of a kind of tropical Nazism here, with France, with Canada, with the United Nations who stood by and let negroes kill other negroes? They're the real murderers, but they're out of my reach. No, all I want is to know, then tell the story."

He inspected every nook and cranny of Modeste's house and found only a red scarf, perhaps the one Gentille was wearing the morning of April the tenth. The neighbours too had fled, and the neighbours' neighbours. Émérita's mother repeated Victor's version word for word. She thought Modeste and his family had gone to Ruhengeri, then probably Goma in Zaïre where the government leaders and soldiers had taken refuge. The area around Goma had become an immense depository of haggard, suffering humanity. The soldiers and militiamen, who had taken a large portion of the population with them in their retreat, were reigning over a new republic of cholera and tuberculosis. They had already re-created their former world. They were fleecing the humanitarian organizations, extorting, raping, killing. The power they had lost in their country they were now exerting over these hundreds of thousands of refugees squatting in the filth of their own excrement.

A hundred dollars distributed amongst a few intermediaries brought Valcourt to Modeste, who had been promoted to lieutenant by the government-in-exile and who controlled the beer trade out of Kisangani. He didn't remember Valcourt. He was a handsome man who looked you straight in the eye and never raised his voice. Why care about the disappearance of a single person when an Anglo-Saxon Protestant plot was going to eliminate every last living Hutu? And that because all Whites except the French hated the Hutus. Fortunately the French had intervened to save them from extermination, enabling them to take refuge here and prepare their victorious return.

Propaganda is as powerful as heroin; it surreptitiously dissolves all capacity to think. Valcourt was talking to a Hutu propaganda addict. Modeste did not know a Gentille and did not remember having intercepted a UN convoy on the Boulevard of the Organization of African Unity. Women, beautiful women, he had them coming to him every day looking for protection or pleasure. The whole district of Sodoma knew his virility.

Valcourt produced a blue workbook out of the bag he was wearing slung across a shoulder. "Today I am shut up in a little room in Sergeant Modeste's house." He continued reading in a low voice, weighing each word and letting long silences hang like shadows, during which he stared with his tired eyes into Modeste's. He read this way for several minutes, the way the clerk of a court reads in a voice devoid of emotion the particulars of an indictment for an especially gruesome crime. "He asked me if I was still bleeding and I told him yes. He doesn't want a bleeding hole." The lieutenant did not flinch. He opened another beer, the third, and he spat on Valcourt.

"I don't know if your wife's dead, but if she is, thank heaven and the Hutus. Your wife was a whore, like all the Tutsis, the worst I ever met, the most immoral. Imagine. She never once said no, never once resisted. Nothing but a whore."

"She didn't want to get hurt."

Valcourt stayed at Victor's while workmen were refurbishing the hotel. His friends kept an eye on him for

fear grief would lead him to excesses. Yes, he was drinking more, but of course one imbibes more when one is
alone. Zozo was reassured; Valcourt had done his
mourning. He was working diligently. He was helping
journalists, all as ignorant as tortoises, who arrived in
Kigali for a few days. The city lay like a gigantic
corpse. Every street had its common grave in which
masked workers dug as the cameras whirred. Valcourt
would guide the journalists from one grave to the next.
He might see the long graceful neck, or the wedding dress
that she was holding under an arm, or Paul Éluard's
Oeuvres complètes, or her blue skirt. When he went back
to Victor's he would settle in a far corner of the restaurant and read and reread his notes, like a stumped
detective who has no *corpus delicti*, or witnesses, or
suspects, but knows he's very close to a body and murderers, maybe they're round the next corner. He would
sometimes fall asleep at the table, more from mental
fatigue than too much beer, and stay there until Victor
gathered him up and took him home.

"You should go away, my friend, at least for a
while."

"No, my friend, not before I find out."

Why was he so determined to write about Gentille's
end? He didn't really know but he had made it a duty,
an obligation, a promise. So he carried on, rather like a
sleepwalker, or a blind man advancing slowly in darkness. He was not desperate or bitter. He bore his grief
like a weightless, transparent garment and kept assuring those he spoke to of the beauty and generosity of
life, which, he said, amply outweighed the horror whose
magnitude people were now realizing. The new Tutsi
rulers, so well educated and organized, frightened him.

He could see a new martial, arbitrary order being set in place, one very like a dictatorship from his childhood in Quebec, the Duplessis régime. Life had never let him down. Men, yes, who so often let life down. But with Gentille, and before her with the two women he had loved, with each woman he had made a pact with life. Each time he had died a bit, and each time life had been given back to him. Not many men are lucky enough to live three times, or even once, after thinking they were dead. Gentille had been his last contract with life. Grief and loneliness were not gnawing at him. They resided inside him, peacefully. And then through all those weeks of happiness he had lived with one certainty: he would lose Gentille—she would leave him one day, that being the usual way of things; but he should have realized that she would be carried away by the relentless course of the coming extermination. Why had he not got her out of there while there was still time? She hadn't wanted to give up, because until the last minute, like himself, she had believed all the prophecies, analyses and signs coming from men were wrong, and her brothers and sisters would not kill her brothers and sisters. If you want to keep living, Valcourt thought as he walked along a row of market stalls that were recovering their former colour, you have to believe in things as plain and obvious as brothers, sisters, friends, neighbours, hope, respect, solidarity.

The cheery cries of merchants at their stalls could be heard again. Valcourt did not recognize any of the women selling tomatoes, nor any of the men selling potatoes. In fact, in this city now full of people from Uganda or Burundi, some of whom stopped him and asked for directions, he hardly knew anyone anymore.

This particular day he was with a German television team that wanted to do a quarter-hour human interest piece on life after the genocide. Where a thousand people had been jostling, shouting, arguing three months earlier there were now perhaps a hundred all told, merchants and customers together. At the butchers' stalls there was more beef than goat or chicken. No one was manning the long, magical counter where little pots of golden saffron and ground peppers had been displayed like explosive flowers. The tobacco sellers should have been visible just behind and, at the end of the line, Cyprien's angular face, his prominent shoulder blades and feverish eyes.

The Germans were tired of these traditional African market pictures. And Valcourt of his memories. Then, in a bright ray of sunshine, Valcourt saw the white cover of a book, with a photograph inset in its centre. A tobacco seller wearing a broad-brimmed straw hat was reading Paul Éluard's *Oeuvres complètes*.

He approached and recognized the back of the neck, then as he bent over her, the hands holding the book.

"Gentille."

"Yes."

She closed the book and placed it on the tobacco leaves. He squatted in front of her, placed his hands on her shoulders and drew her gently toward him. She recoiled in what seemed to be fear. He withdrew his hands and gently asked her to look at him. She bent her head even lower.

"Gentille, speak to me. I've read the workbook. I love you. Nothing's changed . . . You knew . . . you knew I'd come back . . . why, for heaven's sake . . . Come. We're going to leave here, come . . ."

Gentille's voice was very weak, barely a breath, interrupted by a racking cough.

"No, no. My darling, if you love me as you say—and I believe you, I believe you—you'll go away. I'm not the Gentille you loved and that you think you still love. Bernard, I'm not a woman anymore. Don't you smell the sickness? Bernard, I don't have breasts anymore. My skin's dry and tight like an old drum. I can only see with one eye. I probably have AIDS, Bernard. My mouth is full of sores that keep me from eating sometimes, and when I can eat, my stomach won't hold anything. I'm not a woman anymore. Do you understand what they've done to me? I'm not human anymore. I'm a body that's decomposing, an ugly thing I don't want you to see. If I left with you I'd be even sadder than I am now because I'd see in your eyes as you look away that what you really love is your memory of me. Bernard, please, please, if you love me, go away. Go now and leave the country. I'm dead."

She drew a finger along his hand and apologized for having touched him.

"Go, my love."

Valcourt obeyed without a word and entered a second period of mourning. He did not know if he could bear this one. He went back to Victor's and drank and drank.

Victor, relieved to be set free of the lie he had been asking forgiveness for every day, explained to him how Gentille had gathered all his friends together and made them take an oath on the Bible. Since she had ceased, in her words, "to be a woman," Valcourt must not know she was still alive. Since then, the friends had been taking turns driving her from Émérita's mother's brothel, where she was still being cared for, to the marketplace. There she would spend every day but Sunday reading

Éluard and transcribing his most beautiful lines into another school workbook.

They had all come, Victor, Zozo, Stratton, Doctor Jean-Marie, Émérita's mother. Bernard thanked them for respecting Gentille's wish. He asked them now to respect his.

The next morning, Victor told Gentille that Bernard had already left for Brussels and would continue to Montreal. She thanked God.

Every day Valcourt went to the prosecutor's office and listened to the examinations of defendants and witnesses, hoping to learn who had ordained that Gentille and thousands of other women should be consigned to the purgatory of the living dead. Each time as he left, he would smoke a cigarette, standing on the topmost step. Below, thirty metres away, the sun would reflect strangely on the white cover of a book and a hat of golden straw.

Six months later, a lightning-fast attack of pneumonia carried Gentille off in only a few days. She is buried under the great fig tree that shades the hotel swimming pool.

Bernard Valcourt is still living in Kigali, where he works with a group that defends the rights of people accused of genocide. Recently the government, now dominated by Tutsis, threatened to expel him. When ignorant and slightly drunk foreign journalists ask him to explain Rwanda, he tells them the story of Kawa. He lives with a Swedish woman his own age, a doctor who works for the Red Cross. They have adopted a little Hutu girl whose parents have been condemned to death for their part in the genocide. Her name is Gentille. Valcourt is at peace with himself.

Sources

p. 100 "I speak from the depth . . .": Paul Éluard, "Du Fond de l'abîme," *Le Dur Désir de durer.*

p. 102 "I am not afraid . . ."; "this absurd expanse . . .": Éluard, "Du Fond de l'abîme," *Le Dur Désir de durer.*
"A smile challenged . . .": Éluard, "Un Seul Sourire," *Le Dur Désir de durer.*

p. 186 "We are the first cloud . . .": Éluard, "Du Fond de l'abîme," *Le Dur Désir de durer.*

p. 229 "By day the house . . .": Éluard, "Par un baiser," *Le Dur Désir de durer.*

p. 241 "I no longer wish . . .": Albert Camus, *L'Envers et l'endroit.*

p. 244 "I am daughter of a lake . . .": Éluard, "De Solitude en solitude vers la vie," *Le Dur Désir de durer.*

p. 247 "Nothing have we sown . . .": Éluard, "Puisqu'il n'est plus question de force," *Le Dur Désir de durer.*

p. 249 "Sweet future, I am . . .": Éluard, "Un Vivant parle pour les morts," *Le Temps déborde.*
"I am in earth . . .": Éluard, "Un Vivant parle pour les morts," *Le Temps déborde.*
"We shall not grow . . .": Éluard, [untitled], *Le Temps déborde.*

GIL COURTEMANCHE is an author and journalist in international and Third World politics. Among his recent nonfiction works are *Québec* (1998) and *Nouvelles douces colères* (1999). When *A Sunday at the Pool in Kigali* was originally published in French in 2000, it spent more than a year on Quebec best-seller lists and won the Prix des Libraires, the booksellers' award for outstanding book of the year. Rights have since been sold in thirteen countries, and movie production is under way with Lyla Films. Gil Courtemanche lives in Montreal, where he is a political columnist for *Le Devoir*.

PATRICIA CLAXTON is one of Canada's foremost translators, winning her first Governor General's Award for translation in 1987 for *Enchantment and Sorrow* by Gabrielle Roy, and her second in 1999 for François Ricard's biography of the same writer, *Gabrielle Roy: A Life*. She has also translated the work of, among others, Nicole Brossard, Jacques Godbout and Pierre Elliott Trudeau. She lives in Montreal.